In Defense of Good Women

IN DEFENSE
of
GOOD WOMEN

A Novel

MARILYN J. ZIMMERMAN

Copyright © 2025 Marilyn J. Zimmerman

All rights reserved. No part of this publication may be reproduced, distributed, or transmitted in any form or by any means, including photocopying, recording, digital scanning, or other electronic or mechanical methods, without the prior written permission of the publisher, except in the case of brief quotations embodied in critical reviews and certain other noncommercial uses permitted by copyright law. For permission requests, please address SparkPress.

Published by SparkPress, a BookSparks imprint,
A division of SparkPoint Studio, LLC
Phoenix, Arizona, USA, 85007
www.gosparkpress.com

Published 2025
Printed in the United States of America
Print ISBN: 978-1-68463-318-0
E-ISBN: 978-1-68463-319-7
Library of Congress Control Number: 2025901784

Interior design by Stacey Aaronson

All company and/or product names may be trade names, logos, trademarks, and/or registered trademarks and are the property of their respective owners.

This is a work of fiction. Names, characters, places, and incidents either are the product of the author's imagination or are used fictitiously. Any resemblance to actual persons, living or dead, is entirely coincidental.

NO AI TRAINING: Without in any way limiting the author's [and publisher's] exclusive rights under copyright, any use of this publication to "train" generative artificial intelligence (AI) technologies to generate text is expressly prohibited. The author reserves all rights to license uses of this work for generative AI training and development of machine learning language models.

For David,
and for all the women charged with infanticide
whose behavior has been prejudged and misunderstood.

ONE

October 2016

EVEN IN HERE, I SENSE ITS PRESENCE. IT FLOWS, DEEP and determined, behind this jail and the county courthouse next door, swirls around the peninsula where my cottage stands, and flows beyond the place where the baby's body was discovered. You might say the river's the reason I'm here, but that makes what happened sound like an excuse, a defense to my behavior, when I don't mean that. So perhaps I'll just tell the whole story, starting not from the beginning but from where I am now, inside this cell. Maybe then you'll understand what so many people don't.

It's miserably hot. Instead of what I usually wear—some version of a silk blouse, worsted suit, and three-inch Ferragamos—I'm wearing floppy grey panties, limp orange scrubs, and splintered plastic slippers. COUNTY JAIL is stamped across the back of my shirt, as though anyone, least of all me, needs to be reminded where I am. I'm sweaty, and the lenses of my glasses are so greasy it's like looking into the river after a heavy rain before the silt's had time to settle. I squint and will my eyes to focus, to adjust to the fuzzy darkness surrounding me. I make out a few menacing shadows in the hall, the iron bars, and the outline of the rusted, open toilet in the corner of my cell.

My diamond wristwatch, a gift from my dad the week I started law school, is missing. The sour-faced deputy tossed it in a clear plastic bag along with my clothes when she processed me. In its place are the dark swipes of nascent bruising. Similar marks surround my right wrist. I finger the contusions, evidence of the handcuffs the bondsman forced on me before he shoved me into the trunk of his Lexus, although I'd begged him to wait, to bring her with me.

"Fool me once," he'd snapped.

I breathe on the lens of my glasses and rub them on the hem of my baggy shirt, then slide them on my face again. It doesn't help. The odor of unwashed women, like rancid meat, is pervasive and mildly nauseating, maybe because, unlike past visits, I won't be able to call a guard and leave when I'm finished with my business.

On the edge of the metal sheet that passes for my bed I half-sit, elbows on my knees. I'm strategizing, as though I'm still the one in charge of my life. I think about phoning a reporter at the *Sentinel*, a woman would be best, and giving her an exclusive, spilling everything I should have said months ago. I could, at long last, expose the truth about my client, the points that, hard as I tried, I was never allowed to speak about in open court. I mentally outline what I will tell this savior/reporter/woman before it dawns on me that, instead of Callie, I'd be the story she'll want to showcase. No one will understand what caused Callie to do what she did.

A woman in another cell yells something crazy; I can't tell whether she's lost in her dream or, like me, living some sort of bizarre TV show. The wheels of a metal cart squeak, and a deputy barks loudly enough to wake anyone who might still be sleeping. When a plastic breakfast tray scrapes beneath the bars of my cell, I stay where I am. The only thing I might be able to keep down this morning is hot coffee, and I'm betting the swill on that tray will pass for neither.

Sometime later, in another cell, a toilet whooshes and a thick body in a brown uniform appears outside my cell. It's Art Jones, the burly undersheriff, the man in charge of this place. He switches on the fluorescents; the hall lights buzz and snap to attention, and he steps back, rocks on his heels and watches me. Despite the oppressive heat, I feel a chill.

"The prosecutor's here," he says in a low voice.

Barrett?

Josephine, the day-shift matron, appears in my cell, removes the untouched tray and returns, holding a chain and a pair of handcuffs. "Use the toilet." She's a large woman who pronounces her words sharply, loud enough for Art to hear. "There's none where we're going."

"Move it, Counselor," Art says. "Just get yourself in those cuffs."

I stand, raise my chin and square my shoulders.

Josephine points to the floor in front of her. "Arms up. By your face."

Stepping closer, I raise my arms and clasp my hands together. She wraps the chain around my waist and loops the handcuffs through. I start when the metal touches my bruises.

"What happened?" she asks.

"A present from the bondsman."

Her eyes don't leave my face when she locks the metal bands, giving the key an exaggerated twist. Not tight enough to rub. "He prob'ly just didn't want you to slip away. Again." Spoken so Art can hear. I wonder if she's on my side in all this, but I don't trust her enough to ask. Women, in particular, seem to have strong feelings about what I've done.

I silently mouth my thanks, and she cradles my elbow with her hand as she propels me forward, following Art past the other women's cells, most of which are empty. A toothless woman in one grins at us; her pasty arm reaches into the hall and points ominously at our little parade.

We reach the men's block, and Art unlocks a heavy door, slams it behind us, then leads us through the periphery of cells. There's hollering, the giggling of perky hosts on a local morning TV show, a series of doors to be unlocked and resecured. We reach the rear of the building, the side facing the river, and Art nods toward the opening of a dingy room. When he flips a light switch and points, I step inside, resisting the urge to jostle my chains as I walk past him. Art's a cog in this screwed-up machine, but he's not the reason I'm in here.

A beat-up metal desk, a couple of wooden chairs, and a grimy, barred window await. The room's chilly; there's no heat other than what leaks from the corridor. In a corner of the dingy glass, a thick-bodied wolf spider stops working. Beyond the lacy strands of its web, the river's thick, grey water reflects threatening skies. On the opposite shore, behind the Ontario petrol plants, a series of large electrical towers stride toward Toronto like an alien chain gang.

In the twenty years I've practiced, I never showed up to promote a client's cause without being meticulously prepared. Unlike my father, extemporaneous speeches were never my forte, so I outlined and memorized each and every point I planned to argue to a prosecutor, a judge, or a jury.

But I haven't done a single thing to get ready for this morning's meeting. This time I only have one argument to make, and it's not legal, it's personal. Besides, Barrett already knows what I have to say.

I sense the weight of the chains around my waist, the handcuffs rubbing the thin bones of my tender wrists, and I reflexively shudder. My eyelids feel heavy; suddenly, even thinking seems a burden I'm not sure I can manage. I need to be certain Barrett understands the consequences of all this, but can I find the words? What if he calls my bluff? These days I don't know who he is or what he's capable of.

I could also say the same about me. I was a big-shot attorney in a small town, a success according to all my aspirations, the very definition of the word until Callie came into my life. Then somehow my principles got fuzzy and confusing. I began questioning, then crossing every boundary I'd always valued: professional, legal, personal, even geographical, it didn't matter.

My thoughts drift to her, a seventeen-year-old girl who's counting on me, and uncharacteristically I whisper a prayer, pleading with God to keep her safe. I know I'll sacrifice myself if I have to, but I refuse to let her down. Not like I did before.

In the hall, Art and Josephine are making small talk. The spider resumes its spinning, oblivious to my presence. I take a breath and swallow what little saliva I can muster. Then I lower myself into the chair behind the desk and wait.

TWO

Four months earlier
June 2016

A RAZOR-TOPPED FENCE SKIRTED THE JAIL'S ASPHALT lot. On the other side of the fence was a grassy public park that spilled to the St. Clair River, the natural boundary between Michigan and Ontario. The river was a brilliant blue that day, reflecting the summer skies. North of the park, the magnificent steel archway, aptly named the Blue Water Bridge, spanned the river at its narrowest point.

The park was teeming with people taking advantage of the cool breezes hovering along the deep water. Picnickers positioned themselves in folding aluminum chairs and rested on blankets as a lake freighter slid by in the shipping channel. Floating silently past, as though on cue, it resembled a skyscraper lying on its side. On shore, a group of elderly tourists raised their arms and waved. The lone sailor on deck ignored them and repeatedly shot a basketball through a rim fixed to the front of the pilot house as the freighter pushed northward into the deeper water of Lake Huron.

I wore massive Chanel sunglasses instead of my prescription lenses, but when I turned, I still saw them: beyond the scrim of chain link, not ten feet from me, were six women and six angry, red words on a massive poster board: ABORT ROE VERSUS WADE, NOT

In Defense of Good Women

BABIES. The women stood next to the sign, staring in my direction. Although I couldn't see their faces, I sensed they were judging me and that I was not faring well. People often equated me with the acts of the people I defended, so I was accustomed to getting the cold shoulder and dirty looks from the public. But this was different: these women looked both at and through me.

I squared my shoulders and strode to the jail's entrance. Once inside, I told myself I was being paranoid. I'd been appointed to represent the girl less than an hour ago. Word travels fast in this county, but not that fast.

I'd started my day at the county courthouse where, after some negotiation in a DUI file, I put a sweet plea deal for an elated client on the record. I'd planned to drive back to my office, give Gail the client's certified check for two grand, then catch up on some research before my afternoon appointments. But as I was leaving the courthouse, Circuit Judge Henry Osbourne's bailiff caught up with me in the hall. "Judge wants to see you, Victoria," he'd said. So I'd followed him up the wide marble staircase.

Inside Osbourne's chambers his secretary thrust a document in my direction.

"What's this?" I sputtered after reading enough to catch the gist. "The girl already has a lawyer. What happened to George?"

"*Had* a lawyer, Victoria." The response came from the corner chair beneath a tall window on the opposite side of the high-ceilinged room. The glare from the sun obscured him, but I recognized Osbourne's raspy voice. "Deering petitioned to get out this morning," he said. "I granted his motion. He claimed the girl wouldn't have anything to do with him. I decided she might be more cooperative with a female."

"But there are plenty of women lawyers in this county—"

"This will be the last major trial I preside over, and I want a clean record. No basis for appeal."

"But your honor, Henry, *Judge.* I don't take court appointments any more. I'm not on the list. Joyce Ballinger—"

"Apparently you haven't noticed. She's pregnant again. Due to deliver any day from the looks of things."

"What about Helen?"

Osbourne's shaky voice lowered to a sidebar whisper. "Helen Buchowski will file every crazy motion in the book, regardless of merit."

"This case—"

"This case what?" Osbourne pushed out of his chair and grinned at me. He looked like the quintessential jurist he'd always been: sparkling blue eyes, a head of white hair, plus the warm smile that got him reelected more times than most people could count. "You're not afraid of a homicide file, are you, Counselor?"

"Of course not." I'd bristled at his inference. "But—"

"As my Irish mother used to say, 'Don't borrow trouble.'" He patted my arm solicitously before shuffling to his courtroom.

I'd stood there, thinking about all the things I wished I'd thought to argue: that criminal court appointments were gifts to *young* lawyers, those who needed the experience and the county's measly paychecks while they established their reputations and their practices. Or to older lawyers whose practices had never taken off. Guys like George Deering, who'd been an attorney for years but had the reputation of being unable to fight his way out of a paper bag. I'd practiced twenty years. I had plenty of clients, and I didn't need the county's charity. Particularly this case.

I'd tried to think of another local female lawyer whose name I could offer. It had to be someone with experience, someone thorough. But I couldn't come up with a single name. I swore softly and scanned the paper again; it was an Order of Appointment, a binding court order, naming me as the girl's lawyer. Damn. It didn't help my situation that once Chief Judge Henry Osbourne, aka the Great and Powerful Oz, made a decision, he almost never changed his mind.

And this would be his last big trial. He'd had emergency bypass surgery a few months earlier and after he returned to the bench, his secretary, Cynthia, became a regular Cerberus, barring everyone from his chambers unless Osbourne specifically invited them inside. She also replaced the usual office coffee with a watery decaf and kept the office lights so low it felt like some kind of cheesy lounge instead of a judge's chambers.

Cynthia whispered, "Judge's doctor told him if he wanted to come back to work, he had to avoid stress. I'm glad, for his sake, that George is out and you're in. You'll do a good job."

I scowled and shoved the order into my purse. Clutching my briefcase with my other hand, I spun on my heel and stormed down the hall and out of the building.

It was another in a long line of humid summer mornings. Despite the lined pencil skirt I wore, the black leather seats of my Mercedes scalded my legs when I slid inside. I did a half-seated dance, and when my thighs stopped burning, opened the windows and punched the AC. Peeling from the courthouse lot, I narrowly missed a lagging red pickup whose driver laid on the horn and cursed me.

Heading to my office along the road cresting the riverbank, I continued to fume. I already knew plenty about my new client. Primarily, she was seventeen and had been charged with murder for drowning her newborn in the St. Clair River. The girl's crime was, by far, the most notorious in the county's history, in part because the publisher of the area's only newspaper, the *Port Huron Sentinel*, latched onto her story like it was his last chance to rescue his daily from the swamp of internet oblivion. During the past two months every edition of the *Sentinel* seemed to lead with a story tied to her, regardless of how remote or sensational. The articles touched on the girl's church, her minister father, and the sexual habits of teenagers in general. Most had little to do with the legalities of the case, but the public sucked them down like cold beer on a summer afternoon. Not only had the paper's circulation risen exponentially since the girl's arrest, but now some of my regular clients, big-deal felons with their own problems, wanted to spend the retainers they'd paid me talking about the girl's troubles instead of their own.

Soon after the *Sentinel* began its crusade, reporters from down-state dailies and national tabloids began swarming the courthouse. That very morning I'd seen three of them, hovering in the halls with outstretched iPhones, quizzing anyone who'd talk about what they called the "unspeakable act by the preacher's kid."

How would I get an impartial jury in this county? Or anywhere else? I slammed the steering wheel, hard, with my hand, cursed, and slowed for a large Diet Coke with extra ice at a drive-thru. I'd finished it and was halfway to my office when I phoned Gail and gave her the news. Then I made an illegal U-turn and headed back to the jail.

As usual, that morning the recirculated air in the dingy lobby was thick and heavy. Cushions on the plastic teal couch were torn and crusty and the green-grey cinderblock walls gave the place a cavernous, yet claustrophobic feel. On a bulletin board, sullen faces stared back from a dingy FBI MOST WANTED poster whose edges curled away from the thumbtacks working to keep it in place.

I shoved the appointment order beneath the glass of the admissions booth and the deputy inside smoothed the paper, then picked up a telephone. While I waited, I tried not to think about those women in the park and their sign. I'd changed my sunglasses for trifocals when the deputy nodded, slid the order back to me, and reached beneath his desk. A buzzer sounded, and I yanked open the steel entry door then let it slam behind me.

Down the hall, the county undersheriff pointed to a molded plastic chair beside his desk. Art Jones leaned back in his padded leather seat and laced thick fingers across his ample stomach. "Madame Counselor. You're here to see your girl?"

"I am."

"She's a lucky girl. Most lawyers don't give two hoots about their clients. But not you. Peg and I always say that if we ever get divorced, our biggest fight will be over which of us gets to hire you."

Art knew I was strictly a criminal defense lawyer. Still, I said, "Tell Peg she and I will take you to the cleaners, big time."

He grinned and lifted one heavy foot, then the other, to the crest of a massive pile of paperwork on his desk and paused. I knew he was waiting for me to share some juicy piece of courthouse gossip with him. I'd disclosed a few questionable rumors with Art during previous visits. That was part of the give and take of my job, building a relationship with someone from whom I might need a favor sometime. Plus, I liked Art. He was a bit of a buffoon, but he seemed fair to both the lawyers and the inmates in what he referred to as "my little piece of paradise."

"Coffee?" He held up a Styrofoam cup.

"It's too hot for coffee. What's with those women in the park?"

"The ones with the sign? They're from her father's church. Been holding vigils most every day since she was arrested."

"What does abortion have to do with what she did?" I waved my hand in front of my face in a futile effort to cool off. The thermostat in this old building was always out of whack. I'd been here less than ten minutes, and already my silk blouse clung to my stomach like a second layer of skin.

"Don't you read the *Sentinel*? That op-ed piece about how abortion and infanticide are the same?"

"I don't suppose anyone's told those women abortion happens to be legal."

"Some people say abortion leads to infanticide." He shrugged. "You're gonna have your hands full on this one, Counselor. Her own father washed his hands of her. Crime like this, I understand why. I assume that's why he won't post her bond, either." Art shifted his feet, and the mass of paperwork beneath repositioned itself. "You pay attention in this joint, you get so you can see the reasons why people act like they do. A crazy mother, a father who drinks, stuff like that. But this girl's a puzzle. Comes from a good family. Mother's dead, so she lives, *lived*, with her father. When she left the hospital, she stayed with the youth pastor from her dad's church 'til we found the baby's body."

He slid his feet from the desk, tossed his empty cup on the mound of papers, and watched it settle. "The youth pastor visits her in here every now and then. According to him, she was the perfect child. 'A student, sweet kid, obeyed the rules, no drugs or alcohol.'" His phone buzzed. He answered it and hung up, then pushed himself out of his chair. "Ready?" he asked.

I followed him into the bowels of the building, past the muffled shouts of male inmates, inarticulate hollering that bounced off the hard surfaces. Occasionally, metal on metal echoed as a cell door opened or slammed shut, a jarring noise like the ring of a cracked bell. We reached the entrance to the women's area, and I waited for Art to unlock the steel door.

This old jail was built when problem women were more likely to be sent to a state mental institution rather than locked up in here. The women's block was a warren of tiny, dark cells, smaller than those in the men's block. Except for replacing the iron beds with what looked like massive cookie sheets a few years ago, the county never allocated money to upgrade the women's quarters. Nor did they build separate visiting rooms where female inmates could meet with their lawyers. Security in the women's section was lax, too, especially for local attorneys. Art hadn't checked my purse or called a female guard to pat me down, which, unlike jails in other counties, was standard procedure here.

"You okay seeing her in her cell?"

Sort of a moot question, I thought, since we were, by then, standing outside it. "Sure."

THREE

THE GIRL SAT SIDEWAYS ON HER METAL BED, KNEES to her chin, her shoulders hunched, a pudgy lump in her jail scrubs. Oily blonde hair hid most of her chubby face. I'd seen photos of her in the papers, but I was surprised at how young she appeared in person; if I hadn't known better, I'd have said she looked twelve, maybe thirteen years old at most, not seventeen.

"This is your new attorney, young lady. Miss Stephens." Art dropped one of the county's ubiquitous plastic chairs on the concrete floor, then stepped out and locked me in.

The girl didn't move; she appeared to be staring ahead, at something, at nothing. I listened to Art's receding footsteps.

"Calliope. Named for the littlest hummingbird?" I was surprised I remembered this bit of trivia from my own childhood.

She slowly swiveled her head and looked toward me from between strands of hair. Porcelain skin and thin, pale lips revealed themselves before disappearing when she turned away. Despite her size, she struck me as fragile, like the first skim ice that coats the swampy edges of the river on frigid winter mornings.

She persisted in her silence, so I pulled my phone from my purse and checked emails, efficiently deleting all but three of the seventy-two from my inbox that had appeared since I left my office that morning. I dropped my phone into my bag and resumed watching her.

She sat motionless.

I glanced at my watch, remembering the research I'd planned

to finish before my afternoon appointments. "Are you going to talk to me?"

Nothing.

So much for Osbourne's theory about this girl opening up to a woman. I stood and unstuck my blouse from my stomach, considered asking one final time if she was going to talk to me, but it was so damned hot I dismissed the thought.

Besides, I was by then forming a strategy to get out of her case. I'd dictate a petition to be excused as her lawyer and have Gail schedule the motion for immediate hearing. Osbourne would have to let me out, as he had George, because she wasn't talking to me, either. If she wouldn't cooperate in her defense, how could I help her? Let Osbourne appoint some other woman as this girl's lawyer, I reasoned. Maybe some young chick right out of law school could convince her to talk. Meanwhile, I'd get back to my real law practice, to the clients whose retainers made it possible for me to pay off my Mercedes and splurge on three pairs of Manolo Blahniks last month.

I glanced her way again. She hadn't moved. I reminded myself she wouldn't be my problem for long, and suddenly it didn't seem so miserable in here. Pulling my iPhone from my purse, I started to call Art. I'd have to skip lunch to get my research finished in time, but if I hustled I could get to my office and get back on schedule.

"My father picked my name."

When I turned, she hadn't moved. She still stared at the wall, but she spoke again, her words little more than a whisper. "He told me I was a little bird sent to our family from God. Like the holy spirit."

"Calliope—"

"I go by Callie," she said.

A woman in a nearby cell cackled and a television blared, then faded to a dull murmur.

"Okay. Callie." I dropped the phone in my purse. "Callie? Do you understand you're charged with a very serious crime?"

She faced me then and flipped thin strands of hair behind her shoulders. Her eyes were dark and set deep, black pools in an ivory field. Her pale skin glistened in the heat. "Do you think you could talk to him? To my father? Ask him to come and see me? He won't take my calls."

A drop of sweat wandered behind my thick glasses and trickled into my right eye. I blinked away the stinging saltiness. Although she hadn't answered my question, she had talked to me, which meant I couldn't attest otherwise to Osbourne.

I did a quick recalculation. If I talked to her dad, maybe she'd open up to me, tell me what really happened. Maybe I could resolve her case with a quick plea. More maybes than I was comfortable with, but as long as I got rid of her file I was willing to give it a little of my time.

I said, "Okay, kiddo, I'll make you a deal. I'll go see your daddy, and then you and I will talk about what happened."

"I'm not a kid," she said, "and he's not my daddy, he's my *father*. Oh, and be sure to make an appointment before you go. He doesn't like it when people just show up at his office."

I took a slow, long breath of the stuffy air, raised my chin, and said, "Do we have a deal?"

"I believe we do," she said, and turned away from me.

I redialed Art's number and was counting the rings when I heard her say, "He always calls me his best buddy."

When I returned to my car, the church women were still in the park. Despite the searing sunlight, I'd kept my prescriptions on so I could get a better look at them and their sign, maybe even return their stares with a wicked glare of my own, but none of them were watching me now. Their sign rested against the rough trunk of the big maple, and all six stood quietly with eyes wide open, lips moving in silent prayer, hands grasping as if forming some ridiculous chain to bind the world's sin.

I momentarily considered stepping to the fence and calling them over, telling them what I'd told Art: that abortion was legal. For emphasis, I'd add that I was just doing my job. But the county was paying me peanuts to handle the girl's case, and I wasn't going to get a penny more for taking on these zealots. I climbed in my car and left.

FOUR

HIGH ABOVE MY COTTAGE, THE EXPANSIVE WINDOWS OF elaborate McMansions stare across the blue water at the Canadian shore. Their manicured lawns slope toward the river like green waterfalls, and their oversized boathouses hang over the steel seawalls that bracket the river, protected from the swift current and spring ice jams by clusters of pilings driven deep into the river's clay bottom.

My cottage, a miniscule collection of rooms resting on a low bubble of glacial till, sits between and beyond two of these boathouses. Unlike the McMansions, my place is below the road, hidden. I too have a boat well, but it's not a separate building from my home. My boat well is tucked beneath my living room, on the downriver side of my cottage, a dark cave where the water slops and splashes against the cement block walls whenever a large powerboat surges past.

My cottage was constructed during Prohibition by bootleggers who used it to store crates of whiskey rowed across the river from Canada or dragged on sleds over the ice—booze that likely ended up in one of Detroit's blind pigs. My dad obtained title to this place as payment for defending the grandson of the original owner on a Murder Two charge. Over time, Dad exchanged more legal work for construction and eventually moved into the house with my mother and two-year-old me. Mom died five years later.

After Dad died, this drafty cottage, with all its faults, became my sanctuary, the place where I returned each night, however late, for privacy and refuge from my busy law practice. It was my runaway truck ramp, a version of those sandy highway spurs that brought out-of-control semis to a dead stop. Although I could easily afford a nicer place, I've never been interested in moving.

I haven't changed much about this place over the years, although I did cover its walls with my mother's art. After Dad was gone, I rescued her paintings and sketches from a cupboard in the basement where he'd stored them and hauled the moisture-ravaged canvases and a few moldy drawings to a guy in Detroit who specialized in restoring damaged artworks. He did what he could to save her oil of the great blue heron, her studies of buffleheads, her half-finished painting of a Canada goose, and her sketches of tiny wrens, sparrows, finches, and hummingbirds. I hung the salvaged works throughout the cottage, hiding drywall puffy from the river's relentless humidity.

I also saved Mom's cookbooks, her bird books, her art books, and my dad's one indulgence outside of his work: countless dog-eared paperbacks with tales of courtroom dramas and heroic, always male, lawyers. His favorite was *Anatomy of a Murder*. He owned three copies of the book, all autographed by Robert Traver, the former Michigan Supreme Court Justice who resigned from the bench to get back to his first love, fishing, in Michigan's Upper Peninsula. My parents' collections still lined the shelves in my tiny living room, and though I didn't cook or sketch and couldn't be bothered to read any fiction these days, I maintained a sentimental attachment to these old books. Besides, they were a cheap alternative to insulation, helping stave off the icy winds that funneled down the river every winter from the wilds of northern Canada.

My favorite spot in my cottage, winter or summer, was a lumpy cabbage rose chair in the corner of my living room, next to my stone fireplace. I liked to sit there, watch the river traffic, and think.

I'd done some of my best strategizing for my cases on that comfy perch, and after a long workday, I'd been known to fall asleep there.

The day I got stuck with the girl's case, it was dark by the time I got home. In my cellar, I yanked the chain for the bare bulb and listened to water slopping inside my boat well. Though I hadn't checked on the *Margaret Ann* in weeks, I was certain she'd be laced with cobwebs and overrun by river spiders with bodies the size of quarters. Earlier in the year, I'd resolved to take her out more as soon as the weather warmed and had even had her outboard overhauled at the local marina in preparation. But so far that summer, as in years past, I'd been so swamped with work I'd never gotten around to it.

I momentarily considered pushing open the wooden door to the well, clearing the cobwebs with a stubby broom and heading out, floating among the swampy flats and marshes downriver, trying to chill, to forget about that new case I'd been assigned. But I couldn't stop picturing the girl sitting in her jail cell, correcting me, giving me orders, and my jaw reflexively grated, like spring ice on splintered wooden pilings. I surveyed my so-called wine cellar and chose a bottle of oaky California Chardonnay instead.

Back upstairs, beyond my window, an enormous freighter, one of the few thousand-footers that routinely navigated the Great Lakes, headed north, the lights on its rail glowing like an oversized tennis bracelet. A few small fishing boats motored in the opposite direction, unzipping the black water, their wakes spreading behind their sterns like paper fans. I guessed these were walleye fishermen, some of them former clients of mine, poachers catching more than their limit to sell to unquestioning chefs and fry cooks along the river. It was probably time for another DNR sting. Barrett Michaels, the county prosecutor, never went too hard on the guys who made their living on the river. Years before, his dad, a Detroit cop who'd survived an on-the-job shooting, took a disability retirement and

In Defense of Good Women 21

moved his family up to Riverside so he could fish full-time, and Barrett used to say that the walleye from this river financed his college education.

I nestled in my corner chair and munched on the turkey sub I'd picked up from the grocery store deli on my way home. What had Osbourne said? That I was afraid of a murder case? Why hadn't I pointed out that I tried three of the last four murder cases in this county? That all three resulted in acquittals? I took my first swallow of wine as a small powerboat raced past.

"Baby killer," the papers called the girl.

Leftover ripples from other powerboats danced across the darkening water, and I finished my sandwich as I thought about what else I'd heard and read about her case.

Last March, north winds had pushed chunks of ice the size of boxcars from Lake Huron into the river. The massive bergs clogged the surface of the water, even taking out a few scrappy docks and pilings on their way south. By April, remnants of spring ice still littered the surface, chips that by then had shrunk to the size of communion wafers. They floated downriver, propelled by the swift current. That's when the *Sentinel* reported that a girl who had passed out at Riverside High School was rushed to a Port Huron hospital, where the doctors determined she'd recently given birth. Two weeks later, a baby's body was discovered by a couple of fishermen down in Algonac. By then, the girl had been released from the hospital and was living with her youth pastor and his wife because, according to the *Sentinel*, her father refused to let her return to the parsonage. When the rushed DNA test results came back, she'd immediately been arrested. The obvious conclusion was that she'd hidden her pregnancy from her teachers, her friends, the people at her church, even and especially her own father. Worse, that she'd taken the baby to the icy river to kill him and hide his body, just as she'd hidden her pregnancy.

Outside my window, a snub-nosed tug pushed a barge carrying dredging equipment upriver, its engines working against the relentless current. I took another swallow of wine.

A guilty verdict in the girl's case would not only make local headlines, it'd be the lead story in all the papers fixated on this crime, not to mention the internet news links that flashed daily updates. I'd worked my ass off to earn a reputation as a top-notch criminal defense attorney. If I lost this one, which, from what I could tell so far, was a strong possibility, I'd be remembered as the criminal defense lawyer who failed to win the county's biggest case. What would that do to my reputation as a hard-ass, winner-takes-all lawyer?

I topped off my goblet, took a large swallow, and sat in the dark. It was clear to me I'd been tapped for this case so that after she was convicted, Osbourne and the rest of the county powers that be could tell themselves the girl had the best defense around. To add insult to my injury, the county's fee schedule would barely cover my office overhead while I worked on her file.

Around midnight, I finished a third glass and tottered to my bedroom, then undressed and tossed my clothes atop a growing pile I planned to take to the dry cleaners when I found the time. I lay on my narrow bed, listening to the soft clicking of the ceiling fan above and picturing those women in the park—how they'd concluded that abortion and infanticide were the same. Not for the first time, I wished I'd deviated from my pre-law curriculum as an undergraduate to enroll in a psychology course. Maybe then I'd have some understanding of why women thought like that. And maybe I'd have some idea why a teenager would commit such an unthinkable act.

I tossed and turned in the slow breeze. There was something else about this case, this girl, that bothered me. It was more than the feeling the county was using me, more than concern about my reputation, and more than the crime the girl was charged with. But that night, half-buzzed, I couldn't put my finger on it.

As I drifted toward sleep, I kept telling myself that this girl, this Callie, was just another file, that this feeling I had was probably nothing, that I'd work out a deal with the county prosecutor, get rid of her case quickly and quietly, and get back to representing the rest of my clients.

Besides, I'd known the local prosecutor a long time, and we worked well together. He'd offered me plenty of good deals for my clients. I told myself this case would be easily resolved like all the others.

FIVE

THE FOLLOWING DAY, A COUNTY DEPUTY DUMPED AN enormous parcel on Gail's desk. I watched as he stood there, grinning, while she opened the package, removed its contents, then leaned sideways and eyed the monstrous pile, her long, grey braid brushing the floor beside her chair.

"Barrett Michaels said to tell you he wants to push forward. Get this over with." He mock-saluted the two of us and left.

Gail sat up tall and flipped her braid behind her shoulder. "This one won't be a gimme, Vic," she said, "but I guess you figured that out."

Gail was my dad's secretary long before she began working for me. When he died, she agreed to stay long enough to help me get my practice up and running. In the early days there'd been times when she could have sat quietly by and watched me drive blindly off the legal malpractice cliff, but she didn't. She always rescued me before I did anything too stupid. And though I like to think I'm much wiser these days, Gail's still here.

I stared at the pile of papers. Elastic bands stretched to their limits around what I knew would be investigative reports and court documents. Seeing them, I realized I'd still been hoping for some kind of dispensation, some magical reprieve that I now recognized was not going to take place.

"Want the good news?" Gail interrupted my thoughts. "Danielle White agreed to make payments on the balance her low-life son owes. Plus I threatened Sam Munson you'd withdraw if he didn't bring his account current. Weasel has money for that gas-guzzling cigarette boat he races up and down the river but can't pay his attorney? I don't think so."

She lifted a stack of thin envelopes from her lap, tapped their edges, then shoved them, along with a zippered bank bag, in her bulging tapestry purse. "I'll make the deposit on my way home." She hoisted her bag to her shoulder and her slender body leaned into it. "You look tired. Why don't you knock off early for once?" She nodded at the massive pile of papers on her desk. "I'll organize that behemoth in the morning. Any idea why Barrett's in such a rush?"

"The election's five months away."

Barrett was one of two candidates running for Osbourne's seat. I mentally added that to my list of reasons why he'd want to give me a quick deal. It had to be a huge distraction during a busy campaign. According to the *Sentinel*, Barrett and his competitor Jim Anderson, a popular personal injury lawyer, were within a couple of percentage points of each other in the polls.

"First thing tomorrow," I added, "I need you to make an appointment for me to visit this kid's dad."

I locked the door behind her when she left, then scooped the files with both hands. In my office, I dropped the load on my desk and jockeyed the bands until the paperwork came loose. I turned pages, one at a time initially, then in clumps, as if I were in the lobby of my dentist's office thumbing through one of her yachting magazines, checking out photos of lavish hundred-footers with helicopter pads and Jet Skis while I waited for the hygienist to call my name. I flipped past police reports, witness statements, the autopsy report, copies of petitions, court orders. At the bottom of the pile, I found the warrant.

> That on or about the 5th day of April, 2016, in
> the County of St. Clair, in the State of
> Michigan, Calliope Faith Thomas did, with malice
> aforethought, willfully and deliberately cause
> the death of a full-term male infant born on or
> about April 5, 2016, said death being the result
> of drowning, contrary to MCL 750.316.
> Punishment: Mandatory Life imprisonment.

Barrett's unmistakable signature punctuated the bottom of the page, letters resembling a tall-masted sailboat, sharp edges and pointed spires.

Murder One. Mandatory Life.

If nothing else, the charge Barrett authorized was absolute. It made a statement to the voting public about his position on this crime. It also spoke to the strength of his evidence.

I stood and watched, through the small, barred window behind my desk, a plastic shopping bag skitter across the municipal parking lot. When a cloud slid over the sun, my reflection emerged in the dingy glass: a round face dissolving into a receding chin, tiny eyes I hid behind oversized, black-framed glasses, a too-long nose, and unruly blonde hair.

I was aware I wasn't a beauty, but I splurged on expensive suits, dozens of pairs of Italian leather pumps and flats, pricey salon haircuts and colorings, plus acrylic nails, to emphasize both my presence and my success as an attorney. I was also well aware that what really mattered was winning cases and getting the word out, but I excelled at that, too. I spent plenty on local radio ads. Graphics with my signature black frames, office phone number on one lens and the words HIRE A WINNER! on the other, were on every grocery store shopping cart in the county. The chic clothing and the spa treatments I splurged on, not to mention my speedy little Mercedes, were essential pieces of the image I projected to get to and stay at the top of my profession.

From my bottom desk drawer, I retrieved a red spiral notebook. The details of every jury trial I'd defended were recorded on these pages; the listed crimes read like an index of Michigan's Penal Code: Breaking and Entering, Drunk Driving, Larceny, Uttering and Publishing, Safe Cracking, Murder, Negligent Homicide, Kidnapping, plus a litany of Controlled Substance violations. After each verdict, I'd made a meticulous, handwritten account of the charges, the witnesses, my defense strategy, and the outcome. In twenty years, I'd tallied fifty-two wins and just five losses.

I was proud of these accomplishments. Hard-won, this notebook was a criminal defense lawyer's dream curriculum vitae. I'd given up plenty for these victories: never married, no children, no pets. I didn't belong to a health club, and I had no hobbies. I'd focused on one thing: winning cases. This notebook was proof of my success. It told the story of the professional life I'd built, the one I'd been drawn to since childhood.

I dropped my notebook in the drawer and pushed it shut with the toe of my silver Ferragamo, then slipped off my pumps, removed my silk jacket, popped the top on a Diet Coke, and readied myself for a long night. Normally I didn't mind working late. I could focus better without the distraction of ringing phones or other interruptions. But that night the office seemed too quiet, too empty. Not for the first time, I wished Dad were there with me. I wanted to run the details of my new case by him. I could almost hear his deep voice, his shared wisdom, reverberating in my head.

"There are no shortcuts, Victoria," he would say. "The trick is to keep examining the rock wall you're facing. Look closely, then closer still, then raise your magnifying glass and look again. Eventually you'll find a tiny crack, a hairline fracture. That's where you insert your wedge and start chipping."

If I pled this case, it wouldn't become part of the record of my wins and losses. That record chronicled only jury trials. And as much as I wanted to add another acquittal to my resume, it didn't appear this case was one to take before a jury. The girl's crime, if proved, was so dreadful that the likelihood a jury would convict her of Murder One was too much of a gamble.

I'd have to convince Barrett to deal.

I knew from experience that Barrett never offered a plea in a case he was certain he'd win. That meant I had to find a weakness, something that would cause him to doubt his chances before a jury. I needed to find the chink in his armor. I opened a second Diet Coke and started searching.

SIX

I READ EVERY SINGLE WORD ON EVERY PAGE IN BARRETT'S FILE three times.

From the police reports, I learned that on the morning of April 5, around seven o'clock, Callie's father left her at the parsonage and attended a monthly church breakfast meeting. He got a ride to the meeting with Craig Arnold, the youth pastor at his church, and Craig's wife, Rebecca. Afterward, the Arnolds dropped Reverend Thomas off at New Life in God Church, around six miles from the parsonage. About ten o'clock, Callie drove her father's car to Riverside High School. When asked why she was late for school, she told the office staff she hadn't felt well earlier but by then she was fine. Shortly after her third hour class began, Callie asked the teacher for permission to use the lavatory. When she didn't return, another student was sent to check on her. Callie was found in the bathroom, passed out in a pool of her own blood.

At the hospital, the doctor who examined Callie determined she'd given birth sometime that morning. Because Callie was a minor, the hospital called Callie's father. Neil Thomas got a ride to the hospital and once there, signed the necessary consents for an ob-gyn to perform an emergency D&C on Callie. During surgery, it was discovered that a piece of placenta stuck to Callie's uterine wall had caused the bleeding. When questioned by hospital personnel both before and after surgery, Callie denied giving birth and insisted there was no baby. Concerned for a child's welfare, the hospital called the police, who immediately searched the parsonage, the Thomas car, Callie's school locker, all the school lavatories, and even the school's garbage cans. No baby was found. They questioned Callie's friends and asked any student who knew anything about a birth to come forward, but no one did. Two weeks later, a couple of fishermen pulled a pink parcel from the St. Clair River. Inside were the remains of an infant's body. The police returned to the parsonage and again searched Callie's bedroom. The bed in her room was missing a top sheet, so they removed the fitted sheet and sent both the sheet and a swatch of the pink fabric found in the river to the state police lab in Brighton. The lab's conclusion was that the two textiles were identical.

I noted a couple of questionable inferences in the reports, read and reread the lab's conclusions, and reviewed a stack of witness statements. Four hours and three Diet Cokes from the time I started, I recapped Dad's Waterman and tossed it on my desk. Not only had I failed to find anything helpful; on the contrary, Barrett's case was stronger than I'd feared. He had DNA tests confirming that the dead baby was Callie's, hospital reports proving she gave birth a short time before she was taken to the hospital, and the medical examiner's conclusion that the newborn died as a result of drowning in what the state police lab positively concluded was river water.

It was past midnight by then, but I was determined to find *something* before I called it a night. I tried another tactic I'd used successfully in other challenging cases: listing all possible legal defenses, no matter how far-fetched they seemed, and any facts that might support them.

I started with the obvious:

1) *Callie didn't commit the murder:*

 + Barrett has no confession.

+ Barrett has no positive ID. A witness reported seeing "short, plump female wearing dark hooded raincoat" carry pink bundle to boat launch and drop it in river on April 5. Not a conclusive ID but description fits Callie's build. Barrett hasn't found this raincoat. Consequential?

+ Query—Was Callie the only person present during the birth?

+ Query—-Did Callie take the baby to the river?

+ Query—Police searched boat launch two weeks after witness sighting and found no forensic evidence (blood, hair follicles, etc.). Consequential?

2) Self-defense:

With an infant victim? I crossed off this one.

3) Defense of others:

There was no evidence to support this so I crossed it off, too.

4) Duty:

Nothing to support this one, either. Another one I eliminated.

5) Insanity:

I slid Dad's Waterman back and forth in my fist as I considered this one. A local district judge, in response to a motion by George Deering, had already ruled Callie was competent to stand trial. That ruling was limited to Callie's mental state during trial preparation.

An insanity defense would be different. An insanity claim would focus on Callie's behavior and state of mind at the time the act was committed. If I filed an insanity notice, the law would require me to prove that Callie suffered from a mental illness when she committed the crime and that because of her mental illness she either lacked the capacity to appreciate the wrongfulness of her act or conform her conduct to the requirements of the law.

In short, I'd have to prove Callie was mentally ill when she killed her baby.

In a witness statement, the Riverside High principal stated that during Callie's junior year her GPA hadn't dropped below the 3.7 she'd maintained the previous two years. During her junior year, she'd also taken two Advanced Placement classes at Port Huron's Community College. On its face, it appeared Callie was a normal, mentally healthy teenager.

Around three in the morning, I concluded I had two preliminary, although admittedly very weak, defenses:

1) *Callie hadn't acted alone.*
2) *Callie was insane when she killed her baby.*

Although I'd found nothing in Barrett's file to support either and though both were based on hunches, I didn't have anything else. I took off my glasses and massaged the bridge of my nose. I wanted to go home and get some sleep. Instead, I circled the word *insane* in black ink.

Experts at the criminal defense seminars I attended preached that most of the public viewed the insanity defense as a cop-out. Asking a jury to find a defendant not guilty by reason of insanity was, they stressed, the same as asking them to put a guilty person back on the street. The statistical reality was that the insanity defense was rarely raised and it was almost never successful when it was.

If I wanted to deal Callie's file, I'd have to convince Barrett that Callie was likely to be acquitted. But like me, Barrett knew how juries felt about an insanity defense. We'd discussed it at length years earlier, back when I was a law student and he was a young assistant prosecutor. Unless and until I could convince Barrett that Callie fit the statutory requirements for insanity when she killed her baby, there was no way he'd offer me a deal.

Tired to the bone, I turned out my office lights and headed home.

SEVEN

A MASSIVE ASPHALT PARKING LOT SURROUNDED NEW LIFE in God. The grey metal roof of the modern white worship space morphed into a white cross that stretched skyward. The rear of the building, a long, low structure, resembled the tail of an oversized reptile.

New Life in God was vastly different from the church I attended when growing up. The largest Catholic Church in Port Huron, St. Anne's was built when towns along the St. Clair River were flush with lumber and shipping money. It was a grand, gothic structure with tall panes of intricate stained-glass renderings of saints and an organ whose pipes dominated its immense balcony. Once enrolled in St. Anne's boarding school, I'd become a diligent and devoted student who attended daily mass and sang in the girls' choir. On the rare occasions I thought about those days, I missed the nuns and lay teachers from St. Anne's who'd taught and counseled me, but I'd long ago given up on God and hadn't set foot inside a church in over two decades.

On my drive to New Life, I'd mentally reviewed a list of people who might have assisted Callie in hiding her pregnancy and/or covering up the birth. So far, I'd come up with the possibilities of:

1) a girlfriend of Callie's and/or
2) the baby's father.

I'd considered including Callie's father on the list, but he wasn't a strong candidate, I'd decided, mainly because it didn't appear he was present when the baby was born and also because the ER doctor had told the police Neil Thomas appeared genuinely stunned ("incredulous" was the doctor's word) when told his teenage daughter had given birth. In addition, the nine other people from New Life who attended the breakfast meeting said he seemed perfectly normal that morning. I couldn't rule him out, but he wasn't a likely accomplice.

There were several cars in the church lot. I tried the main door to the sanctuary but it was locked, as were the building's other doors. I crossed the manicured lawn and squinted through a window in the building's tail into a low-ceilinged hall lit by tubular fluorescents. I checked my watch again and banged on the glass with the side of my fist.

Eventually a slender brunette turned a window crank and called to me through the sliver of an opening. "May I help you?"

"I'm here to see Neil Thomas."

"It's *Pastor* Thomas," she said. "And you are?"

"I'm an attorney. His daughter's lawyer."

"Wait here." She cranked the window closed and disappeared.

A few minutes later, a door opened and she motioned me over, holding it just wide enough for me to slip through. After securing the lock, she briskly led me down a long hall. We passed a number of classrooms, all of which appeared empty save one, where several adults sat in a circle on folding chairs quietly talking. Near a lettered sign on a block wall that read, THEY'RE THE TEN COMMANDMENTS, NOT THE TEN SUGGESTIONS, the woman abruptly stopped, turned to me, and whispered, "It's the first time we've ever had to lock our church. But those reporters were so disrespectful. One of them—he didn't say he was a reporter of course—told us he wanted to join our church. Once he was here, all he did was pester our members for information. About *her*."

Before I could muster any response, sympathetic or otherwise, she turned her back and started walking again, the clicking of her low-heeled shoes echoing down the otherwise empty hall. Finally, she turned into a large windowless kitchen and pointed to an open cabinet beneath an industrial-sized sink. A man's shoes and body protruded from the cupboard. A pile of oily rags and a wrench lay nearby. "She's here, Pastor," the woman said.

The man pushed himself out slowly, wiped his hands with one of the rags, and stood. He was thin, pale-complexioned, with a trim, dark beard. His soiled navy sweatshirt read, AT YOUR SERVICE, LORD.

"Pastor Neil," he said. His voice was deep, resonant. "Pardon me if I don't shake your hand." He held up his grease-smeared palms. "The plumber I called this morning didn't show up."

"Victoria Stephens," I said. "I'd like to talk to you about your daughter. Is there somewhere more private we should go?"

He leaned against the sink, elbows clamped against his sides, palms up. His eyes were the same as Callie's: dark and piercing. "Anything I have to say I can say in front of my flock. And my God."

The brunette was gone by then, and I glanced around. There was no one else. I said, "I understand you haven't visited her."

"That's correct."

"Is there a reason?"

His greasy hands became tight fists and his eyes narrowed.

I said, "She seems very . . . fragile . . . and I think it might make a difference if she knew you were supportive."

"I cannot condone what she's done."

I knew I needed to make some kind of connection with him to persuade him to visit his daughter. "I don't condone what she did, either," I said, "but when I saw her at the jail, she was intent on talking to you." As an afterthought, I added, "Maybe she wants to ask your forgiveness?"

"It's not me who forgives, Miss Stephens." His hands closed

into fists again and then reopened. "Only the Lord can forgive."

"Okay, but, maybe, at this point, you're the one she wants to see. Perhaps you can help her ask for forgiveness?"

He chewed the inside of his cheek, as though he were scraping off words and pushing them to his tongue. But he didn't speak them.

"I think . . . if you let her know you still care about her, she might open up. She needs to talk to me if I'm going to defend her."

"I *know* what happened—" he began quietly.

He knows? I leaned toward him, poised to hear what he would say, but just then, as if on cue, a group of women burst into the kitchen, chattering and laughing like a flock of noisy birds. Each held some kind of dish in front of her. One in particular, a short, plump woman in a dreary blue dress that hung loosely on her lumpy frame, eyed me closely. The others glanced over and then made themselves quietly busy, turning on stove burners, opening cupboards, and pulling out stacks of plastic plates and cups.

"Time to get organized, Rose?" he called to the woman in the blue dress.

"It is." She turned toward him, her round face beaming. Her eyes disappeared when she smiled, as though she could display teeth or eyes, but not both. "I hope we're not interrupting anything, Pastor Neil."

He picked up a clean rag from the counter, tried wiping his hands again, then folded it carefully before placing it where he'd found it. "This woman was just leaving. And I think I've just about got your sink unclogged." Without so much as a glance in my direction, he lay back down on the floor and his head disappeared inside the cabinet.

"We're hosting a salad luncheon to raise money for an orphanage in India that our church sponsors," the woman named Rose said sweetly. "It costs ten dollars for a ticket. You're welcome to join us if you like."

I couldn't think of anything I'd enjoy less than lunch with a bunch of church women, and now I could only speculate about what Callie's father had wanted to tell me. "Thanks, but no," I told Rose. I gave a final look toward what I could see of him before I left.

On my way out, I passed three men on step ladders talking quietly and hanging a banner from the hallway ceiling. SHALL WE GATHER AT THE RIVER? was hand-painted in flowing blue script. New Life in God was sponsoring an immersion baptism service in the St. Clair River in August. Anyone wishing to be saved was welcome.

I walked beneath the banner. At the end of the corridor I let myself out and listened to the snap of the lock behind me.

EIGHT

THAT SAME NIGHT I SPRAWLED IN MY CORNER CHAIR, still wearing my cream linen suit but minus the four-inch Jimmy Choos I'd kicked off when I walked in, a mixer-sized bowl of buttered popcorn on my lap and a half-full goblet of Sauvignon Blanc on a small table beside me.

I kept picturing Neil Thomas's fists, how they'd clenched and unclenched when we talked. I got that he'd been stunned when he showed up at the hospital and was told his teenage daughter just gave birth. And he must have gotten a second shock when they told him her baby was missing. Still, all that stuff occurred before the baby's body was discovered and before Callie was charged with murder, which meant Neil Thomas made up his mind that day, the day she gave birth, that he wanted nothing more to do with her. Besides the obvious, was there something else that made her father so unforgiving, so angry?

Callie told me they'd been close. What exactly did that mean?

My father and I had been close, at least once I declared my intention to become a lawyer. Dad took me with him to his office during that Christmas holiday, me toting the school library's copy of *Harriet the Spy* that I planned to read while Dad met with his client. After he brought his client back to his office, he didn't close the door. I heard snippets of conversation but didn't pay much attention to them until I heard my father's voice, loud, forceful, and frustrated. "It doesn't add up, Helen. It's like you woke up one morning and said, 'Heads I bake cookies, tails I shoot Arnie.' And Arnie lost the toss." I closed my book and leaned forward to hear the rest of the conversation.

On the drive home along the river that day I'd blurted, "She shot her husband?"

He blinked, as though he'd forgotten I was there, and nodded solemnly. "While he slept. Between the eyes."

"And you don't know why."

"This stuff is privileged, you know," he'd said, so I zipped my lips with my thumb and index finger. Once home, to my surprise, he'd outlined the facts of his case for me as I sat like a statue, hardly daring to breathe. He'd talked about the legal theories he'd considered, and rejected, the cul-de-sacs he'd gone down (after explaining what a cul-de-sac was), the prosecutor's unyielding position, and his own dwindling defenses. I understood very little of what he said, but his voice was soothing. Besides, he'd said so little to me since my mother died the year before that I'd likely have been captivated by anything he told me.

But that night he talked law.

After that, on the rare occasions I was home from St. Anne's, I pestered him to tell me about all his cases. One Sunday afternoon, as I was packing to go back to school, I'd stuffed two of his old law school texts into my duffel. Three months later, when I was home for the weekend, I surprised him by reciting from memory the legal principles in the first ten chapters. My interest in the law quickly evolved into a game the two of us played when we were together.

"Name the six elements that constitute a larceny," he'd say. (*A taking, and carrying away, of tangible personal property, of another, without their consent, with the intent to deprive the owner of it permanently.*)

"What's the difference between an assault and a battery?" (*Assault is defined as placing another in fear of a battery, which is the unwanted physical touching of another.*)

"Explain the Rule in Lord Mansfield's Case." (*The husband of a married woman is presumed to be the father of her child.*)

Nights in my dorm room I preferred reading Dad's casebooks to my regular classwork, not that he would have tolerated anything less than A's on my report cards. By the time I entered St. Anne's ultra-competitive high school, I entertained Dad and his courthouse colleagues by reciting legal definitions and terminology the way my classmates chanted the lyrics to their favorite Bon Jovi or Radiohead hits or, in my best friend Molly's case, the racier poems of Catullus.

Later, as an undergrad, I routinely made the dean's list, and as a freshman at Michigan's law school was invited to join law review. By then, my dad regularly bragged about what a great team the two of us would make, how our criminal defense work would be legendary. But as my second year of law school drew to a close and I was making plans to return to Riverside and help out in Dad's office, Gail phoned. She told me that a couple months earlier Dad developed an aphasia he'd initially blamed on overwork. When she'd finally convinced him to consult a doctor, he was diagnosed with a malignant brain tumor. He hadn't said anything to me because he didn't want to interfere with my studies. "But I think you should know, honey," she said. "I'm so sorry."

Dazed and distraught, I raced through my last final and rushed home, planning to postpone my third year of classes to stay there, take care of Dad, get him through this nightmare. But when I arrived and told him what I'd decided, he exploded. He dressed down Gail because she'd told me and then railed against me. Nothing, absolutely nothing, was to interfere with my law school education. When he finally stopped ranting, he had to gasp for air and his strong hands trembled. Terrified I'd cause more harm if I didn't concede, I promised to return to school in the fall if he agreed to hire a home nurse, follow the dictates of his oncologists, and talk to me every night while I was away.

That summer, I helped out in Dad's office and at home, as much as he would let me, and in the fall I reluctantly returned to school. During our nightly calls, Dad refused to talk about dying and stressed that once he recovered, the two of us would be the greatest father-daughter legal team ever. But by the following spring, he'd lost the ability to speak clearly and to walk without staggering. In October, my bar exam results arrived in the mail, the letter of congratulations, plus the car rental discounts, credit card applications, and computer deals that came with it. Dad was in and out of the hospital by then, so at first, I didn't tell him I'd passed. I wasn't sure I could say the words without breaking down, and I was determined that he not see me cry.

When I finally steeled myself and told him, Dad rallied and ordered me to have his best suit cleaned and pressed so he could move my admission to the bar. With his black pinstripe hanging from his shriveled shoulders and his head covered in post-chemo fuzz, he managed to prop himself on the podium in Osbourne's courtroom and detail the reasons why I was a perfect fit for the profession I'd chosen. His always clear diction was muddled and twice he'd paused, so long that I'd held my breath, my heart breaking, until he continued.

Two weeks later, he died.

My iPhone buzzed; I wiped my eyes, tracked down my purse in the kitchen, checked caller ID, then swiped the screen with a greasy finger. "Hey, Molly."

"You work too damn much."

"That the best you got?"

She giggled, that contagious laugh of hers I can never resist. She's been telling me I work too hard since the first grade, which is when we met. Although we don't see each other often, when she calls to chat she never fails to bring up my long hours and how I don't eat right or get enough sleep.

"How are Jake and the girls?" I said, to distract her.

"Busy, crazy, the usual. Emma's in another play at the community center. Vanessa's working at a nursing home this summer. And Jake's determined to finish that math textbook he's been working on for two years, which means he's like a groundhog: every six weeks he emerges from his den, squints into the light, and then disappears again."

"What are you up to?"

"Finalizing this year's trip. Ten girls and three chaperones, including me, so far. Four chaps if you come along. I was thinking: you could lecture the kids on Roman law, then write off the trip. That's legal, right? *Vivere mement*, Victoria."

"Remember to live."

"Bravo." Molly was the only person I knew who still used our high school Latin, mostly because she'd made a career out of it, teaching classics at a large Catholic girls' high school in Toronto during the academic year and leading tours for her students to Rome and Florence during summer breaks. Her latest invitation wasn't a surprise. For the past several years she'd pestered me to come along as one of her chaperones, but I always turned her down. For starters, I could never leave my practice for two weeks. And though I'd love to see Florence and Rome, my idea of a vacation didn't include hanging out with a bunch of teenage girls.

"When's the last time you took a vacation, Vic?"

"It won't be this summer."

"These girls would love you. They're practically adults; they mostly look after themselves. Plus you can practice your high school Latin," she teased.

My only B in high school had been in Latin class, and Molly never let me forget it. "*Viri sunt viri* and *Stercus accidit?*" I said.

She giggled. "Men are slime, and shit happens. *Quid quid latine dictum sit, altum videtur.*"

"Anything said in Latin sounds profound." It was my turn to laugh.

"Will you at least think about it, Vic?"

"My summer's already spoken for. By a teenager. How's that for irony? The court stuck me with a murder case—a seventeen-year-old charged with drowning her newborn."

"Ouch. That's horrid. Can't you refuse to take it?"

"Nope. Besides, everyone deserves to be represented, no matter what they've done." It sounded like the cliché it was, but that didn't mean I didn't believe it.

"Is this one of *his* files?"

"Yup."

"So . . . you have to deal with the asshole."

"His name is Barrett, Molly."

"He's an ambitious son-of-a bitch with lousy timing."

"That was a long time ago, Molly."

"He dumped you when your father was sick. That makes him a jerk."

"Molly—"

"Okay, okay. But Rome?"

"Not this year, Molly."

She said softly, "I worry about you, Vic."

"I know."

"*Cura te ipsum*, okay?"

Take care of yourself. It wasn't the first time she'd said that to me. "I always do," I said, before pushing the red button on my phone.

Back in my chair, I finished my popcorn and downed a first then a second glass of wine while I gazed at the river. Molly was my closest friend at St. Anne's during all twelve years of boarding school. Unlike me, she'd continued to be a serious Catholic, attending morning mass and making novenas whenever things got tough. I knew I'd disappointed her at times, like when I chose not to have a Catholic funeral for my dad. Still, that didn't keep her from kneeling beside me at the seawall when I rinsed the last of his ashes from my fingers. And afterward, she stuck around to cook for me and make sure I'd be okay before she headed back to Toronto.

A few weeks later, when I was clearing up Dad's estate, I'd phoned Molly to tell her I'd found my mother's death certificate among his papers. He'd always maintained her drowning was an accident, but the document in his safe deposit box listed her cause of death as suicide. Over the next several days, Molly spent hours on the phone with me, trying to help me make sense of things. In the end she convinced me that Dad thought he was protecting me by hiding the truth.

I poured myself a third glass of wine, then slouched in my seat and watched the buoy on the north side of my tiny peninsula flash its single red light. Years ago, Molly christened this navigational mark. "Sister Phillip Ignatius can look after you when I'm not here," she'd declared before she moved to Toronto to marry Jake.

Sister Ignatius had been a crotchety but fair-minded old nun, the principal at St. Anne's. Now she swayed, a sort of nod, then opened her single red eye and closed it as a lone sailboat pushed upriver, its mast light bobbing high above the water. Across the river, a Canadian power plant glowed yellow against a black sky. Steam rose above the warm water flushed into the chilly river from the plant's coal-fired furnaces. During the day, hordes of gulls would circle above the discharge, mewing like cats as they swooped and dove for the small fish gathered there.

I drained my glass as my thoughts drifted back to Callie's father. Was he overly strict? Unreasonable?

My own dad set high standards for me, not only in my classes but in my dress, my grammar, and my manners. He often reminded me that people were judging me, not just as his daughter but as myself. Sometimes I complained, but I didn't mind, not really. If he didn't criticize me, how would I have known he cared? Back then, I was desperate to please him, to make him proud of me.

Had Callie been doing the same thing?

NINE

THE SECOND TIME I WENT TO SEE CALLIE, A DIFFERENT CREW was in the park. One woman held a poster board that read, CHIL-DREN ARE GOD'S WAY OF SAVING THE WORLD, and her companions seemed to be praying, their eyes closed, their lips mouthing words I couldn't hear. They paid no attention to me, but their presence was irritating.

Meanwhile, the jail lobby was the usual stew of thick, smelly air. The booth deputy said Art was busy, so I waited on the plastic couch, feeling increasingly like the spaghetti dinner I'd tried to make the night before, a sticky blob I'd thrown in the garbage before settling for a bologna sandwich washed down with two glasses of Chianti.

When I was finally admitted to Art's office, he apologized for making me wait. "Damage control." He pointed to my usual chair. "You know Eddie Larson?"

Everybody knew Eddie. He was a blowhard Detroit lawyer who bragged that he only took cases in St. Clair County if he got paid an obscene amount of money. His patent wingtips, shiny suits, brusque manner, and brash courtroom style didn't impress the local lawyers. "I know Eddie. Why?"

"Last night around eleven, he rolls in here and insists on meeting with his newest client. My guys tell him visiting hours are over. Eddie throws a fit, threatens to wake up a judge and get a court order if we don't let him in. Apparently it was a zoo in here, a slew of mean drunks plus a boating accident on the river, so we were even more short-staffed than usual. Anyways, eventually my guys let Eddie see his client but tell him he'll have to meet the guy in his cell because they don't have time to escort him and his client to the conference room. Which, I'm told, Eddie agrees to. Since he's not a local, my guys frisk him, hang onto his cell phone and brief-case, and take him back." Art's upper lip curled.

I saw where this was going and grinned.

"Claims he hollered, but my people never heard him. Eddie tells his client to make some noise, too, but the guy ignores him and crawls into his own bed. Around one thirty, Eddie gives up, climbs into the only empty cot in the cell. Used his cashmere sport coat for a pillow."

I was laughing now, big snorts that matched Art's. He wiped his eyes with a brown bandana he extracted from his hip pocket. "Course Eddie was madder than hell this morning, threatening to sue the county for false imprisonment and see to it that everyone on duty last night gets fired. Plus me. I told him not to do me any favors. He might get an apology from the sheriff, but that'd be it. Still, we're covering our bases. I've been taking statements and photos of the quote, unquote, crime scene, since six this morning."

He gestured toward one of several stacks of loose papers on his desk. "The sheriff wants a full-fledged investigation of everybody who was anywhere near this jail last night. Including the prisoners. I haven't even had lunch. And I'm getting too damn old for shit like this." He paused, took a breath. "So, I assume you're here to see your girl?"

"As long as you let me out when I'm finished."

He smirked. "Making progress?"

"Sure."

"The press getting to you?"

"Me? Heavens no," I said. But four of the twenty-three new

emails I'd gotten that morning were from reporters looking for a story about her case. It was far too early to make a statement. I still hadn't decided whether I had a defense or what it would be.

"Well, other than a few nightmares, your girl's behaving."

"How's that?"

"The night matron says she cries out in her sleep. Wakes up the women in the other cells, she yells so loud."

"Has Dad been here?"

"Nope. Besides you, her only visitors have been the youth pastor from her church and some lady came by yesterday to drop off a Bible." He raised his eyebrows. "Seems a little late for that."

"You mind sharing their names?"

Art shuffled through one of the stacks. "I've got 'em here someplace." He slid a spiral notebook from the pile and opened it. "Here they are. Got a pen?"

Callie faced me, an improvement from the last time I was here. Her feet hung over the edge of the single metal bed in her cell. An open Bible was on her lap, but she didn't appear to be reading it. When she saw me, she closed it and laid it beside her on the cot, then patted its cover with her hand.

"He didn't come," she said as soon as Art was gone. It felt like an accusation. "I thought maybe he would. He must be really angry." She began tracing an imaginary design on the pant leg of her orange scrubs with an index finger. Some kind of large flower, a tulip maybe. Or a bird.

"Callie?"

"Yes?" She raised her finger, touched her chin.

"You said if I spoke to your father, you'd talk to me."

She tapped her chin with a finger.

"Let's start with what's called the attorney-client privilege."

She was looking past me, over my left ear, at nothing in particular.

"What that means is that I can never tell anyone what you say. Not unless you first give me permission. The reason for that is so you can tell me the whole truth about what happened. You with me so far?"

She nodded.

"I was hired by the county to defend you. I'm here to help you. Okay?"

Another nod.

"I need you to tell me what happened back in April."

She sat up taller, touched the tips of her fingers together.

I said, "Okay, I'll start. There's a DNA test that establishes that the infant's body that was found in the river was yours. Do you know what a DNA test is?"

She pushed her fingers together, then her palms. "We studied those in biology class. The police use them to solve crimes." Her voice was distant, dreamy.

"Right. DNA testing is pretty reliable. Conclusive even. What's also conclusive is that you gave birth on April fifth, two weeks before your baby's body was found."

She resumed her tracing.

"I want to help you, but I can't do this by myself, Callie. You have to talk to me."

Her fingers stopped moving. She said slowly, "A policeman said I had a baby boy. And that I took him to the river and drowned him. But I didn't."

"Okay . . . I don't want you to tell me what the police said. I want you to tell me what you remember."

She was quiet for a long time, and I felt her drift away, like an untethered rowboat.

"Callie?"

"What?"

"I need to know what you remember."

"I woke up in the hospital. I went to live with Pastor Craig and Rebecca."

"That was later. After the baby was born."

Nothing.

"Callie, you passed out in the girls' bathroom at school. You were bleeding. They called an ambulance. Do you remember any of this?"

"The police said I took a baby to the river."

"Did you?"

She leaned forward, raised her knees to her chin, became a hunched orange ball. Her head moved slowly back and forth.

I said, "The morning, that morning, when you gave birth, was anyone else with you at the parsonage?"

She raised her head, squinted, and shook it from side to side. "I didn't have a baby."

"A girlfriend maybe? A boy?"

Nothing.

"Callie, somehow he got to the river. And he was wrapped in one of your bedsheets."

Silence.

I inhaled the thick air and felt sweat beading along my upper lip. "When you got pregnant—"

"I wasn't pregnant."

"You can't have a baby without being pregnant, Callie."

"I wasn't pregnant." Soft but defiant.

I shook my head, decided to change topics. "Who is Rose Walker?" Art said she'd delivered Callie's Bible.

"Nobody. A lady who goes to our church."

"And your youth pastor is Craig Arnold?" The other name Art gave me.

"Why?"

"And you lived with Craig and his wife? After the hospital discharged you?"

"Rebecca. That's Craig's wife."

"Did you tell them, either of them, anything about what happened to you?"

She flipped open her Bible and ran her finger down a random page, then looked up, but not at me, squinted. "There was nothing to tell."

I rubbed the back of my neck and checked the time, made a quick calculation. I'd been away from my office nearly two hours. Callie had yet to tell me anything I didn't know. "Do you remember anything about the birth? Or that morning? Anything at all?"

No response.

I dug in my purse, found one of my business cards and scribbled my cell phone number on it. "If you think of anything, ask to use a phone here and call me. Any time."

She took the card and laid it on the cot beside her.

On the way to my car, I remembered that the woman I met in the church kitchen a few days earlier was named Rose. *Was she the same Rose who delivered Callie's Bible?* Callie said she was no one special. *While you're at it, Victoria, why not interview every member of her father's megachurch?* I mentally crossed Rose Walker off my list and turned the corner. As I did, one of the women in the park hollered, "We're praying for you, Counselor!"

I grimaced and climbed inside my car, then slammed the door, hard. I wanted to know exactly what occurred at the parsonage that April morning. Unless the prayers of these women could make that happen, they needed to leave me the hell alone.

Flipping the AC lever to maximum, I shoved my favorite Adele

CD in the player, revved the engine, and shot out of the lot, weaving through slower traffic on the highway that crested the riverbank.

How could she not know she was pregnant? Or that she gave birth? Was that even possible?

Below me, on the river, the lake freighter *Lee Tregurtha* pushed a bow wave as it worked its way up the shipping channel toward Lake Huron. Alongside the freighter's ochre hull, a kid skipped his Sea-Doo, hopping waves like he didn't have a care in the world. I'd never seen the boy on the Sea-Doo before, but it occurred to me that I knew as much about him as I did Callie. Which was nothing.

TEN

GAIL WAS FINISHING A SANDWICH AT HER DESK WHEN I got back to the office. She said, "I had a slow morning so I read parts of that new file. And I've got a question." She balled up her lunch bag and tossed it into the wastebasket beside her desk. "When my oldest had Marissa, her cervix didn't close because some of Marissa's placenta got stuck. She never got out of the operating room before she started bleeding. She lost so much blood so quickly she almost died. Your girl gets herself cleaned up, gets rid of the baby, and drives herself to high school. But no one finds any traces of blood besides in the school bathroom?"

"You're saying there should have been a trail of blood?"

She shrugged. "I only know what I know."

Back in my office, I googled a couple of websites that explained birth complications. It was unusual for a woman to seem fine following a birth and later experience cramping and bleeding, but it wasn't unheard of. I called my ob-gyn up in Port Huron, a former classmate of mine at St. Anne's.

"It happens," Susan Hart said, after we exchanged pleasantries and I asked my question. "It's more likely to occur with an older mother or a mother who's given birth multiple times. I had one of those cases a while ago. A patient called complaining she was cramping a month after she'd birthed. By the time she got to my office, she was hemorrhaging. I followed the ambulance to Port Huron General and performed an emergency D&C. Sure enough, I found the tiniest piece of placenta stuck to her uterus."

"As far as I know, this was a first birth."

"It's still possible. I read in the *Sentinel* that the docs performed a D&C on her."

"You've been following this case?"

"Who hasn't?"

Craig Arnold's smiling face and cell phone number were prominently posted on New Life in God's website. That same afternoon, I phoned him and explained who I was. "I understand you've been visiting Callie at the jail. And that she lived with you this past April?"

"Excuse me," he said to someone, and I heard a door close. He said softly, "*With my wife and me*, that's correct."

"I'd like to ask you a few questions." I didn't know what, if anything he knew that would be helpful, but I knew it was easy for a potential witness to blow me off over the phone. I wanted to talk with him in person. "I'm happy to stop by the church—"

"That's not a good idea," he said quickly.

"It won't take long. I'm gathering information for Callie's case—"

"What is it you want?"

"Perhaps you could come to my office. It's not far." When he didn't answer, I offered, "Or we could meet someplace else, like a restaurant."

There was a dramatic pause, so long that I thought he might have hung up on me.

"Hello?" I finally said.

"There's a coffee shop on River Road just north of Algonac. River Brews and Views. You know the place?"

An out-of-the way dive that wasn't likely to be busy on a sweltering summer afternoon. "Sure," I said. "When?"

"I'll be there in fifteen minutes."

The single redeeming feature of Brews and Views was a gigantic window that showcased the river. Unfortunately, that afternoon cobwebs shadowed both sides of the glass. When I entered, a couple of other customers sat at a dingy counter near the entrance, but all six booths were vacant. I found one that looked reasonably clean, sat down, and positioned Dad's Waterman beside my legal pad on the red linoleum table. A waitress appeared beside me with a mug and two coffee pots, and I pointed to the one with the orange lid.

A few minutes later, the wiry, thirty-something man in the website photo scanned the room and nodded in my direction. His face was boyish and his head shaved; a tiny diamond adorned his left earlobe. Before he sat, I offered him one of my business cards, which he dropped in the pocket of his rumpled Oxford shirt without a glance.

"Thanks for coming, Reverend."

"It's Pastor. Or just Craig."

He ordered decaf from the waitress, then turned back toward me. Elbows on the table, he straightened his index fingers and tapped them together, reminding me of a game Molly and I played years ago. "Here's the church. Here's the steeple."

He stopped tapping. "I shouldn't be here. This . . . situation . . . is difficult for our entire church. Pastor Neil is very well liked, well respected."

"How long have you known the Thomas family?"

"God called me to New Life four, no, three years this November. That's when I met Neil. And Callie."

"You're the church youth pastor?"

"Right."

"But you've been visiting Callie at the jail?"

"I see others, too," he said. "My job description reads youth pastor, but when Pastor Neil's schedule gets crazy, I take on the jail ministry for him. And whatever else I can do to help out."

The waitress plunked down a mug in front of him and poured from the pot with the brown lid. "Cream's on the table," she said, and refilled my mug with the other pot.

"Callie lived with you and your wife for a couple weeks last April. How did that come about?"

He blew across the surface of his coffee, took a sip. "It wasn't my idea. I was at church. Rebecca said Callie called in hysterics, so she drove to the hospital to try and calm her down. One thing led to another, and Callie ended up at our house."

"Her father refused to let her come back to the parsonage?"

"That's what I was told."

"Did he object to Callie staying with you?"

"I don't think he was thrilled, but he didn't say anything."

"She was arrested while she lived with you?"

"That's correct."

"Do you think Neil Thomas knew his daughter was pregnant?"

"I'm sure he didn't."

"What makes you say that?"

"Neil adored Callie. He bragged about her all the time, made sure everyone knew what a good daughter she was. She and her friend Stella even started a chapter of the Chastity Club at our church."

I blinked. "What's that?"

"The members publicly take an oath to remain a virgin until marriage. There's a candlelight ceremony for the girl and parents of anyone who joins. It's a pretty big deal."

"And Callie started the club?"

"With her friend Stella. They used to talk to girls in the community about their choice and try to convince them to do the same."

I made a few notes. "Do you know why her father refused to post her bond?"

"I can't speak to that." He took another sip of his coffee.

"Did you offer her a place at your home after she was arrested?"

"When Callie was with us earlier, reporters snooped around, talked to the neighbors, knocked on our door at all hours." He fingered the diamond stud in his ear. "Plus, two weeks before Rebecca invited Callie to stay with us, we found out Rebecca was pregnant. She'd already had one miscarriage, and our doctor told her to avoid stressful situations. So, no. I put my foot down on her coming back."

"Did Callie ever tell you she was pregnant? Or that she'd been pregnant?"

"Neither."

"Did she ever mention anything about giving birth?"

He shook his head. "Rebecca said she mostly stayed in her room. I was at church a lot those days. Our people were looking for answers, and I was trying to help, so I got home pretty late most nights. I think Callie mostly showed up for meals and prayers."

"Does Neil Thomas know you see Callie at the jail?"

"He doesn't ask, and I don't mention it."

"Before this . . . event . . . were you or your wife close to Callie?"

He tilted his head to one side and squinted. "Close? Callie was in the youth group, so she and I spent time together. A lot of our women mothered Callie back then, including Rebecca."

Back then. I pictured those women outside the jail with their damning signs. "Did Callie confide in Rebecca?"

"Rebecca said they talked, but she never mentioned anything special."

"How about friends? Who did Callie hang around with?"

"Mostly Stella Kohler. And the Girls' Club members."

I made a note. "Where does Stella live?"

"Maxwell Road, I think that's the name of it. Not far from the parsonage. She and Callie used to ride the school bus together."

"Did Callie have a boyfriend?"

"Neil didn't approve of her dating. He said she was too young."

"He told you that?"

"Sure." He took a large swig of his coffee.

"Do you have any idea *how* Callie might have gotten pregnant?"

"Besides the obvious? What Callie tells me when I meet with her at the jail is confidential, but I *can* say we've never discussed it."

"Is there anyone you think could be the baby's father?"

"If I knew I'd be the first in line with the rope." He glanced at his wristwatch. "I should be getting back."

"I only have a couple more questions. Where were you early in the morning of April fifth? The morning of the birth?"

"Rebecca and I picked up Pastor Neil at the parsonage and drove him to our weekly church breakfast meeting."

"What time was that?"

"Just before seven."

"Your wife attended this meeting, too?"

"Rebecca helps manage our church thrift shop. She gives reports on that ministry."

"Do you usually drive Neil Thomas to these breakfast meetings?"

"No. But he said Callie was tired of being the oldest kid on the bus, so he'd been letting her drive to school. Rebecca and I only live a mile from the parsonage, so it was no trouble for us to give him a lift." He glanced at his watch again.

"Can I call you if I think of anything else?" I said.

He patted the pocket that held my business card. "How about I call you?" He laid a five-dollar bill on the table, slid wordlessly from the booth, and left.

ELEVEN

TWO DAYS LATER, I PARKED IN FRONT OF A TIRED STOREFRONT in downtown Port Huron. The city's business district had been hemorrhaging stores since the big mall north of town opened ten years before, and the once-thriving area was lined with vacant buildings, most of which displayed FOR RENT or FOR SALE signs in their windows. But Second Chances was open for business, so I walked inside. "Hello?" I called out when I saw no one around.

A short, blonde woman emerged from the back, her arms loaded with hangers of clothes. She hefted the pile on top of a glass and chrome display case that held costume jewelry, leather purses, and shoes.

"Good morning and welcome," she exhaled. "Can I help you find something?"

"I'm looking for Mrs. Arnold."

"You found me."

I extended my hand. "Victoria Stephens. I'm defending Callie Thomas. I spoke with your husband—"

She froze and reflexively curled an arm around what I now saw was an obviously pregnant stomach. "He told me."

"I'd like to ask you a few questions." I retrieved a small notepad and the Waterman from my purse. "I won't keep you long. I'm just trying to get to know who Callie was, what she was like, that sort of thing, before—"

"I don't really know who Callie was." She pulled a box of tags and a pen from the cabinet and inspected a dress on the top of her pile.

"She called you from the hospital when her father wouldn't let her come home?"

"That's right."

"And you drove over and picked her up?"

She laid her pen on the glass case, sighed. "When we first moved here, my husband was always at church. I'd worked retail to put myself though college, so I volunteered to get this shop up and running. Callie used to help me out. She sounded so upset when she phoned, I didn't know what else to do."

"So you'd spent some time together? Before all this happened?"

"I felt sorry for her because she'd lost her mom before they moved here. I thought I could be a sort of big sister to her. That we could share secrets. When I miscarried two years ago, I told her what happened. She brought me flowers and a cheeseburger." She smiled wistfully.

"Did she tell you she was pregnant?"

"No."

"You had no idea?"

"None."

"Did she have a boyfriend?"

"Not that I ever knew. I used to tell her she'd find her handsome prince someday. A man like my Craig."

"When Callie was in your home, did she say anything about her pregnancy or giving birth?"

"No."

"Did she tell you what happened to the baby?"

"The only time she spoke was during prayers."

"Did you ask her where her baby was?"

"I wanted to. But Craig was so worried about me. And I was afraid."

"Of what?"

"Of finding out what really happened."

Gail found Archie Kohler's name and address in a Port Huron phone directory, so when I left the thrift shop, I followed my GPS directions to an address on Maxwell Road. The name *Kohler* was stenciled in black on a silver mailbox. A long gravel drive led to a double-wide plunked in the middle of what was once a farm field. The grass surrounding the home was stubbled and brown, and the front porch was a concrete slab on which sat a black vinyl and chrome kitchen chair.

I knocked and a heavy woman with puffy grey hair opened an inside door. She spoke through a cloudy screen. "Yes?"

"My name is Victoria Stephens. I'm representing Callie Thomas." I dug for a business card in my purse and held it up, but the woman didn't move. "I'd like to speak with Stella. Are you her mother?"

"What's this about?"

"May I come inside?"

"Here is fine." She reached forward and locked the screen door, then refolded her arms across her broad chest.

"I'd just like to ask her a few questions."

"Stella doesn't want anything to do with Callie."

"If I could just speak with her—"

"She doesn't want to talk to you, either." I saw movement behind her, but the woman moved in front of whoever was there.

"Stella?" I blurted, but the door closed.

TWELVE

"YOU NEED TO SEE THIS ONE, BOSS."

Gail tossed the latest issue of *People* on my desk. Her fascination with tabloids and television gossip shows was an on-again, off-again battle between us. Apparently, Dad never questioned the periodicals she chose to order and display in his office. But when I took over the practice, I instructed her to cancel our subscriptions to *Us Weekly* and *People*. They didn't fit the image I wanted to project.

At the time she didn't argue with me, but I noticed that the magazines continued to appear. When I confronted her a second time, she'd simply said, "I'm paying for these subscriptions," as though cost was my ultimate concern.

"That's not the point," I'd persisted. "They're trashy and gossipy and I don't like seeing them here."

"It helps clients to know other people have troubles, too," she said, as though that settled the matter.

I'd continued to raise the issue every so often, and finally Gail made the tiny concession of placing her tabloid collection on the edge of her desk rather than displaying them on the tables with the *Newsweek*s and *New Yorker*s I subscribed to.

Now she said, "Maybe you should have taken that reporter's calls," when I reached for the magazine.

On the cover, a picture of Callie was juxtaposed beside a photo of Suri Cruise and Katie Holmes. Orange caps that barked KILLER

TEEN? were splashed beneath what looked like Callie's yearbook photo. In this picture, Callie's dark eyes appeared sweetly innocent, her sleek blonde hair cascaded in front of her shoulders, and she looked much older, like a serious student, not the baby-faced kid I'd been visiting at the county jail. At least I could be grateful this wasn't a mug shot; I'd yet to see one of those that didn't make a defendant look guilty. Unfortunately, the article inside was replete with comments from Riverside's mayor, the local Methodist minister, and two women from Callie's father's church, all of whom obviously thought stoning was too good for Callie.

"Shit," I said, when I finished reading.

"That reporter called six times last week."

"And what exactly was I supposed to tell him? This damn case." I tossed the magazine back to Gail and said, "Get George Deering on the phone for me, will you? I want to pick his brain."

"That'll be a short conversation." She flipped her braid over her shoulder as she headed back to her desk.

George yawned into the phone. "Hey, Victoria. The Tigers got hot in the ninth last night. Extra innings. I stayed with it to the bitter end. You catch the game?"

"I called to talk about the girl."

"The Yankees drilled one in the twelfth. Actually, you didn't miss much." He yawned again, louder this time. "You mean the Thomas girl, I assume."

"Right."

Another obnoxious yawn in my ear. I punched the speaker button and plunked the phone on its stand.

"The 'killer teen'?"

"I know what the media calls her. I need to know what you found out."

In Defense of Good Women　　　65

"Well, let's see. The kid was an honor student, a Sunday school teacher. Before this."

"Any motive?"

"No clue. You probably heard she wouldn't talk to me. It was like last year when I cut up my wife's American Express card. Did I ever tell you about that? Marsha didn't speak to me for six weeks. Made up a bed for me in the guest room. You know what she bought? A seventy-five-dollar dress for our granddaughter. Megan's two. Two. What two-year-old needs a seventy-five-dollar dress?"

"There was no confession—"

"My wife never apologizes."

"The *girl*, George."

"Oh, *her*." George snorted. "No. No."

"I see you asked for a competency exam." I shuffled through the file, found the petition and yanked it free.

"Oh, yeah. CYA, you know," George continued. "That sure backfired."

"Because?"

"Well, the shrink says she's sane, so naturally I petition for an actual hearing, bring in the state's doc. You know all those TV attorneys who criticize those of us out here slogging in the trenches? I'm not sure some of them even graduated from a real law school. The *nicer* ones called me crazy. You didn't hear about this?"

Plenty of local lawyers had mentioned that George's tactic bordered on malpractice. "How about you give me your version?" I said.

"Well, at the hearing, the state's psychologist said plenty that's not in his report. Like, she's malingering. Said he watched her in his lobby through a two-way mirror before he talked to her. Saw her chatting with a boy who came in. He couldn't hear what they were saying, but he said she seemed to be friendly enough. But when she got in his office, she clammed up.

"The know-it-all press says, 'What was that guy thinking when he brought in the doctor?' 'Why didn't he just leave well enough alone when he got the report?' The media is like a dog with a bone on this one. A *rabid* dog." He took a breath. "The thing is, I wanted to help her. She wouldn't let me."

I made a note. *Malingering?* "Did you talk to her dad?"

"Nope. Finally I decided I needed all this bad publicity from an appointed case like I needed another hole in the head."

"Did you find out who the baby's father was?"

"Does it matter?"

"It might. What if he were complicit in the baby's murder?"

"For all I know this was a virgin birth."

"And you waived the prelim?" I'd been stunned when I saw George's signature on the form in the file. No one ever waived the prelim in a big case like this.

"Less bone for the dogs to chew."

"Any reason you didn't petition to suppress the autopsy?"

"Never occurred to me."

Weeks before, I'd read the *Sentinel*'s article summarizing the baby's autopsy. The condition of the newborn's body had been described in graphic detail. As if finding twelve unbiased jurors in this county wasn't challenging enough, I'd have to find twelve citizens who wouldn't already know every sickening detail about the baby's death. I pinched my lips with my fingertips to keep from saying what I was thinking: that a first-semester law student would have filed a petition to keep the baby's autopsy out of the papers.

Damn George. He never bothered. And then he waved the prelim? I knew getting angry at George wouldn't solve a thing, but still. Damn George.

"If there's nothing else, Victoria, I gotta run. I'm due in court," he said and hung up.

I drummed my desk with the Waterman and considered what

seemed to be my increasingly dwindling options. I'd had no success in finding out what happened at the parsonage the morning of April fifth. I needed more than a hope that Stella Kohler knew something helpful in order to get a warrant to force her to talk to me. And neither Craig nor Rebecca Arnold had said anything useful.

I thought about filing a Change of Venue motion, getting Callie's case moved to a different county. But Change of Venue motions were almost always denied; my dad used to say they just brought more attention to already notorious cases. And even if Osbourne granted a change, how likely was that to make a difference in the ultimate outcome? From what I'd seen so far, the evidence was, and would be, overwhelming, no matter where Callie's trial took place.

I drew a series of lines across a legal pad as I mulled over my choices. The afternoon before, in the county clerk's office, I'd overheard one of the women tell a co-worker that a conviction in Callie's case was the crux of Barrett's judicial campaign. Although, when Barrett announced his candidacy two months ago, I'd written his campaign a hefty check. Shouldn't that give me some clout with him, some influence? If I could convince him to focus his campaign on something other than this murder case—maybe get him to publicize his record of service in this county and all those other convictions he'd secured over the years—maybe he'd consent to adjourn this trial until after the election.

Or maybe I could persuade Barrett to let Callie plead to some lesser offense, a deal he and I could both accept. Then we could wait until the election was over to make our agreement public. Meanwhile, Barrett could keep up his tough guy image during the campaign.

More maybes. But what else did I have?

I scribbled:

Plan A: Convince Barrett to agree to adjourn Callie's trial until after the election.

Plan B: See what Barrett will give me to make this go away.

THIRTEEN

THE FOLLOWING AFTERNOON, I JOINED A BEVY OF DEFENSE lawyers in a small room at the courthouse. Part of the conglomeration of tiny rooms in the back halls of the old building, the space doubled as a pretrial conference room when not in use during jury deliberations. I was there to plea bargain a larceny case, but I also hoped to speak privately to Barrett once everyone else finished their business. While we waited for Barrett to show up, a couple of colleagues asked how my murder case was progressing. I deferred, said it was too soon to tell. I needed to keep a low profile if I wanted Barrett to quietly deal this file.

When Barrett strode in, his arms loaded with red files, the room hushed. I noticed he'd put on a few pounds since the start of his campaign. Because he's tall and broad-shouldered, he could handle the extra weight; it softened the edges of his prominent jaw and made him look more judicial. He was still as handsome as ever, just more distinguished these days. He'd always had a face the voters would trust, one they had trusted when they first elected him as the county's chief prosecutor eleven years ago and reelected him six years after that.

"Time for 'Let's Make a Deal,'" he said, and lowered the stack to the table where it spread like a deck of slippery playing cards.

A heavily pregnant Joyce Ballinger stood and tossed her empty Big Gulp cup into a nearby wastebasket. She leaned over slowly and pulled one from the splayed mess while other lawyers hovered nearby, searching for the files they needed. "That the best you can do?" she quizzed Barrett. "My gal has no priors."

Barrett said, "Your gal held up a liquor store with a shotgun. Priors have nothing to do with it."

One of the male lawyers snickered; Joyce shot him a hormonal "Don't mess with me" look, and his smile wilted.

Meanwhile, I found my client's file and opened it. Scrawled inside was an offer to plead to a misdemeanor—a sweet deal Barrett didn't need to give me. I slid the file across the table to Barrett, nodded, and he filled out a plea form, signed, and slid it back. I strode to the hall, told my client, and we joined the queue in the busy courtroom to put the agreement on the record.

By four thirty I was back in the conference room, listening to Joyce make a last-ditch effort to convince Barrett her client was an otherwise good girl who got mixed up with the wrong crowd. When Joyce surrendered, snapped at Barrett to set her case for trial, and stormed out, he looked at me and rolled his eyes.

"Walk you to your office?" I asked.

"Sure." He gathered what was left of his files, and we strolled through the courthouse lobby. Except for a couple of teenaged boys loitering on the brass county seal imbedded in the granite floor, the place was empty.

We climbed the stairs and reached the landing. Barrett pointed to a long wooden bench, so I dropped my briefcase and sat. He sat down a few feet away, surveyed the empty staircase, then turned back to face me. "How've you been?"

"Never better. You?"

"My life is off-the-charts crazy," he said. "Trying to manage the press in this murder case on top of the campaign. And Tate's first football scrimmage is tonight. He's starting center on the varsity team. You'd think it was the Super Bowl." He chuckled. "I can't believe he's sixteen." He shook his head, looked away. "Plus Melissa's pregnant again."

"Congratulations," I said quietly.

"It was a surprise. But we're okay with it." He looked out the tall window facing the water. Upriver, a lake freighter pushed through the rushing water beneath the bridge. "So, Counselor." He turned back, all business. "How can I help you?"

"I need a deal in the Thomas case. It must be a distraction with all you've got going."

"That's true. But that doesn't mean I can deal it."

"She's only seventeen. Murder One is—"

"Have you read the investigators' reports?"

"Of course—"

"Then you should understand my position. Murder is murder."

"This is me you're talking to, Barrett. Me," I said, more calmly than I felt. "You could give me a break. It's an appointed case." I took a breath. "And I've got a suggestion. How about you play tough during your campaign, but you give me a deal quietly, on the side? We won't make anything public until after the election."

He said, "You know I've always tried to work with you, Vic. Help you, help me. But honestly, things aren't going too great with this campaign. For starters, I've spent all our savings on it, not that we had much to begin with. Remember that cottage my aunt left me in Canada? Even that's mortgaged to the hilt. My dad may have been just a fisherman, but he never owed anybody any money. He'd turn over in his grave if he knew how far I'm in hock." He shook his head. "Today's *Sentinel* says Jim Anderson is ahead in the polls. Sonofabitch is the new savior around here. He's the star at every prayer breakfast in the county."

"You can't sacrifice this kid's life to win an election—"

"That's not what I'm doing. Look at the reports. Even you must have trouble defending her."

"I'd take Involuntary Manslaughter with a sentence cap."

"You're not serious."

"Okay then, do me a small favor, Barrett. Stipulate to postpone the trial until after the election."

He lowered his chin, and his green eyes dazzled in the light from the big window. "I'd like to help you, Victoria. But I can't. Not this case. The paper's still moaning that I waited too long to arrest the girl. Like it's a crime I made sure I had a body before I issued the warrant."

"The *Sentinel* runs your office these days?"

His face tightened. "Anyway, you know how Osbourne is. He won't adjourn anything. And if the defendant's in jail, living off the county dime, forget it."

He was right about that. Osbourne perpetually spouted off about how much it cost to house someone in what he called "the county's largest bed and breakfast."

"I'm sure he'd make an exception if both you and I agreed—" I paused as Judy Solomon, a district judge resembling a large dumpling, walked by, nodding at the two of us.

"Judge." We spoke in unison as she passed. Judy's orthopedic black shoes squeaked on each step and continued across the lobby floor until she pushed through the revolving front door.

"I can't put this trial off. I'm sorry, Victoria." He stood.

"But Barrett—"

"I have to go. Tate's game's in Flint. I promised Melissa we'd get there before kickoff." Before I could say anything more, he hustled up the steps and was gone.

At five o'clock, I was still sitting on that bench as the county employees, notorious clock watchers, filed out of offices and streamed down the stairs. Most ignored me, but a few waved or called to me on their way past. I followed the last of them to the parking lot.

On the drive back to my office, I passed two billboards pro-

In Defense of Good Women 73

moting Barrett's election bid. It occurred to me that my campaign donation probably paid for both of them and maybe a couple of others somewhere in the county as well. TOUGH JUSTICE, one read. PROTECTING THE HELPLESS, said the other. On both, Barrett was larger than life, smiling sincerely, Melissa and their two boys beside him.

That night I pulled a half-empty bottle of pricey French Burgundy from my fridge to drink with the club sandwich I picked up from the grocery store deli. While I ate, I dissected my encounter with Barrett. I hadn't expected him to be a pushover, but I'd been sure he'd work with me; we'd figure out a reasonable solution, one that'd be good for both of us. Maybe I should have begun our discussion by promising I'd arrange for Callie to start counseling so we could all get some insight into what happened. But when he'd been so rigid, I'd been stunned, unable to recover. Damn.

An ocean-going salty headed downriver, toward the swampy flats, a heavy rope ladder hanging from its bow. Under maritime law, there had to be a designated river pilot on board for this leg of the trip, someone to assist the foreign captain through the tricky channels and marshy places, a pilot who'd climbed the ladder in Port Huron and would depart to a waiting skiff in the Detroit River. Last summer when the river was high, I'd watched a salty and a lake freighter collide. Their bows screeched metal and sparks flew as they bounced against and receded from one another, then continued on. A few days later, I'd read in the *Sentinel* that the freighter captain had been trying to keep from making a wake that would push the already high river water above the seawalls, like the one that protects my cottage. He'd slowed so much he lost control of the ship's steerage.

Barrett's inflexibility was something I'd experienced only once before, years ago. As the lights on the stern of the salty diminished in the night, I topped off my glass of wine and sat in the darkness. I needed a new plan.

FOURTEEN

I WOKE AT DAWN IN MY CORNER CHAIR, MY SILK SUIT rumpled and skewed, a wine glass in my lap and the empty bottle on its side beneath my bare foot.

A horn blew softly and thirty seconds later sounded again, this time louder. A thick blanket of marine fog enveloped my cottage, obscuring the river. As the approaching freighter continued its blasts, I became aware of a personal fog, one brought on by too much alcohol and what I recognized was resentment. Despite my aching head and queasy stomach, I was still furious at Barrett for his dismissive treatment of me the day before.

After a hot shower, I downed four Extra Strength Tylenol, and around nine thirty, slid past Gail on the way to my office kitchen where I finished two cups of strong black coffee. At my desk, I answered some client emails and then, as my fog faded, retrieved Callie's file from my credenza. I fiddled with the stylus of Dad's Waterman and tried to recall everything I'd ever heard or read about infanticide.

There was a novel by George Eliot I'd read in undergrad English Lit class: *Adam Bede.* I didn't recall much about the story— something about a young girl who was hanged for killing her newborn. I poured myself another cup of strong coffee and logged onto my computer to search for information about three more recent infanticide cases I'd heard about.

The Prom Mom: Melissa Drexler was a high school senior who hid her pregnancy and gave birth inside a stall in the girls' bathroom at her high school on prom night. She'd stuffed the baby's body in a garbage can and returned to dance with the baby's father. She'd pled to aggravated manslaughter and was sentenced to fifteen years.

Susan Smith drowned her two toddlers in a pond when a man she wanted to marry told her he had no interest in being with a woman with children. She was serving a life sentence for the murders.

Andrea Yates, who drowned her five children in a bathtub, had an obvious preexisting mental illness. A jury found her Guilty but Mentally Ill and the judge sentenced her to life in prison.

I tapped the pen on my cheek and considered, then reconsidered. What did all this mean, if anything, for my case? I'd subpoenaed Callie's school records. They showed no evidence of any preexisting mental illness. Did that mean she'd spend the rest of her life in prison? Or that I had no defense?

I asked myself what my dad would advise and knew immediately: despite my reservations, I had to investigate the insanity defense, even if it led to another dead end. Because then, if Callie were convicted, I could at least have the satisfaction of knowing I'd tried everything possible to help her.

On my computer I kept detailed listings for every expert witness I'd ever retained, along with my comments and critiques about their thoroughness, their preparation, their persona, and their trial performance. Under the letter *P*, besides psychologists and psychiatrists, were lists of pathologists, phlebotomists, polygraph operators, and private investigators. I perused my list of shrinks and decided on Samuel Stringer, MD, PhD. Sam was a retired forensic state psychiatrist who these days testified as an expert witness in criminal defense cases. Six years ago, he'd examined a client accused of arson and opined that the man possessed a seriously suggestive personality. According to Sam, when my client was questioned by the veteran arson detective, he would have confessed to whatever crime the officer suggested, "including but not limited to assassinating Abraham Lincoln," as a smiling Sam explained to the jurors. The ten men and two women on the panel had liked Sam, and my thirty-eighth Not Guilty verdict was proof of that.

"This the one I've been reading about in the papers?" Sam asked when I reached him by phone.

"Correct. I'll file a motion and arrange things if you're agreeable."

"I have to tell you, I don't hold out a lot of hope, given what I've been reading. What your client did is actually neonaticide, the killing of a baby within twenty-four hours of its birth. There are plenty of these cases, with supposed good girls who can't face the fact that they played around and got caught. They hide their pregnancies and then try to get rid of the evidence. Anything you can do to reduce the charge?"

"It's called prosecutorial discretion. Barrett Michaels can charge her with whatever he wants. I know it may be a long shot, but I'd still like you to interview my client, read her file, see what you think."

"Be happy to help, Victoria."

FIFTEEN

OSBOURNE GRANTED MY PETITION FOR A PSYCHIATRIC examination but ordered me to arrange it "with all due haste." Outside the courthouse, I phoned Sam from my car, and he made room in his schedule to see Callie three days later. His exam would take place in a private room at the jail. He promised to phone me with the results as soon as he finished.

The day before Sam was to meet with Callie, I sat at my desk fumbling with a new ink cartridge for the Waterman, scribbling circles to force the ink through the nib. I was uneasy, still trying to convince myself I'd done the right thing petitioning for this exam. That morning, I'd met with Callie at the jail to encourage her to tell Sam what really happened.

"Will you be in the room when I take the test?" she asked me.

"That would make the test results unreliable. You know, in case I was sending you signals about how to answer the questions," I joked, but when I saw she was serious, I said, "Sam's a nice man."

She shrugged.

Still nagged by the possibility that Callie hadn't acted alone, I asked, "When's the last time you saw Stella Kohler?"

"That day at school. She's in my second hour class."

"Did she know you were pregnant?"

"I wasn't pregnant—"

"But she was your best friend, right? You rode the school bus together?"

"We were the oldest kids on the bus. We hated it."

"Any chance she was at the parsonage the morning of April fifth?"

"No."

"I thought you didn't remember what happened."

"Stella wasn't there."

"It's important that I talk to Stella, Callie. I went to her house, but her mother wouldn't let her speak with me. I thought maybe you could call her—you could use my phone."

"She won't help me. She hates me. They all do."

"What makes you say that?"

"Everyone thinks I'm evil."

"Even God?"

"Especially God. Sometimes I think you do, too."

"I'm not here to judge you. I'm here to help you. My personal feelings are irrelevant."

She didn't seem convinced.

At my desk, I looked at the legal pad in front of me and saw I'd scribbled the word *insanity* with the pen, which was working smoothly by then. I pulled another file from my credenza and tried proofreading an appellate brief I'd been working on, but I couldn't focus. I was too keyed up about Callie's exam. I remembered an uncorked bottle of California Merlot in my cellar and envisioned a full pour and settling into a chair to watch the river traffic, maybe even taking the *Margaret Ann* out for an evening cruise.

I was halfway to my lobby when Gail approached and waved me back. In my office she whispered, "There's some old lady here who insists on seeing you."

"Can't you get rid of her?"

"Believe me, I tried."

I scowled and followed Gail out front. An elderly woman was sprawled in one of my lobby chairs, the toes of her tooled leather cowboy boots pointing in opposite directions. She wore a long paisley caftan and chandelier earrings that brushed her sloped shoulders. Her wiry grey hair looked like she'd combed it during a convertible ride. She was knitting, something purple and so enormous that the bottom of whatever it was pooled on the carpet beside her.

"Can I help you?" I asked.

"You're Victoria?" She didn't wait for my answer before pushing out of her seat. "I'm Jean Burley. An attorney from Detroit. I've been following your case."

"And?"

"Give me ten minutes of your time." She glanced over at Gail, who had, by then, ducked behind her computer screen. "In private."

Gail peeked out and pointed a finger at the phone, her eyes wide, our longtime signal to phone the police. I shook my head. This woman was odd, but I didn't feel threatened. I'd give her a few minutes and then usher her out and head home as I planned.

Meanwhile, she'd started for my private office, talking to me over her shoulder as she waddled ahead. "I've been reading the articles in the *Detroit Free Press*. The prosecutor in your case is being a real asshole."

"He's running for an open judicial—" I said to her back, then paused. Whatever my frustration with Barrett these days, I wasn't ready to malign him to a stranger.

"I see. He's one of those," she said. In my office, she settled into a chair, extending her short legs and once again displaying her cowboy boots. Then she resumed knitting.

I stood behind my desk and crossed my arms. "What exactly do you want?" I asked.

"Your prosecutor is someone who puts a wet finger up to see which way the wind's blowing." Her grey eyes narrowed. "I should have guessed that." She shook her head and her earrings tinkled. "I used to work in the public defender's office in Wayne County before I retired. I know all about those kinds of people."

"He's not so bad—"

"You don't think so?" She waved a hand in front of her face and said, "Do you realize that over thirty first-world countries have a separate category in their homicide laws for a mother who kills her child while under the influence of the birth? But not a single state in the United States has a provision like that. Most people don't know that. Canada, just over there"—she pointed in the direction of the river—"is light-years ahead of us on this issue."

I knew nothing about Canadian infanticide laws. But Callie was charged under Michigan law, which meant that neither Canadian law, the law of any other country, nor the law of any other US state, was relevant. I said, "Michigan allows the mother to be charged with murder, or any lesser crime, at the discretion of the prosecutor."

"That doesn't bother you?"

"It wouldn't do me any good if it did. The law is the law."

"You sound more like a prosecutor than a defense lawyer." She scowled up at me. "If you understood the reality of infanticide, you might be able to help your client." She rearranged her stitches, letting her hands guide her work while her rheumy grey eyes stayed on my face. "I spent the last eleven years following every infanticide case in this country. If the case is in the Midwest, I attend, take notes, and talk to the defense lawyer—or try to. Most won't listen."

Her deftly moving needles were hypnotic. I blinked and reminded myself that I was the one in charge of Callie's case, not this old woman. "Exactly what is it you think I need to do?"

"You can begin by hiring a good shrink, not that quack you hired. I read about him in the *Detroit Free Press*, too. He's the real reason I'm here."

"What's wrong with Sam Stringer?" I removed my glasses and rubbed the lenses on my blouse, then slid them back on as she finished a row and distributed the stitches evenly on the needle, flipped her yarn to the back and started over. Her hands, loose skin over swollen knuckles, abruptly stopped.

"My last file was a case like yours. I was appointed, too. Angela Lee was a junior at Wayne State, an honors English major who wrote poetry and liked to read Victorian novels. She planned to teach at a university after she got her PhD." She took a breath, exhaled. "Angela's neighbors complained of an odor coming from her apartment. When the super came inside to check, he found a deceased newborn in the closet. The police picked Angela up in the university library. She was charged with First-Degree Murder.

"The prosecutor in my case wouldn't budge. Like yours. And Sam Stringer worked as the state's shrink back then. It was before he retired and started his so-called private practice. I expected him to follow the party line back then, but he gave new meaning to the phrase closed-minded. His testimony against Angela was venomous. He said he was certain Angela had been lying to everyone about her pregnancy, that she let the baby die in that closet so she wouldn't have to own up to it. Our shrink, some guy who worked cheap since my office had no money for decent experts, was no match for Sam. Outside the courtroom, Sam marched up to me and said that as a woman, I should be ashamed to represent Angela. Real professional, right?"

"What happened to the girl?"

"By the time the trial was done, I thought we were lucky to get a Murder Two conviction."

"She's still in prison?"

"The night she was convicted, Angela was taken into custody. She hung herself in her jail cell."

I flinched. "God."

"No God in that courtroom, honey. Two days later I gave my notice and retired." Her needles were clicking again. "The person you want to hire is Dr. Eleanor Allen. She's with U-M's med school in Ann Arbor. She's the best. The best. You need to take your client to see her, have Dr. Allen examine her."

I had a mental image of that girl, Angela, in her cell. Had she known she was pregnant? Why would she have put the baby in a closet if she were trying to hide it? "I appreciate the tip. I'll consider it," I said.

"Don't just consider it," Jean fired back. "You need to do what I'm asking. And let me know what you find out from Eleanor Allen. I could be very helpful to you." She reached into her cloth knitting bag and rooted around, then drew out a limp business card, laid it on my desk. "Snail mail works fine," she said. "My home address is on the card. I don't have an office per se these days. But I'd be willing to consult."

Gail poked her head in, her face a question mark. "Need anything else, boss?"

"No, thanks. I'll see you tomorrow," I said. I told the woman, "You could have phoned."

"I don't have a phone. And I don't email." She waved a hand, as though those things weren't important to her or to our conversation. "You need to think about what I told you. A girl's life is on the line here, you know."

Suddenly, I wanted to tell her that I wasn't that kind of lawyer, that this wasn't how I practiced, that I was known for *over-preparing* for my cases, not being caught off guard like this. I said, "Thanks, I've got things under control," but I could tell she knew that I didn't and that what she'd told me had unsettled me. I pointed toward my lobby. "I'll walk you out."

She pushed her knitting into the cloth bag. "Don't do to this girl what I did to Angela. I live with that every day."

I peeked between the blinds on my front door and watched as she climbed into a mint-green Cadillac, complete with tailfins, and drove off. Then I dropped limply into Gail's empty chair. After a few minutes, I switched on her computer and watched as photos of Gail's granddaughter Marissa danced across the screen, a smiling towhead showing off for the camera. I googled "infanticide Canada," removed my glasses, leaned my face closer to the screen and read:

> In 2005 the Canadian Parliament made infanticide a special category of homicide, defined as the death of a newborn child caused by the mother's willful act or omission where she had not fully recovered from the effects of giving birth. Punishment for conviction was capped at five years in prison.

So that's what the old woman meant. Prior to 2005, a Canadian woman in Callie's situation could have been charged with murder. But under this new law she would be treated much differently. Had the Canadian government determined there was a deeper psychological explanation for the crime of neonaticide? Canada was considered liberal compared with the United States; still, I couldn't help but wonder what we Americans had missed. More importantly, I wondered, what did *I* miss?

I followed links to facts and statistics concerning infanticide throughout the world, and Jean Burley was right about those as well. The United States was one of the few first-world countries that didn't provide a special category of homicide for either neonaticide or infanticide. Of the fifty American states, not one of them made the exception so many other civilized nations recognized as necessary, as *reasonable*, in situations like Callie's.

I took a breath, my fingers poised above the keyboard, then typed "Angela Lee." On the *Detroit Free Press* website, I found a series of old articles plus several photos. One piece quoted a younger-looking Jean Burley saying, "This case is the worst kind of travesty," after the verdict was announced.

I saw a high school photo of Angela, a smiling, happy girl. Then her arrest photo: a young woman who appeared dazed, confused, and lost. Her suicide happened just as Jean Burley said. After Angela was dead, there were tributes from her professors, her former roommates, her minister, all of whom said she was an outstanding student, a kind and unselfish girl.

So what happened?

I closed out the site and eventually Marissa reappeared on the screen, this time wearing a Santa Claus hat and clutching a stuffed reindeer with a jingle bell on its red nose. I googled "Eleanor Allen" and a host of sites popped up showing photos of a diminutive, silver-haired woman with a CV that read like an encyclopedia index. Following a list of degrees were pages of article titles she'd authored on the topic of neonaticide, plus titles of papers she'd presented at conferences throughout the world. She currently headed the psychiatry department at the University of Michigan's medical school.

I scrolled to the article she'd written titled, "Neonaticide Syndrome: The Only Possible Explanation," downloaded it, and printed it. Once home, I forgot about my wine. Instead, I sat in my corner chair reading, then rereading, the article. I filled the margins with notes and underlined phrases and words to investigate further.

Around midnight, I dozed in my chair, then woke and watched a freighter steadily work its way up the dark river. I felt ashamed and embarrassed and guilt-ridden. The truth was, so far I'd done a lousy job in Callie's case.

Dr. Allen's article said the syndrome had only recently come to light within the psychiatric community. Sam hadn't mentioned it when we talked, and he'd been less than open-minded when he chided Jean Burley ten years before. Sam Stringer might know about neonaticide syndrome, but based on my conversation with him, I strongly doubted it. Had Sam been merely going through the motions to pick up his fee? And when I hired Sam, was I just going through the motions? Would I really have collected my county check in Callie's case, telling myself I'd done the best I could and walked away knowing she would spend the rest of her life in prison?

Why had I not looked into Callie's behavior more deeply? Into her motivation? Why had I not kept an open mind, as I prided myself on in all my other cases? Why was I not giving Callie the defense she deserved?

Around five that morning, I phoned Sam's answering service and left a message. "There's been a change in plans," I said. "I'm postponing your exam of my client until further notice."

SIXTEEN

THE NEXT MORNING, MY SCHEDULE WAS JAMMED WITH appointments: four with potential clients, each of whom, based on earlier phone conversations, would arrive bearing a check or a high-limit credit card for the retainer I'd quoted. Gail was exceptionally cheerful on days like this. She'd record numbers in our receipt book like a big winner cashing out at one of the Canadian casinos across the river in Port Edward, then hustle to the bank with the deposit.

Appointments with new clients gave me the opportunity to impress them, to convince them they'd chosen precisely the right lawyer. I never pandered to or sympathized with them, like some attorneys. Instead, I made it crystal clear that I had the experience and the knowledge to manage what was ahead, and that the client's role, once they'd paid me, was to listen and take my advice, down to the tiniest detail.

But that morning I was shaky and uncertain, my usual confidence MIA. The copious notes I always took during first appointments were sketchy, and several times my attention drifted away from the stories I was being told to my sloppy work in Callie's case. It had been sheer coincidence, not my usual relentless preparation, that saved Callie from Sam Stringer's exam and his potentially prejudged conclusion of her guilt.

I managed to get through the morning and collect four big checks, but as soon as the last client was out the door, I disappeared into my office and typed "neonaticide" on my computer keyboard. One million, eight hundred thousand sites popped up.

In Defense of Good Women 87

How did I miss this?

I began scrolling the pages, skimming titles, dismissing those that seemed political, looking for something that might help me understand the concept I'd read about the night before. Plenty of sites equated neonaticide with abortion, just like that sign those women displayed the first day I visited Callie. Others promoted an obvious agenda, claiming liberals favored neonaticide or that neonaticide was hidden in the programs of Planned Parenthood. I found sites on the history of neonaticide, even references to *Adam Bede*, but nothing as helpful as the article I'd read by Eleanor Allen.

I added "United States" to my search, which led me to sites about contraception, abortion, and Moses Laws, the safe haven laws recently adopted in all fifty states allowing mothers to drop off infants at hospitals or police stations with no questions asked. I scribbled a few notes on a legal pad, then sat back, stretched. Would a teenager who couldn't admit she was pregnant have the presence of mind to take advantage of her state's Moses Law?

By the end of the day, other than the piece by Dr. Allen, the most comprehensive resources I came across appeared to be three books on the general topic of infanticide. I sprung for extra postage with Amazon so *Mothers Who Murder*, *Modern Infanticide*, and *Homicidal, Hormonal Mothers* would be in my hands by the next day. When Gail delivered the box of books to me, I instructed her to cancel the remainder of the day's appointments and rushed home.

In my corner chair, I took pages of notes as I read, then reread, studies explaining the similarities in young women accused of neonaticide. The most common factor in their behavior was hiding their pregnancies from everyone around them, including family members, friends, and teachers. Some of these young women, mostly teenagers, came from good families and were otherwise obedient, respectful girls. Just as Dr. Allen had written, a large percentage of the cases of neonaticide involved young, unmarried women who denied their pregnancies and claimed to have been completely shocked by the onset of their labor pains. None of these girls had a preexisting mental illness. Most often, after the child was born, these otherwise sane mothers did something irrational to hide the infant's body, like placing it in a bathroom vanity, stuffing it in the family refrigerator, leaving it in a closet, or burying it in a shallow grave. Every study I read concluded that these young women had been overtaken by temporary psychoses and that their psychoses were the reason they denied their pregnancies and then attempted to get rid of their babies in bizarre ways. When their babies, the cause of their psychoses, were gone, the psychoses evaporated, and their sanity was restored.

Two days before, I'd been certain Callie's behavior was that of a scared girl who'd had sex and gotten caught. But these studies—by reputable physicians and psychiatrists—were convincing me I'd been wrong. I was now open to the idea that Callie was one of these women I was reading about, that she'd had a psychosis but now it was gone.

When I finished the last of the three books, I poured myself a large glass of wine, then curled up in my chair and stared out at the river. Was it possible I had a defense? One I could sell to Barrett so he'd offer Callie a decent plea? Or if not Barrett, to Osbourne and then to a jury?

I watched a series of sailboats motor upriver in the darkness, their mast lights bobbing as they made their way from marinas in Detroit to the Black River in Port Huron. The annual race to Mackinac Island was scheduled for the coming weekend. In previous years, I'd taken a short break from work and watched the parade of boats cast off. This year I wouldn't make it: I'd be busy preparing my defense.

I had a defense.

The horizon across the river was edged in pink, the precursor to a brilliant sunrise, but I was far too keyed up to sleep. On my kitchen counter was a stack of mail I'd been too busy, or too tired, to open that week. I tossed a pile of catalogs and flyers in the trash before spotting an envelope with festive Italian stamps and familiar looped handwriting. Slicing it open, I pulled out a card. On the front was a print of a painting I recognized from my single undergraduate art history class at Michigan: *The Annunciation of Mary* by Botticelli.

Molly'd been collecting Annunciation renderings since the first year she chaperoned students to Rome, and each summer, she sent me a card depicting her favorite from that year's trip. Among others, she'd sent a da Vinci, a Fra Angelico, a fresco from the wall of some cathedral, and a pre-Renaissance oil by someone whose name I couldn't recall. Just like this year's Botticelli, every card depicted the Angel Gabriel announcing to Mary that she was to give birth to the son of God. In each, the angel handed Mary a white lily, a symbol of her purity.

I studied the picture on the latest card. Mary appeared resigned and serene. But it occurred to me that, virgin birth or not, when Mary learned she was pregnant it had to be a shock. Back then, an unmarried single woman who was pregnant could be stoned by her community. Even now in some cultures, an unmarried pregnant woman might receive the same punishment. They believed an out-of-wedlock pregnancy revealed to the world the kind of person she really was. A fallen woman, she would have been called—someone whose life was ruined.

And nowadays? Plenty of women would see an unexpected pregnancy as a blessing, an opportunity for marriage or for a baby to love, but for others in different circumstances, with different lives, I knew it wasn't like that. An unplanned pregnancy for an unmarried woman could still be a tremendous problem, something she had to deal with.

The pod of sailboats was far upriver now; the water's smooth surface hid the swift current beneath.

Before this, I hadn't seen any similarities between one unplanned pregnancy and another. Maybe, I began to think, maybe I'd been wrong about that, too. I stood the card on the counter and stared at Mary's face.

Every unplanned pregnancy was different, but every unplanned pregnancy was the same.

I glanced out at Sister Phillip. She winked her red light at me, and then I was once again in the dark.

SEVENTEEN

JUDGE OSBOURNE'S PRIVATE OFFICE WAS A SHRINE TO his decades-long career on the bench. Photos of him with three past Michigan governors, plaques from police associations, and a collection of brass gavels sat on walnut bookshelves lining the back wall. Barrett had arrived before I did and sat in front of Osbourne's desk with one foot on the opposite knee. He held his ankle, and his foot jiggled—a nervous habit I once teased him about. I wondered whether he was sizing up the room, imagining how his own mementos would look in this office if he won the election.

"Victoria."

I sat in the chair next to his, facing the judge's desk. Although I was still smarting from Barrett's dismissive treatment of me a couple weeks before, I didn't feel quite so angry now that I had a defense. Although I hadn't had a chance to talk to him about it.

"Osbourne had something to put on the record. He'll be back in a minute." Barrett's foot jiggled again.

"I've been trying to catch up with you, to tell you about some new information I discovered."

I paused as Osbourne flowed in like a small, slow-moving barge, the hem of his black robe fluttering softly behind him. He unfastened the robe with stiff fingers and struggled to hang it on a coat tree in the corner.

"Those new attorneys file every motion they can think of in open-and-shut cases, wasting everyone's time," he told us. "Evidently, they all showed up during the Con Law lecture when their profs talked about the fruit of the poisonous tree." His voice sounded stronger today. He sank down in the tall leather chair behind his desk. "We're here for a pretrial in the Thomas case, correct?"

I said, "I have some new information that may require more time. This case is more complex than I once thought."

"It seems pretty simple to me." Barrett didn't look at me.

"What is the prosecutor's position on adjournment?" Osbourne asked.

"This case needs to be resolved."

"Well, I'd like it resolved, too," said Osbourne, "and I bet you'd like to get on with your campaign, right, Barrett? How's it going so far? Eaten your fill of rubber chickens?"

Barrett's foot wiggled. "You bet."

I said, "There's some recent research that might explain my client's behavior—"

"Like I said, this seems pretty simple to me," Barrett said.

"That's what I once thought, but this psychological research is cutting-edge—"

"Is this illness in the *DSM*?" Barrett asked. *The Diagnostic and Statistical Manual.* The bible of psychology.

"It's not. But that doesn't mean—"

"Then it's not valid." Barrett kept his eyes on Osbourne.

"You can file a motion and I'll certainly consider it, Victoria," Osbourne said. He called, "Cynthia, bring my book, please," and his secretary scuttled in and laid a calendar on the desk in front of him. "I promised my wife I'd take her to see her sister in San Diego this fall. It's the only way I could get her to let me serve out the year. So, I want this trial over soon. How about we shoot for the eighteenth of August?"

I said, "I may file an insanity notice."

Barrett lifted his chin. "I thought you cancelled your exam."

"I did. But that doesn't mean I'm not going to pursue it."

"You got another expert?"

"I'm working on it."

Osbourne frowned and said to Barrett, "That'll mean you need an expert. More money the county will have to dole out. Any likelihood of a plea bargain?"

"The defense isn't interested in our offer," said Barrett.

"Pleading guilty to the charge is hardly an offer."

"You're not offering anything?" Osbourne eyed Barrett. He looked surprised.

"I can't. Not with a crime like this."

"Cut the crap, Barrett," I said. "There's no press here, no voters to persuade. No need to posture. You could at least listen to what I have to say—"

Osbourne's chalky eyebrows shot up. He looked from me to Barrett. "So, you're going to roll the dice in court, Mr. Prosecutor? There's always a risk, you know. Juries are curious animals. They do funny things." When Barrett didn't respond, Osbourne said, "Okay then, let's move everything back. Trial date October eighteenth. My wife won't be happy."

"That's awfully close to the election." Barrett's foot bounced.

"Think of all the free publicity you'll get, Barrett. None of that equal time crap for your opponent. Pretrial motions filed and resolved by October fourteenth. Victoria, you'll have to file your Notice of Insanity by September sixteenth."

I gave my earlier strategy one last try. "I'm happy to accommodate Barrett's request for a postponement, Judge."

Osbourne shook his head. "We'll stay with these dates. Get this thing behind us and move on." He stood and pulled his robe from the coat tree. "Bring your client from lockup, and we'll put these dates on the record. October eighteenth, be ready to rumble, folks."

In the hall outside Osbourne's office, I reached for Barrett's sleeve. "You could at least listen to what I have to say," I told him.

"If I bowed to every defense lawyer with some nutso psychological theory, I'd be a lousy prosecutor."

"There's a prof at U-M's med school who's the expert on this stuff. I could send you an article—"

"File a motion if you have to, Victoria. I'm not going to back down unless Osbourne orders it."

EIGHTEEN

"ELEANOR ALLEN HERE." HER GERMAN ACCENT UNDERSCORED a voice that was all business.

"Yes, hello. My name is Victoria Stephens. I'm an attorney in St. Clair County, and I was appointed to represent a young woman charged with neonaticide. I wondered if you could examine her . . . tell me what you think, whether you could help me. Help *her*. Maybe you've read about her case?"

"My admin didn't return your calls?"

"No."

Dr. Allen sighed. "Our regular is on maternity leave. This one is less than satisfactory. I apologize."

"I have an October trial date and I'll need to file a Notice of Insanity soon. If I decide to go that route."

"This is the Thomas girl?"

"So you've been following the case." I hoped her interest was a good sign.

"I have. And I'm sorry to disappoint you, but I'm not going to be able to assist you. I'm not taking on any new cases just now. I wish we'd let you know sooner. You could have retained someone else."

"But I think my client might be one of those mothers. The ones you write about."

"It's possible."

It's possible? I tapped the Waterman against my palm, and my mind raced. If Dr. Allen wouldn't assist me, I might not have a defense. I blurted, "But how do I know whether it's true? When she tells me she didn't realize she was pregnant? Or that she was having a baby?"

She sighed. "You're wondering how it's possible your client doesn't remember the pregnancy and the birth. Assuming she's telling you the truth."

"Of course."

"Neonaticide syndrome is complicated. Think of it as the manifestation of a form of panic. The mind and body are in shock, and they work in tandem to protect each other. In order to do that, they step outside themselves, go somewhere else until the evidence of the sexual act is gone. Once it's gone, they return. You are aware that in the two jurisdictions where the syndrome has been raised, both judges refused to allow the jury to consider it?"

I'd read those cases. "But neither of those women was tried in Michigan, so those decisions aren't binding in this state. What if . . . what if my client was one of those girls with the syndrome? At first, I assumed she was lying about not remembering what happened, but the more I read about the syndrome, the more I think she fits the criteria. Which means she *is* telling me the truth. But I need the opinion of an expert."

"Ms. Stephens, I am impressed. You have obviously done your homework. So. A couple of colleagues of mine have also studied this subject. I can give you their names if you wish."

Jean Burley had started me down this path. I heard the old lawyer's admonition: *Dr. Allen's the best.* So far, her advice had been exactly on point. I said, "Jean Burley said I shouldn't accept anyone else's opinion. If you say my client doesn't have the syndrome, I'll live with that. But if you could just examine her—"

"Jean Burley?" Dr. Allen chuckled. "Do you know that she attends every one of my lectures on this topic? She's even been known to sneak into my med school classes."

"She says you're the only one who can help me."

"She flatters me." I heard papers shuffling, another sigh. "Hold on."

I squeezed my pen so tight my fingers were becoming numb.

"Ms. Stephens?"

"Yes?"

"I am about to act against my own better judgment. If you hold again, I'll put my admin on the line to give you my address here at the university. Send me copies of everything in your file— police reports, autopsy, witness statements, everything—and I'll review them. Then I'll find some time to meet with the girl here at my office."

"But that's impossible, Doctor. Her father won't post her bond, so she's still in jail. I can't get her down there—"

"That's the best I can do, Counselor. I'm chairing a department meeting in five minutes, so I have no more time just now. Leave your email with the admin, and she'll send my fee schedule to you. Then get me the information and bring your client here. I'll see her and give you my opinion. But I won't promise anything."

"It's not much, but it's something." I settled on the edge of Gail's desk, one shoe dangling from my foot. I'd just told her about my call to Ann Arbor.

"I don't get it," Gail said. "A shrink already found her competent."

"This doctor's going to determine if Callie was sane when she killed her baby. That's not the same as being competent now. I just need to figure out how to get her to Ann Arbor."

"Why not just get a court order? Writ her out?"

"I'd have to file a motion and give notice to Barrett. I'm not ready to tell him the specifics about Dr. Allen."

"Because?"

"First of all, I don't know what she'll conclude. If Dr. Allen says Callie fits the syndrome, maybe I'll have a shot at an insanity defense. And if she says Callie doesn't fit it, Barrett will know about her. Whatever she concludes, she's the clear expert in this field, bar none."

"Why not just do like those other lawyers do? Hire a prostitute to say what you want and be done with it?"

"Hiring someone to say what I want is like suggesting facts to a client. It's unconscionable. It's also suborning perjury, which is grounds for disbarment. Lots of things would be easier if people cheated." I knew I sounded sanctimonious. There were plenty of grey areas within the law, but plenty of others that were black or white. It was the blacks and whites that made the justice system work. I added, "When lawyers mess with the rules, the system falls apart." How many times had I heard my dad say that?

Gail handed me a fistful of messages. "Some of your other clients need your attention."

I took the slips and wandered back to my office. Once there, I shuffled through them, then glanced over the files on my desk. Motions needed to be dictated, evidence reviewed, and potential witnesses phoned. I'd always kept up on these sorts of details, but just then all I could think about was Callie and that syndrome. I turned on my computer and leaned forward.

NINETEEN

WHEN CALLIE WAS ARRESTED, HER BOND WAS SET AT HALF a million dollars, cash or surety. That meant one of two things had to happen for her to be released pending trial. First, someone had to deposit five hundred thousand dollars with the county as security, the bulk of which would be refunded once her case was resolved if she'd showed up for every court hearing. The alternative, the security bond, required that someone pay fifty thousand dollars to a licensed bail bondsman. In exchange for this nonrefundable fee, the bondsman would pledge to pay the entire five hundred thousand dollars to the court if Callie failed to appear.

I pored over LexisNexis, my legal search engine, studying every Michigan statute that had any connection, however tenuous, to the subject of bail bonds. I reread the statute that precluded me, as Callie's lawyer, from posting her bond, then concluded, not for the first time, that there was one person who should *want* to post it, who should be *clamoring* to post it. I wasn't excited about confronting him but couldn't see any other way to solve my problem. I reached for my purse and told Gail I'd be back soon. This time I didn't bother making an appointment.

When I arrived, I pounded on the front door of the church until the same brunette who'd let me in before opened it. When she did, I pushed past her and headed down the hall, toward the clearly marked CLERGY OFFICE, her heels clicking furiously behind me. Inside her office, she glared at me while snatching a ringing phone, covering the mouthpiece with her hand and saying, "He won't be able to see you today. He's a very busy man. You can make an appointment."

"I'll wait." I perched on the edge of the nearest chair.

"Uh-huh, yes. The church is growing so much." Her phone voice was sweet, saccharine. "Uh-huh. Why don't you join us for Bible study? See what you think. Thursday nights Reverend Neil leads it himself. He's very good. And we're a welcoming bunch."

I spotted a Bible concordance on a nearby table and picked it up. I was crystal clear about what the Catholic Church would say about an illegitimate pregnancy, although my religion classes at St. Anne's hadn't included much serious Bible study. We'd mainly focused on church teachings and the lives of the saints: lots of martyred virgins. What did the Bible actually say? The nuns never mentioned it, but I was sure I'd heard something about harlots in the Old Testament. And what about Mary Magdalene?

In the index, I found the word *illegitimate*. It referenced *bastard*, and that led me to Deuteronomy, the book of rules about how the ancient Hebrews were supposed to conduct their lives. I ran my finger down the tiny print, past verses about boundary disputes, rebellious children, and sexual relations. It took me a while to find it, but I did. "A bastard shall not enter the congregation of the Lord; even to his tenth generation shall he not enter the congregation of the Lord." I had my answer. I shut the book and dropped it on the table.

The brunette was off the phone now. She sat stiffly at her desk. When the door to his office finally opened, a smiling Neil Thomas escorted a young couple out, then turned toward me, his expression growing as dark as his eyes. I stood and strode past him, into his office.

It was a modern space, all light wood and white walls, except for the colorful book spines on the shelves and hanging plants, explosions of green leaves diffusing light from a large window. When I heard the door close behind me, I turned back.

"Would you have accepted the child? Her child? If she'd told you she was pregnant?"

"It's a little late to worry about that now, isn't it?"

"Reverend, I know your daughter's behavior has disappointed you. But there's a psychiatrist in Ann Arbor who understands these types of cases. I'd like Callie to meet with her."

"How does that concern me?"

"I need to take her there. Which means she needs to be bailed out of jail."

"Miss Stephens, I cannot—"

"She's your daughter. Whatever she's done, she needs your support."

"Has she admitted her sin?"

"What she tells me is confidential."

"She knew how I felt about promiscuity."

"Then you know how she became pregnant?"

"Not in so many words."

"I don't know what happened either," I pleaded. "The woman I'd like your daughter to see is a very qualified psychiatrist. I'm hoping she can help me understand what Callie did so I can explain it to a jury."

"Miss Stephens"—his voice was so quiet I had difficulty hearing him—"all this psychobabble may help you confuse the issue when you go to court. It may even help you win your case. Isn't that all you lawyers care about? But it won't change the result. Things in the Lord's eyes are clear."

I took a deep breath and tried one more time. "I agree, what's happened is a terrible thing. But we're talking about the rest of her life. She's seventeen—"

"I know how old my daughter is."

"Then please, help me. You're her father. Let's find out what really happened." When he said nothing, I scribbled my cell phone number on one of my business cards and plunked it on his desk. "If you decide to help your daughter, you can reach me here. Please," I repeated, but he was looking out the window, as though I was already gone.

TWENTY

THE FOLLOWING MORNING, I WOKE UP IN MY CORNER chair. Again. My throat was parched, my tongue thick, and my head was throbbing: my punishment for selecting a cheaper bottle of wine from my stash the night before. I still had on the skirt and silk blouse I'd worn when I confronted Neil Thomas, but they were skewed and my glasses balanced crookedly on my face. I made a feeble attempt to straighten my clothes and wiped my greasy lenses against the front of my blouse as I thought back on my evening.

I'd started out on my deck. Angry at Neil Thomas and his refusal to help his daughter, I'd hardly tasted my first glass of Merlot. As fishing boats sped past in both directions, I replayed Eleanor Allen's explanation of Callie's behavior. It sounded so logical, so reasonable. But if I couldn't get Callie to Ann Arbor and I couldn't present it in the courtroom, what good did it do me?

Frustrated, I'd hauled my wine bottle inside, curled up on my corner chair, and poured myself another glass. "Think of her behavior as a manifestation of panic," Dr. Allen had told me, "of the mind and body going outside themselves until evidence of the sexual act is gone."

I was certainly familiar with the concept of panic. Clients of mine routinely reacted badly to frightening situations, desperate to regain control of their lives and undo something they'd done. The result of their panic was often what led them to hire me.

I'd poured myself another glass and thought about those panicked clients, then about Callie and how likely it was that she too had panicked. And as I poured the last of the bottle into my glass, I started thinking about myself, about the time I panicked. By then I was drunk, my chair pulsing and the glowing bulbs on the rail of a passing ship one long blade of light.

Now I glanced at my watch and stumbled from my chair, stepping out of my clothes and into the shower, letting the hot water run over my head, hoping to clear my brain. Walking to my car in the too-bright sunlight, I told myself that the two circumstances, Callie's and mine, were not the same and that I could not, would not, confuse them. I needed to focus on Callie's case, not something I'd done years ago.

Two days later, hordes of Saturday pleasure boaters whipped the river into a lumpy froth. I sat in my corner chair sipping a cup of dark coffee. The night before I'd had too much wine. Again. The empty Pinot bottle, conclusive evidence, sat on my kitchen table.

My cell phone beeped. I shuffled to the kitchen, squinted at the screen, and swiped it. Then I dressed in jeans and a tee shirt, threw a silk jacket over my shoulders, brushed my teeth, and ran a comb through my snarled hair. Despite my hangover, Adele wailed from my car's speakers while I sped to the county jail.

"Well, well. No rest for the wicked, huh?" Art grinned like a jack-o-lantern when he saw me. He pointed to my usual seat. "The prosecutor's on his way. The good reverend's not here yet, but Mueller's prancing around like a kid on Christmas morning. This bond will pay for his new Lexus."

"Did Mueller say why Dad changed his mind?"

"All he said is he got a check, certified. Maybe somebody in Dad's church came up with the money, I'm thinking, but who knows? I do know Earl won't be too happy being paged during his Saturday golf game."

In Defense of Good Women   105

I heard the bondsman's voice in the hall. "Right this way, Reverend. We'll have your little girl out of here in no time." Mueller sashayed into Art's office. "Victoria, I didn't expect to see you here." He turned to Pastor Thomas. "She's the best, didn't I tell you? You're lucky to have her. Most attorneys don't bother with a bond hearing. Just shows."

"Hello again." I offered my hand to Neil Thomas, assuming the two of us had reached some kind of uneasy truce. But he stepped back, his face drawn, dark circles framing darker eyes, so I dropped my hand and turned away.

Earl Norton arrived next, wearing khakis and a red polo shirt; a black robe hung over a beefy arm. "To whom do I give thanks for rescuing me? I was three-putting everything today." He surveyed Art's office. Neil Thomas was staring into the distance. Earl glanced at Art, who raised his eyebrows and shrugged.

Barrett walked in wearing an MSU tee shirt and pair of jeans. He didn't look happy. "Counselor," he nodded at me, "I understand bond has been posted?"

"Right-o," chirped Mueller. "Pastor Thomas, that is, the defendant's father, has taken care of all that. We're set to go."

Down a hall at the jail, Art and one of the matrons escorted Callie into the makeshift hearing room. She wore orange scrubs and her pale arms were handcuffed to her sides by a heavy chain wrapped around her waist. One side of her face had a red crease, as though from a wrinkled pillowcase, and her hair was dirty and uncombed. When she saw her father, her eyes widened. But he kept his eyes on the cement floor in front of him.

"Ready?" Earl punched buttons on his recorder. "This is in the matter of Calliope Faith Thomas, file number 16-007742 FY(O). Present is the defendant, her attorney Victoria Stephens, Prosecutor

Barrett Michaels, Bail Bondsman Edward Mueller, and . . ." Although he looked at Callie's father, Mueller spoke.

"The Reverend Neil Thomas, father of the defendant, your honor."

"I understand bond has been posted?"

"Everything is in order," said Mueller. "I took care of all the necessary paperwork." He grinned at Neil Thomas and nodded again.

"Please state your full name," Earl said to Callie.

I stepped forward and stood next to her. "Tell him."

"Callie Thomas," she whispered.

"Louder. Your *full* name," Earl barked.

"Calliope Faith Thomas."

"Miss Thomas, your father has posted what is known as a surety bond. This means that you will be released from custody, but there will be certain conditions attached to your release. Do you understand?"

Her father leaned forward in his chair, hands clasped, still looking down.

"I understand."

"The first condition is that you must appear on time for each and every hearing in your case set by the court. Do you understand?"

"Yes."

"And you must live at the address the court has for you, that being 4044 Havens Road, Port Huron. I assume that is your father's address?"

"Yes."

"And this is also your understanding, Mr. Thomas?" asked Earl.

"Reverend Thomas?" Mueller nodded as he spoke. "Calliope will be living in your home?" Mueller was still grinning.

"I'm sorry? What?"

"Your daughter will be living in your home while this matter is pending?"

"I'm . . . No. No, she cannot."

Barrett's head swiveled toward the pastor, then back at me. Mueller's grin faded.

"Mr. Mueller, I thought you said the paperwork was in order," said Earl. "Off the record." He punched a recorder button. "Let's get it together, folks. I need a specific address within this jurisdiction. You all know that."

Barrett scowled at me. "Did you know about this?"

"Of course not." I stepped to Callie's father and leaned closer. "Pastor? Callie needs a place to live. We all assumed she would reside in your home."

"She cannot return to the parsonage."

"Maybe you have relatives in this area?"

His eyes down, he shook his head. "I do not."

"How about the home of one of your parishioners? The youth pastor and his wife, where she stayed before she was arrested? I could help you arrange something." I searched his face for an explanation.

"No." He spoke sharply.

"But surely there's someone . . . your congregation is huge . . . maybe one of those women from that luncheon at the church?"

"No," he repeated, this time more firmly.

"There must be some realistic option here. Perhaps a foster home?" I asked.

"The state would never agree to a foster home placement, Victoria," Barrett said.

"I'm not liking how this is going down, folks." Earl slid the sleeve of his robe above his wrist, glanced at his watch. "Mr. Mueller, Ms. Stephens, if you cannot find me a suitable option, I intend to conclude this hearing and get back to what's left of my golf game."

My head reeled and my stomach curdled. Why the hell did

Callie's father post bond if he didn't intend to take his daughter home to live with him? Didn't Mueller explain things to him? Where did he think his daughter would go after she was out? A homeless shelter? A tent in some park? "Pastor Thomas, please—" I said.

Callie watched her father with wide eyes; her lower lip trembled.

"Counselor?" Earl's voice.

I held up my hand. "A minute," I said and closed my eyes, tried to think.

Barrett told Earl he'd been coaching his younger son's soccer practice in McMorran Park when he was paged. "He's got a wicked left foot," Barrett said.

"Great place to be seen," Earl said.

A tear dripped from Callie's chin and a dark orange blot appeared on her shirt. I yanked a tissue from my purse and thrust it toward her.

Earl said, "It seems this little gathering was all for naught. Let's go back on the record."

I felt something grip my insides then, nothing that had any connection with my hangover, something that wouldn't let go. "Wait." I cleared my parched throat, coughed. "Wait," I said again as I frantically tried to figure out exactly what I should do. What I could do.

If Callie went back to her cell, if Dr. Allen couldn't interview her, I might not have a defense. And what if Callie was one of those girls who panicked? I shut my eyes and my breath was shaky. Beside me, Callie wiped her face with the tissue and sniffed.

"Yes?" It was Earl.

I heard myself say, "Calliope Thomas can . . . that is . . . she can live . . . with me." That same voice said, "She can live in my home."

Earl crooked his index finger and motioned Barrett and me forward.

"Victoria, do you know what you're doing?" Barrett whispered.

I kept my eyes on Earl, afraid that if I looked at Barrett, I might change my mind, behave reasonably, and act logically. Anything but what I was about to do. "It would be unlawful for me to post her bond. But I'm not doing that."

"I don't question the legality of your actions," said Earl. "I'm questioning your judgment."

I said, "My judgment is not this court's concern. I would remind you that I am a member of the bar in good standing."

"Vic, come on—" It was Barrett.

"My home, the location where Miss Thomas will reside, is located within and subject to this court's jurisdiction."

"But Counselor, this is an appointed case, is it not?" It was Earl.

I remembered how not long ago I too had thought of this appointed case, this girl, as less than worthy of my valuable time and my help. "Since when are appointed clients not entitled to the same rights as retained clients?" I raised my chin and glared at Earl, then Barrett, back to Earl again.

"This goes well beyond rights, Victoria," said Barrett. "All I'm saying is that . . . no one's ever . . . it's certainly not necessary . . ." I could hear him breathing hard and could tell he was furious. Finally he stepped back.

"I know what I'm doing," I said emphatically.

"I sure hope you do, Counselor." Earl punched a button on the recorder. "Okay, folks, we're back on the record."

TWENTY-ONE

WHEN CALLIE WALKED OUT OF THE FRONT DOOR OF THE jail, two visitors were sitting on a bench in the hot sun, smoking and talking. I waved my hand from outside my car where I was standing, but Callie didn't see me. She stepped back toward the building and seemed to cower in the shade, unmoving. Finally I stepped forward and took her arm.

"Callie? You're coming to my house with me. Remember?"

She looked up at me and nodded slowly, then let me lead her to my car. While she was being processed inside, her father wordlessly deposited two cases beside me, one a hard-sided black Samsonite and the other a large plastic box with a handle, then drove off.

Mueller hustled over now. "I'll help you with these, little lady," he said to Callie. He hefted the suitcase into my abbreviated trunk, then grabbed the plastic box. "Heavy bugger. I'm guessing a boat anchor." He grinned and slammed the trunk closed. "You'll be fine, little lady. You have a good lawyer. Rhymes with warrior, you know." He winked at me over the top of my little car before scurrying away to his Lexus.

When I arrived earlier, I'd looked for the zealots in the park, but they weren't there that morning. In their place was a bevy of grey-haired ladies in sagging bathing suits who'd scuttled along the fence in the direction of the river, toting colorful floats, their faces partially obscured by colorful ball caps and dark glasses. One shouted, "See, Lois? It doesn't matter if you can't swim! Getting from our cars to the river is the scariest part of this trip!"

Now, inside my car, Callie was remote, oblivious to everything and everybody, including and especially me. When I said, "Seat belt?" she robotically pulled her seat belt and snapped the latch in place, then stared straight ahead. I didn't feel like talking, either, so I drove slowly along the river road. I spotted those women on the water, floating lazily in the current, arms draped over the sides of their tubes, fingers dangling. Just then I wanted to trade places with them, join in their mindless leisure, relax, and forget this girl and her problems. What in hell had I been thinking when I offered to bring her home? And what had scared her when she came out of the jail today?

In my driveway, I dragged her suitcase from my trunk, set it in front of her, and pointed down the wooden steps to my cottage. Meanwhile, I struggled with the plastic box, which was almost more than I could carry. Once inside, I let go, and it landed with a thud on my kitchen linoleum. Callie gently lowered her suitcase to the floor and waited, her dark eyes looking over my messy kitchen.

I pointed at the box. "What is this beast?"

"A sewing machine."

"You sew?"

Another one of her shrugs. I caught her eyeing what she could see of my cottage and realized how it must appear to her. Gail kept my office tidy and organized, the image of capability I wanted to present to clients. Here at home, I could and did let things go. There were unwashed dishes in my sink. An onion bagel I'd browned that morning, then didn't feel like eating, still sat inside my dingy toaster oven. The pile of clothes I'd meant to drop off at the dry cleaners that week but hadn't was heaped in a corner. Every horizontal surface was coated with a thin layer of dust, even my kitchen table, where last night's empty Pinot bottle stood like a green beacon. The rest of my cottage wouldn't be any cleaner.

Reaching for my bottle of Tylenol and the mug with the remnants of my morning coffee, I downed three caplets. "I wasn't expecting company," I said, and pointed to her suitcase. "This way. You can leave the heavy one here for now." I pushed it against the wall, out of the way.

She followed me to what had been my father's bedroom. Now his double bed and maple dresser were the only furniture. I jimmied a stubborn window and propped it wide with a slat of wood from the blackened sill, then crushed a fat-bodied spider in a tissue and brushed aside its thick web. "You'll need clean sheets and a pillow," I said, and tried to think what else she might need. Soap? Toothpaste? Tampons?

I shoved open a sticky closet door and pushed my pricey tweed jackets and matching pencil skirts, my cashmere turtlenecks covered in plastic bags, and my dark-hued silk blouses to the back. "You can hang your clothes there." I wrenched open a swollen dresser drawer. "Other things can go in here."

I pointed behind her to the hall and my only bathroom. My towel was slung over the shower rod and dried toothpaste speckled the vanity mirror. The toilet was disgusting, smelly. I said, "Fresh towels are in the hall cupboard. Are you hungry?"

"I guess . . ."

"Maybe you'd like a shower first."

"Yes, please."

I swiped a clean towel from a hall cupboard and handed it to her. "Takes a while for the water to get hot. Let it run."

Cooking, like cleaning, is for me an activity of attrition; I only do it if I happen to have the right ingredients in the house, which is rare, and when there are no other possible options, like pizza delivery or one of the four Riverside delis I regularly frequent. I made a quick inventory of the few items in my fridge: ketchup, eggs, a jug of skim milk that was likely sour, one rock hard navel orange with a growing bruise, eight cans from a twelve-pack of Diet Coke, an unopened carton of cottage cheese, six slices of American cheese, some limp carrots, a stick of butter, and what was left of a loaf of rye bread. I could make a grilled cheese sandwich for Callie, but I knew I should stick with a cold Diet Coke, no ice. The carbonation would calm my queasy stomach.

While the buttered bread sizzled in the pan, I replayed the morning's events. Barrett had been the same rigidly detached guy he was whenever he had anything to do with Callie's case. I smirked, remembering how I'd gotten his attention when I volunteered to bring Callie home with me. Then I heard my bathroom door open, and my smugness evaporated. I now had to live with this girl, this *kid*, until I could get her to Ann Arbor. She'd be with me 24/7, mostly in the privacy of my home. *My* home. What in hell had possessed me?

I lifted a corner of the sandwich with my fingers; it was black. I slid it from the pan to a plate, scraped the inedible bits off, and dropped it back in the hot pan to brown the other side. When the mess was on the plate, I stared at it, then told myself it was probably better than anything Callie'd had to eat at the jail and would have to do.

She appeared in my kitchen. Her blonde hair, still wet, was the color of river sand, and she wore the same clothes as when she'd walked out of the jail: a long skirt that brushed the floor and a long-sleeved floral blouse that covered her knuckles. Neither piece flattered her. I wondered whether she was making a fashion statement or if this was an evangelical version of those awful plaid skirts and white blouses we'd been forced to wear all twelve years at St. Anne's.

"Diet Coke?" I pulled the tab.

Callie shook her head. "No thank you. May I have water?"

I filled a glass for her and sat, then tipped back the can and let the cold liquid do its work.

"Miss Stephens?"

I swallowed. "Yes?"

"I'd like to pray. Before we eat."

It had been a long time since anyone prayed in this house. I plunked the soda can on the table and waited, my eyes open.

"Heavenly Father," Callie began, her hands folded and her eyes squeezed shut, "we invite you into this house and ask that you bless those who reside here and that you also bless this food to our use. Keep us in your care and in the light of your boundless love. Bless my father"—her voice caught, but she inhaled and let out a shaky breath—"and bless Miss Stephens. Amen." She opened her eyes and took a small bite of her sandwich, chewed it slowly and swallowed. "My father posted my bond, right?" She said it to herself, like she was thinking out loud. "That must mean he's not as angry as he was."

"I'm not sure what to think."

"I'm all he has, you know. Since Mother died. We're very close."

When Callie finished her sandwich, she asked to be excused, then carried her plate to the sink and rinsed it before retreating to her bedroom. I assumed she wanted to unpack her things and was relieved I wouldn't have to make conversation with her.

Accustomed to using my weekends to catch up on casework, I headed to my corner chair, laptop in hand, and located my most pressing file: an appellate brief that was due in Lansing on Monday. It wasn't like me to wait until the last minute to polish a brief, but I'd been so caught up in the details of Callie's case I hadn't devoted the time I should to this one. Now I'd have to hire a runner to deliver it to Lansing. I opened the file, scanned the screen, and cringed. My arguments were imprecise, sloppy, wordy, and complicated when they should have been concise and convincing. I made a couple of minor changes and rewrote my opening, but it was still far from satisfactory, so I opened another soda and then took a break. When I stepped outside, I startled a flock of sparrows from the deck.

As they scattered, I thought of my mother. She'd been on my mind, off and on, during the past week. Years before, when I found her death certificate, I'd realized she'd been pregnant with me when she married my dad. I'd wondered, the past several days, how she'd reacted to the news that she was expecting a baby.

The *Margaret Ann*, rocking in the boat well downstairs, had been a present to her from my dad. I now know it had been a last, desperate gift to help her. She'd used it plenty that final summer, taking it out at daybreak as the first birds stirred, telling us she was heading down to the marshy St. Clair Flats to sketch. I'd lie in bed and hear the motor catch and the thrum of the engine each time she scooted away.

After she died, my dad abruptly removed her bird feeders from the deck. When I asked what the birds would do for food, he told me they'd cope just fine. "Besides," he'd said, "you'll be at school, and I'll be too busy to feed them."

I wandered back inside and made a few changes to the brief before closing my laptop. I still couldn't focus on it. I told myself I'd finalize it the next day.

Around five o'clock, Callie came quietly into the living room and stood at the window, staring out at the river traffic.

"Hungry?" I asked.

"I guess..."

I poured myself a glass of wine and tossed a freezer-burned boxed pizza into the oven. When it was sufficiently toasted, we sat at the kitchen table, and I waited while Callie recited the same grace she had before lunch. While we ate, our sparse conversation was awkward; I asked whether she'd unpacked her things, and she said she had and politely thanked me.

When I refilled my goblet from the open bottle on the counter, she said quietly, "My church doesn't approve of drinking."

"To each her own," I said, and added, "My house, my rules." Then a question I'd been meaning to ask her came to mind. I said, "Something outside the jail yesterday frightened you. What was it?"

She answered in clipped words. "Nothing."

"Was it those men?"

"I hate cigarette smoke," she mumbled, and I thought she shuddered slightly.

"Any reason?"

When she didn't answer, I concluded smoking was probably another sin in her church. One of a long list. "It's certainly un-healthy," I said, and the silence continued.

When the pizza was gone, I toted both bottle and glass to my chair and plunked down to watch a tall-sparred touring sailboat bounce in the wake of a snazzy cigarette boat. A massive powerboat sliced through the water, like something from an early James Bond movie, slanted dark windows in a sleek hull. I replayed the jail scene again.

Why had I failed to keep my distance from this girl?

I'd felt sorry when her father refused to take her home to the parsonage. Sending her back to that cell after he posted her bond seemed heartless. My need to have Callie examined by Dr. Allen was a factor in my decision, but there was more. I took another drink and leaned my head against the back of the chair. Had I been drawn in because of what once happened to me?

A flock of Canada geese, like bowling pins with wings, descended and skidded to the river. They stretched their necks and spread their wings, then folded them tightly against their bodies and floated out of sight. I left my wine and strolled back to the kitchen. Everything had been neatly cleared by Callie, counters and table wiped clean before she disappeared into her room. I found her there, sprawled on the bed, still dressed, a pink teddy bear on her stomach.

"Thanks for cleaning up," I said.

"May I ask you a question?" She fingered the bear's ear.

"Shoot."

"Why did you say I could come live with you?"

"Well, the psychiatrist, the one I want to examine you, can't come to the jail. I need to take you to see her. It'll be easier to do that if you're staying with me."

"Miss Stephens?"

"Yes?"

"Those women in jail were sinners. I hope you don't think I'm one of them."

I often said I wished I had a nickel for every criminal client who sat in my office and claimed, "I'm not a criminal." I could have had a good night at the slot machines across the river in Port Edwards. The fact was, most of my clients fit the definition of criminals but couldn't reconcile their self-image with what they had done. It was easier to remain in a state of denial.

I said good night to Callie and drifted back to my chair and my wine. *Those women in jail were sinners.* Sister Phillip opened her eye, then shut it. I reflexively counted the seconds until the next blink. Thirty. Never more, never less. I heard the toilet flush and the door to Callie's bedroom click shut. Outside, a salty pushed its way upriver, its steep bow producing a tall wave that splashed over the top of my seawall, then receded.

Around midnight I heard a noise from Callie's room. Her voice erupted in angry moans, and I crept closer and listened. Should I open the door? What could I say that would help? I was her lawyer, not her mother. When any of my other clients got emotional, my usual response was to slide a Kleenex box across my desk and wait until they got themselves under control.

I decided I'd done enough to help this girl today. I'd invited her into my home, I'd fed her two meals, given her a bed to sleep in, and a bathroom to use. That was enough. Besides, I was dog tired. I crawled into bed and burrowed my head beneath my pillow to muffle the sound.

TWENTY-TWO

THE FOLLOWING MORNING, CALLIE'S MEAGER PERSONAL items lined a shelf against my bathroom wall, like latecomers to a play, waiting to be escorted to their seats when the first scene ended. Callie's bath towel hung neatly over a rod. She must have hung mine up, too, because it wasn't where I usually dropped it, on the tub's edge or the floor. Her bed was made and a pink teddy bear was propped against the pillows. She sat on the opposite edge of her bed, her back to me.

"Morning," I said.

She turned. She wore the same clothes as the previous day. "Good morning."

"I'll figure out something for breakfast in a minute."

"My father and I don't eat on Sunday mornings until after the last service. Miss Stephens?"

"What?"

"I wondered . . . I wondered if you . . . Could you take me to my church? Craig, Pastor Craig, I mean, when he came to see me at the jail, he told me that since I've been away, they've had to combine the second through fifth graders in Sunday school."

"I don't think—"

"Second and third graders study the Old Testament. Fourth and fifth start the New. They shouldn't be in the same class. Besides, my father depends on me. I'm his right-hand girl. That's what he calls me." Her dark eyes filled. "I thought, if he saw I could still help, he might . . . maybe he'd talk to me, maybe let me come home." She sniffed and wiped her nose with her hand.

Was this how it was going to be? Callie in tears, begging to see her father? Nightly outbursts that kept me awake? For a moment, I considered retreating beneath the covers of my own bed and covering my head with my pillow again. I was not going to take Callie to that church or any other church this morning. I didn't do church anymore.

"But if he saw that I was the same . . . that we could get back to the way we were . . ."

I ran a hand through my uncombed hair and straightened my glasses. I had a vague recollection of Molly talking about offering choices to her daughters. Something about options, the illusion of control. I said, "Callie, your choices this morning are a TV church service or . . . having a personal Bible study." It felt strange saying that, like I'd just been handed the script in a play I'd neither auditioned for nor rehearsed. I didn't wait to hear her response.

In the kitchen, I yanked open my fridge, surveyed its contents, then grabbed eggs, milk, and a loaf of bread. To my surprise, Callie emerged from her bedroom and stood in a corner watching me. I pointed to the bread. "You mind making the toast? Butter's in the fridge."

She stepped to my toaster oven and slid in two slices, then stood perfectly still. I stuck my nose in the opening of the milk carton, grimaced, then dumped it down the drain.

"I'm afraid your beverage choices this morning are water or coffee," I told her.

"Water's fine."

"I'll pick up some groceries tomorrow." I slid two rubbery fried eggs on a plate and, when the toast popped, said, "Breakfast is served." After filling a mug with coffee, I sat at the table.

"May I pray?"

"Right. Of course."

She ate as though she hadn't had a meal in days, then wiped her mouth with the side of her hand and said, "My father gets home from morning services around noon. May I call him then?"

When I said, "That's not a good idea," she huffed and held up her hands. I said firmly, "I'd like to use our time together to work on your case," an idea that only then popped into my head and continued, "And I have a question, Callie. What if . . . what if your father . . . believed you had sex?"

Her body stiffened and her dark eyes flashed angrily. "But I didn't. I told you, I . . . did . . . not."

"Okay." I nodded slowly, not in agreement but more out of habit, a technique I use when a client tells me a story I don't believe, when I want to buy time, to look like I'm processing, trying to see my client's side when in reality, I don't. "I'm not accusing you. I'm just asking a question. Hypothetically. You know what *hypothetical* means?"

"I'm not stupid."

"No one said you were. I'm just asking a question. What if he *thought* you had sex?"

When she covered her face with her hands and let out a sob, I swiped a tissue from a box on the counter and held it out, then gave her three more as she continued to cry. If she was acting, she was damn good. When she didn't stop crying, I put a hand on her arm and said, "Why don't you rest for a while? I'll clean up."

"I don't see what it would hurt if I called him."

I handed her the Kleenex box. "My house, my rules, remember?"

She grabbed the box and fled to her room.

Rinsing dishes at my kitchen window, I watched a pack of powerboats race past, skipping across one another's wakes. Sister Phillip rocked back and forth crazily. Based on Callie's reaction to my questions, I had my answer. If her father discovered she'd had sex, he would have been furious.

TWENTY-THREE

AS CALLIE'S SHOULDERS INCHED CLOSER TO HER EARS, I grabbed her arm and pulled her against me. Media types encircled the parking meters outside my office, their cameras rolling. Someone thrust a tape recorder in my face when I tried to pass. I raised my laptop like a shield.

Linda George, the former prosecutor with her own show on CNN, shoved it to the side and planted herself in front of Callie. "Young lady, how does it feel to know you're going to prison for the rest of your life?"

Callie shrank from me.

I stepped between the two of them and glared at Linda. "Stop bullying my client."

Linda bowed dramatically and held up her microphone, then backed away. "Did you get that?" she called to her cameraman.

Callie had covered her face with her hands, so I half-shoved, half-dragged her. Suddenly I noticed the pungent aroma of cigarette smoke. Callie froze and refused to move. I pushed her closer to the door. When we reached it, it popped open and I half-carried her inside. Gail locked the door behind us, then gripped the shade and nearly pulled it off its roller in her haste to cover the window on which my father's and my names were etched in gold gothic letters. "They'll be going through our garbage next," Gail mumbled, but I thought I detected a hint of excitement in her voice.

"I need you to draft a petition for a restraining order. Keep the media fifty yards from this office. And my cottage. They'll be there next. Allege they're interfering with the operation of my law practice."

Gail's eyes sparkled. "Like Jackie O. When Ron Galella harassed her."

"Who?"

"Paparazzo Extraordinaire? If you read the tabloids, you'd know these things—"

"Buzz me when the petition's ready for my signature. I can't have the rest of my clients harassed. Or worrying about being photographed coming to my office. Allege all that. Got it?"

"Absolutely." Gail slid into her chair and switched on her computer, her excitement palpable now.

I turned to Callie, who stood off to one side, her shoulders curled forward and her white Bible against her chest. She was trembling, so I took her arm again, gently this time. "Come with me," I said, leading her to the rear of my office. "You're okay, Callie," I said, but I don't know if she heard me. "You'll spend your days at my office until I can get you to Ann Arbor."

I showed her my private office, the bathroom, the tiny kitchenette, and my law library, a high-ceilinged room with a large table and floor-to-ceiling shelves of leather-bound books. Although I performed nearly all my legal research on my computer, I'd never been able to toss out these old casebooks of my dad's.

"You can sit in this library while I work. No windows. Okay? Callie?" She still wouldn't look at me. "I'll take care of those people. That's my job. To look after you."

She dropped into a chair, still clutching her Bible.

Out front, Gail was leaning into her computer screen, proofing the beginnings of her work. Without looking up, she said, "I thought it was a bad idea to socialize with clients."

I recognized my words and those of my dad. "I'm not socializing," I said. "I'm just giving her a place to live until she sees the doctor. Also, we can both keep an eye on her. She could help you with filing or something."

Eyes still on her screen, Gail pursed her lips and said, "I do my own filing."

At my desk, I phoned Dr. Allen, tapping Dad's Waterman on my desk while I waited to get through. I'd already decided to reschedule my other hearings, do whatever it took, if it meant Callie could get in to see the doctor right away. Once she was evaluated, there'd be no need for her to stay with me. Maybe Dr. Allen could even see her this week.

"Hello?" A woman who identified herself as Dr. Allen's admin answered. "She said if you called, I was to give you a message. The doctor's son fell during a rock-climbing expedition in Switzerland, and she's cancelled everything and flown there to be with him. I'm not to schedule anything until she returns."

I closed my eyes. *Shit, shit, shit.* "Any idea when she'll return?"

"She hopes his condition will stabilize soon, but everything is day-to-day just now. I'll call you when I know more."

I peered between the slats on my window blind. A couple of reporters in the dusty parking lot out back were chatting. A barrel-chested man handed a cup of coffee to a slender guy in a sport coat, then leaned against a white van, a large camera at his feet.

"Petition's ready for your signature." Gail stood behind me.

I scanned and signed it. "You'll run it up to the clerk's office? I don't think I should leave her just yet. The craziness outside spooked her."

Gail said, "I'll lock up when I leave. Oh, and Molly's on the phone. Line one."

"Does she know I'm here?"

"Yup."

I hesitated. Molly kept up with the news back here by reading the *Sentinel* online. What had they printed? And what had Molly read? I took a breath and picked up.

"Vic, hi. I thought I'd need to leave a message. Aren't you usually in court on Mondays?"

"Not today."

"*Perfectus.* I'm calling to see if you'd like a visitor next weekend? Jake's on deadline for his textbook, and the girls are visiting their grandmother in Quebec, so I thought I'd come see you. I have photos from my trip. And I brought you a present from the Vatican Museum. I could be at the bridge by three on Friday."

"This weekend's not good, Molly."

"But the weather's supposed to be gorgeous. We can go tubing, I'll cook for us—"

"Molly, I already have a house guest."

"You?" She knew how seriously I guarded my privacy. "Who's that?"

"The teenager I told you about. She got bonded out on Saturday, and her father wouldn't let her come home. So . . . well . . . the short version is . . . she's living with me."

"Your homicide client? At your cottage? Jesus, Victoria. Have you lost your mind?"

"Maybe. Mostly it's . . . strange having her there. Awkward."

"Strange? Awkward? It's a terrible idea. You're supposed to be defending her, not bringing her home like she's some stray from a shelter. If you're lonely, get a damn dog."

"This whole thing's complicated, Molly. If it's any consolation, it's not much fun having her. For starters, I don't know what I'm supposed to talk to her about. Besides her case. And she won't talk about that."

"If she's anything like my girls, she'll just watch TV or play games on her phone."

"She doesn't have a cell phone. And she hasn't mentioned TV."

"Every teenager has a cell phone. Jesus, Victoria. I cannot believe this."

"Maybe I'm just rehearsing to be one of your chaperones."

"There are better ways to accomplish that. My god, Victoria."

"You don't have to be so upset with me. And I don't need a lecture—"

"I'm not lecturing, I'm—"

"You are, Molly." The office phone rang, so I said, "I've got to grab that," and hung up, then let the other call go to voice mail.

During the coming week, Callie politely, but repeatedly, asked if she could phone her father. Each time I refused her request. Other than that, she didn't say much. At my cottage, she kept to her room, showing up for meals and then silently cleaning up the kitchen before returning to sit on her bed. Nights I often heard her moaning in her sleep; sometimes she shouted an emphatic "No!" One night she wandered from her room and I found her on the deck, staring out at the dark water. When I touched her arm she woke up, eyes wide, and let me lead her back to bed. On the drive to my office the following morning, I'd asked Callie if she wanted to talk about her dream. But she didn't respond, so I dropped the subject.

Gail served the press with copies of the restraining order and continued to keep the front door locked, admitting only known clients for scheduled appointments. I spent much of the week in my car, juggling court appearances in five different counties. When I returned to my office that Friday afternoon, Gail greeted me.

"I have great news," she practically gushed. "I took in a big-time extradition file. I quoted forty thou on the phone—just for grins—and the father said he'd be here first thing Monday with the money. He wanted to know if you preferred cash."

I slumped into the chair beside Gail's desk. I'd been awake

most nights that week listening for Callie. Her nightmares continued, and while I'd only found her on the deck that one night, even that one event worried me. The river could be an escape—from me, from the trial, from everything. Why was she out there?

"I don't know the first thing about extradition," I said now to Gail.

"It can't be that hard to figure out. And you told me you can't get the kid in to see the shrink until who knows when—"

"With a retainer like that I'd have to be available, day and night. And what if Dr. Allen returns?" I shook my head. "Much as I hate to turn this client away, I have to."

"But—"

"I'm pretty sure Joyce Ballinger told me she handled an extradition case once. She must have had that baby by now. Give the client her number."

In the library, I found Callie napping, her head on her arms, her Bible beside her. I touched her elbow and she jumped, as if I'd given her a jolt of electricity. "Callie," I said softly, "It's time to go home."

On the drive I asked what she'd done all day and she didn't have much to say besides that she'd read some chapters of her Bible.

"Would you like me to bring you some library books? Or we could bring your sewing machine here so you'd have something to do. You must be climbing the walls."

"I'm okay." Another one of her shrugs. "But thank you for offering. That's very kind of you."

"Sure. If you change your mind, let me know."

TWENTY-FOUR

ONE DAY THE FOLLOWING WEEK, I ARGUED A MOTION TO Suppress in a felony drug case while a begrudging Gail continued to supervise Callie at my office. The judge worked us through lunch, then took my motion under advisement, promising a decision in two weeks. When I left the courthouse, I could already taste the burger I planned to pick up at the drive-thru around the corner. I tossed my briefcase on the passenger seat and was half-in, half-out of my car when a woman in an oversized floral dress hustled toward me. "Miss Stephens?" she called.

I recognized the woman from the kitchen at New Life in God, the one who invited me to that luncheon. Rose something. "Yes?" How had she known I'd be here?

"I have something for you. I mean for Callie." She pointed to a red Honda nearby. "Callie's father packed her suitcase, but I thought she might like some of her other things. I'm Rose Walker. We met at my church, remember? Callie didn't tell you about me?" She paused expectantly, then took a long breath. "I'm her father's fiancée. Reverend Thomas and I were supposed to get married. This summer. Callie was going to be my maid of honor. Are you sure she didn't say anything?" She looked hopeful.

I said, "I can't say what we talk about."

"Like a pastor. I understand." But her posture and her voice were suddenly deflated. She said, "Well, I'll just get those bags."

She returned with two bulging black garbage bags. "There's a quilt I made her in one of these. The other has some underwear and a few things I thought she might need."

I popped my trunk lid, and she shoved both bags inside.

"How is she doing?" she asked.

"Okay." I nodded. "Okay."

"Well, tell her Rose said hello. You know, I couldn't stand the thought of her sitting in that jail cell. I'm glad she's out. Neil doesn't have that kind of money. But I had a savings account for my retirement."

"You posted her bond?"

"It wasn't easy convincing Neil, but I'm glad I did. Will you tell her that I'm praying for her?"

"Do you want her to know you posted her bond?"

She tilted her head from side to side, smiled. "I guess it wouldn't hurt."

"Rose, do you know why her father won't let her come home?"

She glanced around the lot, then back toward me. "It's not my place to say. He's a very righteous man, our church is lucky to have him."

"But—"

"Neil loves her very much. I know that. But this is difficult. For all of us. I really can't stay. I probably stayed too long as it is." She looked around, then hurried to her car and drove off.

I picked up the burger and ate it on the drive to my office. I thought back to the day I brought Callie to my cottage. She'd insisted she was all her father had, that the two of them were very close. Why hadn't she mentioned Rose? Did it matter?

Gail was thumbing through an issue of *Us Weekly* when I perched on the edge of her desk and told her about meeting Rose. "Why didn't Callie tell me?" I whispered.

"No clue." She slid a brochure across the desk. "But there's a seminar next week in Detroit you might want to attend . . ." She rested her chin on her fist and watched me read the shiny pamphlet.

"'How to Tell When a Client Is Lying'?"

"It's just that you always preach about keeping a professional distance from our clients and now—"

"You think she's lying to me?"

"Or sandbagging you. Maybe. It's one thing to defend a client and another to rescue one. And if she's hiding things from you—"

"Is there something you know that I don't?"

She shrugged. "It's just a feeling I have."

I dropped the pamphlet on Gail's desk. "She in the law library?"

"Should I register you?"

"Not yet," I called back to her as I walked away.

I found Callie dozing, her head on her Bible. When I touched her arm, she jumped. I put my hand on her shoulder. "It's me, Callie. You're okay."

She blinked.

"Did you get any lunch?" I asked.

"Gail gave me a tuna fish sandwich."

"Good." I pulled out a chair and sat. "Callie, does the name Rose Walker ring any bells with you?"

She began fingering the soft leather cover of her Bible.

"She said she was engaged to your father."

Her fingers slid along the book's edges.

"She made a quilt for you."

Callie said, "It's too hot for a quilt," and opened her Bible. She licked her index finger and turned several pages, then bent her head forward and pretended to read.

"Why didn't you mention her to me?"

She shrugged. "Is it important?"

"That's what I'd like to know," I said.

Back at my desk, I absentmindedly flipped through the cache of messages Gail had taken during my absence. I'd always prided myself on being able to ascertain when a client was lying. I couldn't decide whether Callie's failure to mention Rose was a lie, a sin of omission, or an oversight. She hadn't said much of anything to me since she moved in, but somehow this seemed consequential. How was I supposed to know if it was or wasn't? I'd made a note of the word *malingering* when I talked to George Deering. What exactly was going on?

TWENTY-FIVE

THAT EVENING CALLIE HAULED BOTH BAGS TO HER bedroom, but instead of holing up in there as she usually did, she immediately reappeared. I was in my kitchen, sorting through my personal mail, junk mostly, which I tossed in a waste bin beneath the sink. "I'll order dinner in a minute," I said.

She knelt at one of my low kitchen shelves and ran her index finger across the spines of the books there. "You have a lot of cookbooks," she said.

"Uh-huh."

"Do you ever use them?"

"Never."

She pulled a tattered *Joy of Cooking* from the shelf, flipped through it. "This sounds good. Poached salmon." She lifted the book to show me the recipe.

"Too many ingredients. My cutoff is four," I said.

"Four ingredients? Why?"

"I'm not interested in cooking. I tried a few times. But it was always a disaster. I even screwed up Stove Top stuffing. That box mix?" I'd tried to surprise him with a home-cooked dinner. Peach soup in a crust instead of peach pie. Watery stuffing. I'd aced two years of law school classes; I didn't think I needed to read the instructions on the back of the stuffing box.

Callie said, "I used to cook for my father and me. I could make dinner for us sometime. I'm up to seven ingredients."

I grinned at her, then tapped Mario's phone number into my phone. Some new kid answered and put me on hold. I pushed the speaker button and uncorked a bottle of Chardonnay. *Callie used to cook for her father.* I poured myself a glass and took a swallow. Finally, someone came on the line and took my pizza order. While we waited for the delivery boy to show up, I told Callie, "Make a list of ingredients, and I'll pick them up tomorrow."

A week later, Callie fussed in the kitchen while I sat nearby with a glass of wine and a legal pad. Ever since I'd confronted Callie about Rose, she'd been slightly more talkative. Was this her way of apologizing for something she shouldn't have kept secret, or was it a coincidence? And she prepared all our dinners. I let her cook whatever she wanted; her meals were what I'd call homestyle—spaghetti, pork chops, roasted chicken, that sort of thing. Nothing gourmet but they were surprisingly tasty. I hadn't stepped on my bathroom scales for a while, but my suits were getting a bit tight.

I flipped to a previous page on my legal pad. That afternoon I'd jotted down a question, a major concern I was certain jurors would have. I'd have to answer it to have any chance of convincing them my defense made sense:

- *What would cause a mother to kill her own newborn?*

Even if Dr. Allen were allowed to explain neonaticide syndrome, I was sure some jurors would have trouble getting beyond their instinctive beliefs about how mothers behaved.

Now I wrote:

- *A mother would instinctively try to save her child.*

- *Maternal instinct would overpower a mother's desire to conceal the birth of her baby.*

"*Question the premise.*" I heard my dad's voice. "*Keep digging.*" I added:

- *What exactly is maternal instinct?*

While Callie chopped onions, I googled "maternal instinct" and passed over cutesy photos of mother lions and mother bears with their young as I searched for serious studies on the subject of human mothering.

I came upon a paper by a prominent sociologist who'd written, "All human females have maternal instincts. But the degree varies widely. In fact, many mothers do not exhibit a full-blown commitment to their infants immediately after birth. Instead, the bond unfolds gradually. Maternal instincts are not an all-or-nothing proposition."

A second study concluded that maternal instincts were not absolute. "Because society craves the ideal of the Madonna and child, it claims that nurturing comes naturally to all women. Women to whom it does not are looked upon as aberrant females, unnatural creatures. The experts on this topic all agree that isn't the reality."

A third site said the percentage of women who resolve to give up their babies for adoption and then change their minds was inversely proportionate to the amount of time they held their babies following birth.

A fourth study said women who committed neonaticide did not see their infants as babies, but rather as objects to be gotten rid of.

I needed to go over this information with Dr. Allen and ask how we could incorporate it into her testimony. I made some notes before Callie called me to dinner. She offered a blessing over the meatloaf and carrots she'd prepared.

I said, "The dinners you make are all great, Callie. Every one. We'd never eat like this if I were cooking."

"You practice law. You don't have time to cook, too. I've been thinking that maybe I could help out more here. I did the cooking and cleaning at the parsonage. And I could wash your clothes when I do mine."

"That's not necessary—"

"But you're taking care of me, letting me stay here. Wouldn't it help you?" she asked. "You'd have a lot more time to work on my case. On all your cases, I mean, not just mine," she said. "And I could make our lunches to take to the office."

I considered. "I guess you could do some of that. Or all of it if you want. But only if you want. That's not why you're here."

"I know. I'm here because you took me in and my father doesn't want me." She sniffled.

I asked, "Why don't you like Rose?"

She scowled and rested her chin on her hand, covering her mouth. "Who says I don't?"

"Well, you never told me about her. And you didn't seem too excited when she sent you that quilt she made. Did you know she put up the money so you could get out of jail?"

"I don't need another mother."

"She tries to mother you?"

She shrugged. "So can I start doing the cleaning around here?"

"I guess. Although I don't have a lot of cleaning supplies."

"I already made a list of what I'll need," she said.

That same night, after Callie disappeared into her room, I opened my laptop and googled Neil Thomas. Copies of his sermons were posted, along with invitations to join New Life in God, in several online sites. I added "Indiana" to my search and found an old church website, much simpler than New Life's, with fewer photos, one that apparently hadn't been updated in a while. On it was a photo of Callie standing next to her parents. Sheila Thomas was an attractive blonde.

I added her name to my search and found a short obituary plus a lengthy news article that described a double fatality outside the parking lot of a Days Inn in Indianapolis. Sheila Thomas's car was T-boned by a semi. There'd been another victim, a male passenger, in her car, so I searched for his obituary.

Harry Stillman was a member of Neil Thomas's church. Nothing in the article offered an explanation of why the two had been together at this motel. No church conference or meeting was mentioned.

Were Sheila Thomas and Harry Stillman having an affair? Did Callie know? Or had Callie's father hidden this from her? Was this the reason they'd moved here from Indiana?

Heading to bed that night, I peeked into Callie's bedroom. She was clutching her teddy bear and snoring softly, her mouth open. As I watched, she sniffed, turned on her side, and settled into a sound sleep.

TWENTY-SIX

"I FEEL LIKE A DAMN JAIL MATRON." GAIL FLIPPED THE pages of the latest issue of *People*.

I'd been in federal court in Detroit all day, and I was spent. I'd only stopped in to pick up Callie and head home.

"She and I are locked up together all day in this office."

"I know." I sank into the chair beside her desk. "I don't suppose Dr. Allen's office phoned—"

"The only thrilling communication today was this piece of crap." She handed me an envelope on which PERSONAL AND CONFIDEN-TIAL had been written in bold ink. "Someone slid this beneath the door. Naturally, I opened it."

I unfolded the paper inside, read.

NOW SHE'S LIVING WITH YOU? THERE'S A SPECIAL CHAMBER FOR BITCHES LIKE YOU IN HELL. I HOPE YOUR DISGUSTING EXCUSE FOR A SMELLY SOUL ROTS WHILE YOU WRITHE IN PAIN, NEXT TO YOUR WHORE OF A BABY KILLING CLIENT.

A chill skipped through me. In all the cases I'd defended, even other murder trials, I'd never received a single piece of hate mail. I crumpled the paper and threw it, hard, into Gail's metal wastebasket. "Any other surprises?" I asked.

"Not exactly a surprise, but something you might be interested in." She handed me the day's *Sentinel*.

On the front page was a picture of Barrett shaking hands at a pro-life rally. The caption didn't say he'd spoken at the rally, but thanks to the photo his support for the pro-life cause was clear. It was also clear that he was determined to try Callie's case in the court of public opinion. If the voters wanted to link abortion to neonaticide, he was more than happy to let them.

"Great." I dumped the paper into the wastebasket and headed to my office. I found this latest tactic of Barrett's offensive, but effective. BARRETT MICHAELS FOR JUDGE yard signs had been popping up like morels during a warm, wet spring. A conviction in Callie's case would seal the deal for him.

Unsettled by the letter and the photo, I told myself I didn't have the luxury of going home as I'd planned. I'd been hoping Eleanor Allen's testimony would provide the crux of my defense; still I didn't want to miss any evidentiary issues. At my desk, I opened Callie's file and read over the search warrant seeking the black raincoat. As far as I knew, the police still hadn't located it.

On a hunch, I stepped to my library. Callie sat quietly; she appeared to be sketching something on one of my legal pads.

I said, "Callie, did you own a black raincoat? With a hood? The police claim you had it on when you went to the river."

"I didn't go to the river," she said without looking up.

"But do you own a black raincoat?"

"Yes."

"Do you have any idea where it might be?"

"Sure."

"Mind telling me?"

"It's in my closet. Well, I mean *your* closet."

"At my cottage? How the hell did it get in my closet?"

Callie pursed her lips and froze. My language sometimes

bothered her, but I'd told myself that was her issue, not mine.

"How the hell did the coat get in my closet?" I repeated.

"I think it was in my suitcase. Or one of those bags from her. I don't remember."

"By 'her' you mean Rose?"

She nodded robotically.

"I need you to give it to me as soon as we get home. First thing."

When she emerged from her bedroom with the coat, she said, "Are you going to give this to the police?"

"God, no. This . . ." I looked it over, checked the pockets, lifted the hood. "This"—I held the coat up to her—"is privileged information. Between you and me. No one else. Understood?"

She tilted her head. "Is that legal?"

"Perfectly. Absolutely." In my bedroom I examined the fabric beneath my bedside reading lamp. No blood was visible, nothing that would link the coat to the baby's birth.

But who sent this to Callie? Her father was present when the police searched the parsonage for it. Later, he'd packed her suitcase. Had he sent it? Was this another stunt from him, like refusing to take her home after her bond was posted?

Or did Rose send it in one of those garbage bags? I should have inventoried their contents, but it hadn't occurred to me. By now I'd seen enough to question whose side Callie's father was on. And Rose seemed to want to help Callie, but not at the risk of angering her fiancé.

I hung the coat in the back of my closet. I'd figure this out later.

TWENTY-SEVEN

DR. ALLEN'S ADMIN PHONED TO SAY THAT HER BOSS WAS back from Switzerland and would make time to see Callie the following week. Which meant I would know soon if I had a defense.

And if I didn't?

I'd once hoped, assuming Callie's diagnosis was favorable, that her father would listen to an explanation of neonaticide syndrome, that he'd accept that that was what caused her behavior, and that he'd allow Callie to come home to the parsonage pending her trial. I no longer thought that. Not since I'd concluded that either Neil Thomas or Rose Walker sent the black coat to Callie and meant for her to wear it in public. I was betting on the reverend, but Rose seemed so loyal to him I didn't feel comfortable trusting either one of them.

That weekend, Callie cleaned up from the chicken parmesan dinner she'd prepared, then curled up on the living room sofa with the legal pad and pencil I'd recently noticed her toting to and from my office along with her white Bible. Although most times I'd peeked in the law library she was staring into space, every now and then it appeared she was writing or drawing something. I was relieved she was doing something to pass what must be interminably long days in my office.

Meanwhile, I went online to read a law review article about neonaticide statistics, surprised to learn how prevalent the syndrome was. When I shut my laptop, Callie wordlessly slid her legal pad on top of its closed cover.

She'd drawn a merganser, one of the ducks that congregated along my seawall earlier that evening. Its comb was striated and the iris in its large eye appeared to reflect the sunlight.

"It's a present," she said, "because you like birds so much."

"What makes you think I like birds?"

"All these paintings and drawings around here—" She pointed to the cottage walls.

"My mother painted those."

She reached for the pad, pulled it away. "Oh, I thought . . ." She flipped the pad over on her lap. "I probably shouldn't be drawing anyway."

I remembered the last argument I heard my parents having before my mother died. She'd shouted at him, "My art is what keeps me sane."

I reached out for Callie's drawing. "This is actually quite good, Callie," I told her. "If it's okay with you, I'd like to keep it."

On the drive to Ann Arbor, I passed a VW bus covered in abstract flowers—lilies and daisies, showy blossoms in teals, magentas, and oranges. When my speedometer inched above eighty, I braked and set my cruise control to seventy-three.

"Dr. Allen knows about cases where girls were accused of the same crime as you. I expect she'll ask you some questions and give you some tests. What you tell her is confidential, just like it would be if you told me something."

Callie sat silently, her white Bible open on her lap. A bumper sticker on the rear of a rusted pickup in front of us read, DON'T LIKE MY DRIVING? CALL 1-800-GOTOHELL.

"Blasphemous," she murmured.

"You can tell her anything, okay?"

"You've said all this. Repeatedly," she said patiently.

"So she can help us."

"I know."

I tapped the steering wheel with my fingers, and Callie reached over and patted my arm.

On U-M's Medical Campus, a petite sixty-something woman in an expensive-looking suit opened a frosted glass door. Her grey hair was in a bun, and large sapphire earrings accentuated the blue in her eyes. "Attorney Stephens?" She shook my hand, then turned to Callie. "And you must be Calliope. I'm Dr. Allen. I'd like to speak with you first."

I pulled a *Drunk Driving Defense Manual* from my briefcase and made a few margin notes in a chapter titled "Breathalyzer Challenges," then set it aside. Next I changed seats so I'd be closer to a large window overlooking the east side of the university's sprawling campus. The leaves on the maple trees were turning soft yellows, precursors to the brilliant oranges and reds that made autumn so beautiful in Michigan. Below me, students hurried past.

I reopened the manual to the chapter titled "Driver's License Revocation," but I was too jumpy to absorb what I was reading. I stood and tried unsuccessfully to focus on the activity below. After a seemingly endless three hours, Dr. Allen appeared with Callie in tow. "Have a seat, Calliope," she said. "I wish to speak with your attorney."

The largest diploma on the wall was from Ruprecht-Karls-Universität Heidelberg, summa cum laude. Other diplomas, plus numerous framed honors and awards from the American Psychiatric Association, surrounded it. Dr. Allen pointed me to a chair, then sat behind her desk.

"How's your son doing?" I asked.

"He's much improved, thank you. For a time, we thought we would lose him. But he will recover." She folded her small hands beneath her chin. "Your client presents an interesting case," she said. "During our interview she was quiet, soft-spoken, and respectful. Until I asked about her pregnancy. At that moment, she became what I would characterize as extremely defensive, almost hostile. She denied that she had been pregnant, and she also denied that she gave birth. I assume this is all consistent with what she's told you?"

"That's correct."

"I asked her about her family and her current situation. She claims to have been very close with her father and involved in his ministry until this incident. She's grateful that you have taken her into your home when he wouldn't let her return to the parsonage. She seems to like living with you." Dr. Allen glanced at her notes. "She says that since her mother died when she was twelve, her father has depended on her for household chores and assistance with the large congregation to which he ministers. She began to cry when I asked what he said to her about the charges, but she didn't answer my question. She seems more interested in his approval than in anything else. But he hasn't spoken to her since her hospitalization?"

"That's correct. But his fiancée posted her bond so she could come here."

"He didn't explain why they did that?"

"Not to me. His fiancée said she couldn't stand the idea of Callie in a jail cell."

"Does Calliope interact with this fiancée?"

"Callie doesn't seem to like her."

Dr. Allen made another note. "And she's been living with you for almost two months now. Have you noticed any behavior that concerned you?"

"She has nightmares, not every night but regularly. She hollers in her sleep. One night I found her on the deck of my cottage just staring at the river. And there's something about cigarette smoke that seems to frighten her. She's almost catatonic when she smells it. Mostly, I guess I'd say she doesn't seem interested in much of anything, although she's begun drawing and sketching. She's quite talented. And recently she asked to cook our meals and clean the cottage. It seemed important to her, so I said yes."

She made another note and looked at me. "So today I administered two significant tests. There is a Checklist for Dissociation and another similar test for children. Because Calliope is only seventeen, I administered the Child Dissociative Checklist. The DES-B, as it's called, helps us determine whether there is a likelihood that the test subject dissociated from reality at some time in the past. I also gave Calliope the Test of Memory Malingering, the TOMM, which can help us determine whether someone has a genuine memory loss or is malingering.

"The notes you sent me indicated your concern that Calliope might be malingering because of her abrupt change in behavior in the state psychologist's office during her competency exam. But having a normal conversation with someone who has no connection with and is not a reminder of the traumatic event does not prove someone is malingering. Quite the opposite. It is the traumatic event that triggers the disturbance.

"Calliope's answers to the DES-B questions, while not conclusive, are within the range of those we find when someone has suffered a dissociative experience at some previous time."

"What exactly is a dissociative experience, Doctor?"

"A dissociative experience occurs when the mind acts to protect itself from what it sees as an unimaginable situation. It doesn't let itself believe the reality that is taking place. You see, when a traumatic event occurs that directly challenges a person's connection to their main attachment, which in Callie's case would seem to be her father, the brain tries to prevent that separation from happening. It's an issue of survival. 'If I remember and others know what I did, I won't have anyone to care for me and I could die.' Do you follow?"

"Yes."

"In your client's case, if she could not cope with the idea that she was pregnant, it is likely she may have dissociated right on through the birth of her child."

"Is dissociation a mental illness?"

"Not necessarily. It depends on the degree of dissociation. We all dissociate. Have you ever driven to work and once there, can't remember how you got from home to the office? Come into a room to get something and then can't remember why you are there? These are mild forms of dissociation."

"Is dissociation different than denial?"

"Dissociation is a much more severe form of denial. Dissociation can have both conscious and unconscious roots. The stronger the unconscious origins, the more profound the denial. In cases such as Calliope's, these young women ignore what might be obvious signs of pregnancy to someone else. Some of these women even continue to menstruate, most don't gain much weight, if any, so there are no outward signs."

"Did Callie talk about these things with you?"

"She was reluctant to talk about her periods, but she disclosed that she had regular menses during the past year. She claimed she gained little or no weight. She's somewhat overweight, so it might have been easy to hide a pregnancy. If she wore baggy clothing, for example. And she has no mother or sisters who would see her without clothing, correct?"

"Right."

"There can be a fine line between conscious and unconscious denial, Miss Stephens. Like your client, some of these girls who dissociate come from what appear to be good homes, good families. They are terrified of the consequences should their pregnancies be discovered. It would be a visible sign to the world that they had sexual relations. They think, 'I'm a good girl, and good girls don't get pregnant. Therefore, I cannot be pregnant.' Becoming pregnant would be particularly traumatic for the daughter of a minister."

"She founded a club at her church where girls could take an oath to remain virgins until they married."

"Yes, she does present an extreme case. No wonder she dissociated. And, based on the results of the TOMM, I found no evidence of malingering. I have concluded that, in my opinion, Calliope's memory loss is genuine."

"Is it likely she will ever remember?"

"It's hard to say. Usually once the baby is born, the mother gets rid of it in some way and then immediately reverts to a nondissociative state. She often remembers being present for the birth but will say it was like she was hovering above the birth, present but not involved. Once the baby is gone, things are as they should be, back to normal, in her mind. So there's little evidence of a mental illness."

"Which is why insanity is difficult to prove?"

"Precisely. Unlike mothers who commit infanticide, most women who commit neonaticide are not mentally ill, per se. Nor do they have a known history of, or current presenting, mental illness. Neonaticide is often committed by teenagers who are frightened, confused, and panicked by their situation. On some occasions, these girls have been forced into sexual relations."

"They were raped?"

"Not just raped as we commonly understand it, but any sexual assault could trigger a dissociative experience. Keep in mind that we have no evidence your client was sexually assaulted. But where there is such profound denial, such inability to remember, as in her case, there is that possibility. The experience of forcible sexual relations can be so traumatic, especially to an immature girl raised with very strict sexual standards, that they receive what you Americans call a 'double whammy.' First, the trauma of the assault, which the young girl cannot bring herself to report, and then the dissociative behavior when, on some level, she suspects she might be pregnant. These girls usually blame themselves for the sexual activity, whether that's the reality or not. So they just want the whole thing to disappear. Ergo, they do nothing until the birth occurs."

Dr. Allen pulled off one of her clip-on earrings, then the other, and placed them in front of her on the desk. She massaged her earlobes with her fingertips. "This, of course, is hypothetical, since we have no evidence that your client was raped or otherwise violated. But. You are here to find out whether you have a basis for an insanity defense. My answer is that there may be not only one basis but three."

Three?

"The neonaticide syndrome, a more specific kind of dissociation, would be strongest, if your judge permitted the jury to learn about it. The second would be dissociation. Unlike the neonaticide syndrome, dissociation *is* a recognized diagnosis in the *DSM-5*. You're familiar with that?"

"The *Diagnostic and Statistical Manual*, yes."

"Since dissociation is recognized in the *DSM-5*, it could form a basis for a finding of insanity regardless of whether the neonaticide syndrome is allowed. However, I don't see this as a strong defense as it may be difficult to convince a jury that a woman who went to the lengths your client did to hide the birth was dissociating. You see, in most cases of this type, the baby is stuffed in a closet or cupboard or tossed over the back fence. There's no outward, rational act to hide the birth or the baby. But a growing number of experts in my profession believe that if a young woman has been sexually assaulted, she may suffer from a severe reactive psychosis when faced with the reality of her pregnancy. And both depersonalization disorder and brief reactive psychosis, which you might know better as post-traumatic stress disorder, are recognized in the *DSM-5*."

"So you're saying if Callie was raped—"

"It would present another insanity defense that's a third alternative to the neonaticide syndrome and dissociation. In the event your judge does not allow testimony about the syndrome, you could argue that she suffered from PTSD. Your client's behavior, including her calculated efforts to clean up any traces of the birth and get rid of the body by taking it to the river, would be explained by the trauma of the assault. If she hid the baby's body and went about her normal routine, she was absolving herself of the experience of being violated. Also, her recurring nightmares and inability to focus are criteria that show alterations in Callie's mood and cognition consistent with PTSD. PTSD might have a chance of being understood by a jury."

I said, "I didn't come across anything that mentioned PTSD as a defense to neonaticide."

"It would be far preferable to present the neonaticide syndrome if we have no evidence that Calliope was sexually violated when she became pregnant. But your judge must allow that testimony and, as you know, no jurisdiction has yet done so."

"And you're saying that PTSD is a long shot, too?"

"It has been offered and allowed as a defense in other cases, but the results have not been favorable. However, it's within the realm of possible diagnoses, so I must offer it to you."

"She's been so adamant that she wasn't pregnant, that none of this happened."

"The DES-B and the TOMM are designed to filter out the possibility that a subject is lying. I saw no evidence that your client was being untruthful, but no test is foolproof. Which means my opinion is just that—an opinion. It is based upon the facts as I currently understand them."

"Does this mean you'll help us?"

She bit her lips together, sighed. "I'll do what I can, but I can't promise results."

"I understand, yes." I stood and grasped one of her hands, as though she'd just thrown me a lifeline, which in a sense she had. "Thank you," I said, "thank you so much."

"If anything changes, you must contact me immediately."

"You're saying I should let you know if Callie remembers anything about what happened?"

"Correct."

"How likely is it that she will remember anything that happened so long ago?"

"Not likely. And it's important that you not try and force her to recall what she cannot. It could result in worse trauma than she is already experiencing. But there is some data that the safer a victim feels, the stronger the chance she'll recall and speak about the events surrounding the trauma. I don't expect it here, but one never knows."

"I understand."

"If there's nothing else, I'll have my report emailed to you within the next couple of days." She tipped her head from one side to the other as she replaced her earrings.

Outside the building I said to Callie, "Let's walk." I lifted her Bible from her arms and dropped it in my briefcase, then locked the case in my car trunk. "I'll give you the ten-cent tour and then take you to a place that makes great sandwiches."

I led Callie across campus. I felt ten pounds lighter, maybe twenty. Eleanor Allen's analysis and offer of help were the best I'd hoped for.

Through a stone archway, sunlight dappled a grassy courtyard at the center of Michigan's law school, an imposing Gothic structure modeled after King's College in Cambridge, England. On the groomed lawn, students talked and laughed, slept, or read textbooks. All appeared to be taking full advantage of one of summer's last warm days. Inside the grandiose library, Callie tipped her head back and studied the intricate ceilings, then tiptoed into one of the alcoves to admire the antique casebooks, their leather covers the color of honey.

"It's like your law library, but so much cooler," Callie whispered.

I laughed and squeezed the back of Callie's neck, led her outside, then north on State Street, past a series of shops. Students wearing jeans and tee shirts wandered past, some with purposeful looks and others dreamy-eyed, like people in love. We walked ahead of a group who chatted about their new classes and complained about the workload they'd been assigned.

"The diner's right up here," I told Callie. "I used to hang out for hours in one of their booths when I wasn't in the law library. I studied and drank pots of tea. I was there so much the owner threatened to charge me rent. I got hooked on their tuna bagels." I stopped mid-stride. Dean's had vanished, replaced by a sporting goods store whose windows were packed with maize-and-blue shirts, hats, and sweats.

Callie studied my face and then said quietly, "Maybe some night I could make you tuna bagels. You'd have to tell me the ingredients, though."

I nodded. "That would be great, Callie. And as long as we're here, let's pick you out a shirt."

Inside the massive store I purchased a hooded Michigan sweatshirt that matched one I regularly wore on cold nights. "You'll need this," I told Callie. "The weather's about to get chillier."

That night, Callie sat on the deck, her new sweatshirt over her clothes. It occurred to me, not for the first time, that this was the same river where the baby's body was found. I might have thought Callie wouldn't want to sit on the deck facing the river if she had any memory of bringing her baby here. Instead, she was quietly drawing; she looked up at me and smiled when I joined her with a glass of Pinot. A freighter slid by, dark but for the string of white lights on its rail, and I peered over her shoulder. She was sketching one of the finches that frequented my deck. Its feathers were perfectly formed, its tiny beak shiny and sharp.

"That's nice, Callie," I said.

She turned to look up at me. "You really think it's good?"

I patted her shoulder. "More than good."

She smiled and resumed sketching while I sipped my wine and thought about what I'd learned today. *If Callie was violated, that would explain everything. She never said she'd been raped, only that she did not have sex. Does she think the two are different?*

She signed her sketch with a flourish, handed it to me, and disappeared inside.

However Callie got pregnant, she must have been terrified. She would have known that her father would never accept her child. She coped in the only way she could.

A series of fishing boats skidded downriver in the dark.

If I send Callie back to her father or to jail, the connection I'm developing with her will vanish. The more Callie trusts me, the safer she'll feel. And maybe, just maybe, she'll tell me how she got pregnant.

TWENTY-EIGHT

GAIL RESCHEDULED MY APPOINTMENTS, AND CALLIE AND I headed south on I-94, following directions from my GPS.

"I want you to meet someone who can help with your case. On the way home, we'll pick up a new bird feeder and some sunflower seeds for the deck. Then you can sketch your birds close-up. That's what my mother used to do. Plus, I think it's time you called me by my first name. Miss Stephens sounds too formal. Especially since you'll be living with me."

"I'm going to stay?"

"I'd like you to."

"My father doesn't want me?"

"It's complicated. Anyway, I decided it would be best for us to spend time together. So we can work on your case. *Our* case. Is that okay with you?"

She smiled, paused, and then said, "This time of year, the birds would be better off finding their own food, *Victoria*." She pushed her hair behind one ear and grinned. "But if they do, they won't model for me."

"The world is full of compromises, dear," I said.

The brick bungalow was one of the few remaining houses on the block. Most of them had either been boarded up or torn down, leaving vacant lots filled with confused collections of dried grass, spindly weeds, and bald patches of grey dust. The lawn was littered with speckled bits of paper, the remnants of litter chopped up and spit out during attempted summer mowings.

I double-checked the address on my phone and told Callie, "You stay here 'til I make sure we're in the right place."

I climbed the bungalow's four crumbling cement steps and pushed a rusty doorbell. Jean Burley materialized in a dark green tee shirt and faded bib overalls, plus the same chandelier earrings she'd worn at my office. She gave me a cursory glance, then squinted at my parked car. "Well," she said, drawing out the word, "don't leave her sitting out there." She waved to Callie and hollered, "Come in!"

Inside, Jean scooped up scattered newspapers from the couch and dropped them in a corner. Several articles about Callie's case, clipped from the *Free Press* and the *Sentinel*, lay in a pile on the scratched coffee table, along with a pair of scissors and a collection of cat hair and dust.

"Sit," Jean said, pointing to the stained couch.

A large tabby cat wandered in, popped up next to Callie, and rubbed against her arm. Callie stroked its thick fur, and it responded with a sound that was more snore than purr.

"This is Frankie. He's the leader of my Rat Pack," Jean said.

"There's more than one?" Callie's hand was still, and Frankie butted his head against her arm until she resumed her petting.

"I have five these days. The rest will show up when they hear the tuna cans open."

Callie scratched the insides of Frankie's ears. "I had a cat," she said quietly. "Her name was Naomi. She followed me everywhere." She looked from Jean to me and back to Jean.

I shrugged quizzically, but Jean chuckled, "Like Ruth's daughter-in-law. In the Bible. 'Whither thou goest.' You still have your kitty?"

"We had to give her away. When we moved here from Indiana. Our church doesn't allow pets in the parsonage."

"That's a stupid rule," Jean said.

Callie said, "We gave Naomi to a family from our church. When she died, they called. They thought I'd want to know." She leaned her face into Frankie's back and rubbed her cheek against his fur.

"You never get over the loss of a pet," said Jean.

"Did you know some churches have pet blessings?" asked Callie.

Jean snorted. "I could see my crew at a church service. If a dog were anywhere near, it'd be a feline swearing contest."

"That's funny." Callie patted her knees, and Frankie crawled on her lap and laid down, curling his front paws beneath his body. He resembled a furry loaf of bread.

"Just toss him off if he bothers you."

"I don't mind." She scratched the back of his thick neck, and he tipped his head back and closed his eyes.

I noticed that Callie seemed more relaxed, more open, that day. Was she happy that Dr. Allen's exam was over or pleased I'd told her she could stay with me? I hoped it was both.

"I need to talk law with Jean," I told Callie. "You stay here."

Jean steered me through a small dining room, past an oak pedestal table with immense claw feet, its surface covered with hanks of yarn, knitting patterns, and mason jars holding what looked like armies of knitting needles. "Retirement hobby," Jean said as she held open a door leading to her kitchen, then let it swing shut behind us.

I sat at her kitchen table, a metal relic from the fifties. The vinyl seats on the matching chairs were scarred, torn, no doubt shredded by Jean's cats. I said, "Eleanor Allen thinks she might have dissociated during the pregnancy."

"That's great news."

"She also thinks that if we could prove Callie was sexually assaulted, it would explain her continued denial of her pregnancy. She could testify Callie had PTSD, which explains why she took the baby to the river and cleaned up the parsonage."

"Do you know she was raped?"

"I don't. So I'll have to do my damnedest to get the judge to allow expert testimony about the neonaticide syndrome."

"A *Daubert* hearing. Bravo." Jean sounded excited. "Even if a jury doesn't buy it, the public will hear about the syndrome."

"The more I read about it, the less I think Callie belongs in a prison cell for this. Lots of unmarried women who get pregnant panic." I paused, swallowed. "Callie's behavior just took a bizarre turn."

"That's one way of describing it. And if you lose the motion?"

"Then we hope Callie tells us she was raped." I picked up a pair of salt and pepper shakers that resembled tiny ears of corn and fingered their crevices. "I'm getting kind of attached to this kid. I'm terrified I'll lose. But I'd like you to work with me if you're willing. I'd be lead counsel, of course, and I'd pay you out of my own personal account."

She took so long to answer, I thought she might turn me down. But she said, "I have some old suits I could drag out of mothballs so I look more . . . conventional." She pushed open the door and leaned out. "You okay, kid?"

"I'm fine," Callie called.

The door swung shut, and Jean stuck out her hand to me. "I'd be thrilled to join your team."

Back in the living room, Frankie dropped soundlessly to the floor and padded toward Jean, who plopped into a chair and pulled a knitting needle from a basket, then scratched his furry head with the tip. "Frankie prefers to be scratched with size sevens, don't you?" She turned to Callie. "So, Callie, do you knit?"

"Me?" Callie looked at Jean, blinked.

"You. Knit. Is that a hard question?"

"I don't."

"I should probably teach you."

My mind flashed to the Murder One case I'd pled six years ago. Barrett offered me a plea to Murder Two with a twenty-five-year cap. Every Christmas since, the client sent me a Christmas card and a potholder she'd crocheted in prison. I had five of them in a box in my closet, all unused.

Jean said, "I love to spread the good news of knitting."

"Good news. Like the Gospels." Callie grinned.

I said, "Callie's an artist. She doesn't sew, and I'm not sure she has time for knitting." From my purse I pulled a small package and handed it to Jean. "Here's a cell phone with preprogrammed minutes. Keep track of your time and bill my office."

I turned to Callie. "Come on, dear. Let's go home."

TWENTY-NINE

IN THE DRIVE-THRU LINE, I SNUGGLED UP TO THE BUMPER of the car in front of mine. By then, Callie had become a welcome housemate. She washed and folded my laundry and collected my dry cleaning, then toted it to my car. She kept track of the food in my house, writing grocery lists in perfect Palmer. She did all the cooking, and she vacuumed and dusted on the weekends, carrying countless spiders in her cupped hands and releasing them on my deck. One night after we walked in the door, she even set out a wine goblet for me. When I asked what that was for, she rolled her dark eyes dramatically and grinned.

The previous night, as we were finishing dinner, I knew I had to get back to business. I anticipated she would balk at my question, but I needed to ask a question I'd never asked her before: Did she know how she got pregnant? As soon as I said the words, her easy smile shriveled and she disappeared behind that curtain of hair, then retreated to her bedroom. I followed her, and she looked so miserable, I told her she didn't need to answer any more questions.

Which wasn't true. If Callie was raped, I needed to know. Callie's father wasn't helping, her mother was dead, and I didn't trust Rose Walker. Who else was with Callie last July?

I paid for my burger and pulled over, then dug in my purse for my phone. Pastor Craig answered and we arranged to meet at the same coffee shop as before. An hour later, he slid into the booth.

"When did Neil Thomas and Rose get engaged?"

He pursed his lips and frowned. "Last June, why?"

"How did Callie react to their engagement?"

"She seemed okay. Maybe quieter than normal." He raised a finger to the waitress and she wandered over with a mug and two coffee pots. "Leaded," he told her and she poured from the pot with the orange handle. "Now that you mention it, when we were in Kentucky, she wasn't her usual self. I figured she had a lot to think about."

"Kentucky?"

"A busload of us went down there to do mission work in July. Callie always did a good job as student leader, but this trip she seemed . . . distracted."

"Did she have a good relationship with her father? Before the engagement?"

"They were very close." He leaned forward, fingered his diamond stud. "Can I tell you something in confidence?"

"Go ahead." I rested my chin on my fist.

"Sometimes I think Pastor Neil blames me for what happened."

"What makes you say that?"

He hesitated. "There were four chaperones for forty kids. But I was in charge. We weren't the only church group down there, but we kept a strict eye on our kids. If something happened during that outing, I don't have the slightest idea when. Or how."

"Callie's father thinks she got pregnant on that trip?"

"The kids slept in the church basement, boys on one side and girls on the other. Chaperones with each group all night. I don't see how it could have happened."

The waitress came by with her coffee pot, and I waved her off.

He continued, "I wasn't much of a math student in school, but I can count. April minus nine equals July. We watched our kids like hawks. And they're good kids."

"So there were boys from other churches down there? Is there anyone you suspect? Anyone at all?"

"Sorry."

"You said she didn't have a boyfriend."

"None that I knew of."

"Callie was sixteen when this happened. That means that if she had nonconsensual sex it wouldn't have been statutory rape. But it still may have been rape. That could make a difference in her defense."

"Rape?" He practically shuddered. "I don't see when . . . or how . . . God help her. And *me* if that happened."

I never suggested the facts of a case to any client. And I'd heard what Dr. Allen said about not pushing someone to remember a trauma they had suppressed. But time was running low and I began to think it might be okay to make an exception. If Callie'd been raped, maybe I could get her to understand that what she'd done wasn't her fault, and then maybe she'd begin to remember what really happened.

That night, while she experimented with a recipe for tuna bagels, I sat at my kitchen table and fingered the base on my glass of Chablis. "Can we talk?" I said.

She reflexively scowled. "About what?"

"Dr. Allen says that there's a possibility you sort of blanked out when you got pregnant, which is why you might not remember what happened."

She pulled the leaves from a head of romaine and ran them under cold water, shook them over the sink and placed them inside a clean towel to dry. "You mean like I had amnesia?"

"Sort of," I said. "Sometimes, when girls have been traumatized, they block everything out. To protect themselves. If a girl is sexually violated, sometimes she doesn't remember any of it. Do you know what sexual violation is, Callie?"

She ripped the lettuce into pieces and laid them on the towel. "Did you say you liked the mayonnaise mixed with the tuna or just spread on the bagels?"

"Mixed. Callie, this is important."

Her body became rigid, her eyes somewhere else.

"It's where the girl doesn't want to have sex but the boy does."

She opened a mayonnaise jar and dipped in a large spoon.

"Something had to happen if you became pregnant, Callie. Since it's been so long and you don't remember, I thought, maybe . . ."

She slopped a glob of mayo on the tuna.

"I talked to Pastor Craig. I think something might have happened when you were in Kentucky last summer."

"You saw Pastor Craig?"

"He and I counted the months and it seemed . . . like maybe you got pregnant when you were in Kentucky."

She churned the mayo into the tuna, her hair covering most of her face. She untwisted the wire on the plastic bag that held the bagels and pulled out two, then grabbed a bread knife from a drawer and used it to split them. With the knife in her upraised hand she said, "Can we not talk about this anymore?"

"Dr. Allen says the reason you don't remember the pregnancy and the birth might be because you were raped."

"But I wasn't—"

"I know. You say you weren't pregnant."

"So why do you keep asking?" She slammed the bread knife on the counter and glared at me. "Why?"

"Because I care what happens to you." I stood and put an arm around her shoulder. Her body felt warm, soft, against mine.

But she pulled away and wiped her eyes with a dish towel. "If you really care about me, you won't keep asking these questions."

That night, when I knew she was asleep, I retrieved the black raincoat from my closet. I sat on my bed, holding it for a long time. Then I stuffed it in a plastic garbage bag and carried it down the stairs.

The *Margaret Ann* rocked quietly, her deck shrouded in spiderwebs. With my old broom, I swept them aside, climbed aboard, and opened the hatch where I stored extra bumpers and boat hooks. After pulling the gear from the locker I shoved the plastic bag inside, then relocked the latch.

Back in my corner chair, I nursed a second glass of Chablis as I watched Sister Phillip blink her single eye. Hiding evidence would fall on the dark side of Sister's black-and-white world. But under the rules of evidence and the ethical code I'd sworn to uphold, I had no obligation to help Barrett prove his case. Hiding evidence violated no rule I'd pledged to obey.

On my phone, I checked the weather forecast. A series of thunderstorms was predicted, rain that would bring some relief from all these weeks of steamy summer heat. On the Lands' End website I found an anorak in a petite, large, that looked like it would fit Callie nicely. I ordered it in pale blue and paid for expedited shipping. She'd also need some conventional clothes to wear in the courtroom, not those outfits that looked like they came from a church rummage sale. I perused a couple of sites and decided on two pleated skirts, three pairs of slacks, six blouses, two complementary twin sets from JCPenney's, plus two pair of ballet-type flats, one blue and one red from Ann Taylor. I arranged for next-day delivery for those as well.

"Is there something wrong with my clothes?" Callie asked when I appeared in the library with the stack of boxes.

"Of course not. It's an image thing. I work with all my clients on how they dress."

"They're different from what I usually wear."

"They're for court. But you should start wearing them so they don't look brand-new."

"What if I spill something on them? Or ruin them?"

"Then we'll buy more. That pink blouse shows off your hair color." I reached over and lifted a lock of Callie's hair. "Maybe we'll get your hair trimmed, too. And try out some make-up."

"I don't wear make-up. And my father likes my hair long."

"I'm talking about a trim, maybe a touch of mascara. That's all. To show off your beautiful brown eyes."

"You think I have pretty eyes?"

"I do. You should show them off."

Gail walked past the library, saw the clothes laid out on the table. "What's this, Christmas?"

"Don't be ridiculous. I have a court uniform, and Callie needs one too."

She curled her lips and nodded, then continued walking.

THIRTY

I WAITED UNTIL THE LAST DAY TO FILE MY NOTICE OF INSANITY and send a copy of Dr. Allen's report to Barrett. His office quickly arranged a date for Callie to meet with the state's psychologist.

Meanwhile, Callie continued to sketch and to cook and clean at the cottage. When she finished her work each evening, she sat on the deck with me, chatting about the river traffic and showing me her latest sketches. But she'd yet to reveal anything that would help me with her case.

A week after Callie saw the state's expert, a deputy delivered his report to my office. James Hayden, PhD, said that nothing in Callie's behavior or his testing supported a finding of insanity. During his interview, he wrote, Callie maintained she hadn't been pregnant and hadn't given birth. Other than that, she refused to say anything about a baby. He quoted from the police reports about how her baby was placed in the river, a five-mile trip from the parsonage, and, just as Dr. Allen predicted, he concluded that Callie's behavior was volitional, that she'd been sane when she gave birth and sane when she killed her baby.

When I finished reading, I handed the report to Jean, who'd been showing up at my office each day with her knitting bag, "ready to help as needed," as she put it.

"Crap," she said now, when she'd finished. She tossed it on the floor and resumed her knitting.

Gail faxed the report to Dr. Allen, who phoned to reassure me that the state shrink's conclusion was not unexpected. "Typical forensic center bullshit" is what she called it, but with her German accent, it sounded almost high church. "Dr. Hayden is correct when he says that mostly we are able to distinguish the difference between a malingerer and someone who fits the dissociative state pattern. Usually, as you and I discussed in my office, the girls who dissociate say they had the sense of being present during the birth, that it was as though they were in a corner of the room, watching. The fact that your client didn't acknowledge anything about the birth to him or to anyone else may mean she's malingering as he says, or it may mean, as we previously discussed, that she has a more severe form of denial. But he has seized on the crux of this case."

"So there's nothing new here. Which is great."

"Nothing new, correct. But I remind you that you cannot expect miracles, Miss Stephens. I will do what I can, but the outcome of your case may not be what you hope. It will no doubt stimulate a debate about neonaticide and that in itself is something good."

"There's nothing new," I repeated.

Each night during the coming week, Callie and I left the office promptly at five. On our way home, I ran into the grocery store with Callie's list while she stayed in the car. One evening she concocted a vegetable stir-fry, fussing in the kitchen, while I sat nearby writing my direct examination questions for the upcoming *Daubert* hearing. The aroma of Callie's cooking transformed my cottage into a cozy, inviting space. She found paper napkins in a kitchen cupboard and set the table. She filled two tumblers with ice water and lime slices, then held up a goblet, as though she were offering to toast me.

When it was time, I waited for her to say grace before picking up my fork. Her prayer was different these days. Asking for help for me but not mentioning her father or his church. I was beginning to think I'd need a miracle so I'd even begun chiming in, "Amen," when she finished. Whether God was listening was another matter. I cut back on my wine consumption, knowing I'd need to keep my wits sharp for the upcoming hearing. Two glasses per night became my absolute limit.

One night Molly called. I'd barely said hello before she started in.

"I thought she was only going to stay until she saw the shrink. I read that piece online—"

"No need to lecture me, Molly. I know what I'm doing." I carried the phone to my bedroom and closed the door.

"How well do you know her, really?"

"Well enough. My job is to defend her, and keeping her here is part of that. You've only read what the papers say about her. And she's very sweet, actually, and helpful. You'd like her. You know those old cookbooks that belonged to my mother? She's been cooking for us from recipes she finds in them. And she likes to draw birds. Don't you think that's interesting?"

"Victoria, I'm only saying this because I care about you. I don't want to see you get hurt."

"I don't see the connection."

"If this girl killed her baby, then she's going to prison, right? And if she goes to prison and you have a relationship with her, she isn't just another client."

"I'm giving her a home. For a little while. That's all. It turns out we both know some things we can teach each other." After a silence, I said, "You still there?"

"I'm here. But I don't have a good feeling about this."

"She hasn't heard word one from her father since he posted her bond."

"How about jail?"

"She doesn't belong back there. She's behaving herself here. Our bathroom is clean and my laundry is caught up. My house hasn't looked this good in years."

"Victoria—"

"What?"

"*Tum podem extulit horridulum.*"

I didn't have to ask her to translate that one. You are talking shit.

Late that night, I pulled a cardboard box from the rear of my closet. I'd packed it years before. Now I untucked the flaps of the box and saw them: a collection of my mother's blouses on which she'd embroidered flowers, birds and vines, grape clusters and tendrils, or tiny schools of fish on the collars and cuffs. My dad never wore anything but fine worsted pinstripes and long-sleeved white shirts, along with impeccably polished black brogues.

I held up a Cossack-style shirt with puffy sleeves. Tiny yellow birds were stitched along the button placket, along with the initials *MAS*. I lifted it to my face, hoping to inhale some hint of my mother, maybe the Emeraude she used to keep on her dressing table. Instead of lilies of the valley, the blouse smelled of mildew and stale tobacco, a remnant of the old cigar box I'd included.

I pulled the cigar box from its nest within the clothing. On the cover, the black-haired senorita in a red dress twirled her skirts and flirted. When I opened it, a half dozen sharpened dark green number 2B's rattled, then settled next to a hunk of tan rubber. A Strathmore drawing pad was next in the pile, its tan cover as familiar to me as if I'd seen my mother sketching on it that very morning. I turned the napped pages one at a time, hoping, foolishly, to find a sketch of me in there. Long ago, I'd wished my mother would draw me, not just all those birds. But the pages in this book were blank.

The next morning, Callie spotted the cigar box on the kitchen table where I'd placed it on top of the drawing pad. "What's this?"

"These belonged to my mother. When she was drawing, which was most of the time, she'd stick one of these pencils in her hair." I grabbed a pencil from the box and demonstrated. "And she'd use another one to draw. She was never without her pencil." I picked up the eraser and squeezed it like I'd seen her do. I was surprised it was still pliable. "And after you get rid of any mistakes, you cover up the lead shavings like this." I folded the rubber over on itself. "This way you get a clean surface that won't smudge your page. It's kind of like kneading dough. That's what she once told me. Anyway, I'd like you to have these, Callie."

Callie fingered the wire spiral that held the Strathmore's pages together. "I'm still not sure my father's okay with me drawing."

"*In loco parentis*," I said firmly. "That means when you're with me, I'm your parent. And I say it's not just *okay* if you draw, it's a *good* thing."

"Then it's a good thing." Callie looked at me and smiled.

That day, she settled into the law library with her art supplies and my mother's copy of *Peterson's Guide to North American Birds*. I'd added that to her pile on our way out the door. Several times I peeked in to see how she was doing, complimented her sketching, and pointed out birds in the guide that I'd seen on the river.

Once, I'd been envious of these birds, not understanding the allure they held for my mother or this fixation that distanced her from me. But I hadn't given these art supplies to Callie because of some memory I had or some hole in my life that needed filling. I'd given them to Callie in hopes that her art might give her some comfort, as it had my mother, at least for a time. Besides, maybe if Callie felt comfortable and secure, she'd begin to tell me her story. Because time was running out.

The afternoon before the *Daubert* hearing, Jean and I reviewed our plan for the next day. When we finished our preparations, I said, "I'm counting on winning this motion."

"And if we don't?"

"If Osbourne doesn't recognize the syndrome and Callie doesn't acknowledge she's been raped, I don't hold much hope. Why would the jury buy that Callie dissociated when I can't talk about the neonaticide syndrome? They'll just see Callie as a scared girl who killed her baby so no one would find out."

"Remember to emphasize that Osbourne has an opportunity to make some new law."

"He's never been a very bold judge."

"Convince him to go out in style, make some legal waves."

"And if he doesn't?"

"Then we fight this tooth and nail during trial. Convince the jury to compromise on a Murder Two verdict."

I said, "Murder Two is a possible life sentence. If only she would admit she was raped."

"If she was raped—" Jean paused and I followed her eyes to the doorway of my office. Callie stood there quietly, listening to us.

"What is it?" I asked her.

"You said to remind you that we need more seed for the birds."

"Right. Wouldn't want the birdies to go hungry." I nodded.

She turned away and headed back to the library.

"She's worried about the birds, for god's sake," I whispered to Jean. I covered my face with my hands. "I don't know what I'll do if I lose. She's a *child*. A sweet, sweet girl. How can she spend the rest of her life in prison?"

"We'll do everything we can, Victoria, but we cannot control the outcome. If nothing else, we'll have brought attention to the neonaticide syndrome."

"That doesn't do Callie a damn bit of good."

THIRTY-ONE

A REPORTER FROM THE *SENTINEL* PLUS A COUPLE OF OTHERS I assumed were media types congregated in the back of the courtroom, chatting and chuckling. Television crews were conspicuously absent. Gail had sent out notices to all the major stations and papers. Now I wondered whether we should have held a press conference, passed out copies of our brief so the press would understand our motion. Should I have sent those people engraved invitations? I'd just assumed they'd show up for this hearing.

Barrett strolled in, accompanied by a slender man with beady eyes who resembled a weasel in a suit. I didn't recognize him and figured he must be a new assistant in Barrett's office. Barrett seemed preoccupied with his file and didn't bother to introduce us.

Eleanor Allen sat behind us in the first row of the gallery. She wore a grey suit with a pink blouse and small gold hoop earrings. Her only notes were in a thin black binder small enough for her to carry in one hand.

When Osbourne took the bench, what little noise there was in the courtroom hushed. I focused on the elderly judge, reminding myself that he was the only person I needed to convince today.

"I've read both briefs on this matter." Osbourne pulled his microphone closer, snapped it on, and his raspy voice boomed throughout the room. "If no one has anything else to add, let's get to the expert testimony."

"A syndrome is a group of behavioral signs and symptoms that occur frequently enough to suggest a common underlying pathogenesis." Dr. Allen oozed professionalism from the witness stand. She leaned into the microphone and her voice projected easily. "A syndrome helps a fact finder or a treating professional understand behavior that most people assume means other than it does. For example, most people assume that a rape victim will immediately report the assault to the authorities. If the victim doesn't, most people assume that when they *do* come forward, they must be lying."

I glanced at the reporters in the back. Their heads down, they appeared to be typing on their laptops, but I couldn't tell whether they were taking notes on the testimony, trolling the internet, or playing solitaire.

"In fact," Eleanor continued, "prompt reporting of a rape is contrary to what happens in most cases. Think about all those former altar boys who did not report their sexual abuse by parish priests until years after it happened. What we once called rape trauma syndrome is a form of dissociative amnesia that provides an explanation for this behavior that might not otherwise be understood by the general public."

"Are there other examples of syndromes?" I asked.

"Battered woman's syndrome, or dependent personality disorder, is another. Most people assume that a woman who is abused will leave if threatened or harmed but, in fact, most do not. Understanding this behavior is necessary if psychologists are to help abused women and if finders of fact are to understand whether to believe a claim of abuse. Over time, psychiatrists and other practitioners have collected data on symptoms and behaviors of rape victims and battered or abused women. This aggregated data has been reviewed, researched, and reported in psychiatric journals and treatises. These two syndromes were eventually accepted by the scientific community and now both are recognized in the *DSM-5*."

Barrett's new assistant was furiously taking notes.

"Dr. Allen, what is the neonaticide syndrome?" I asked.

"Studies of mothers who commit neonaticide reveal that many of these mothers possess a number of shared characteristics. The most significant is pregnancy denial without any prior indication of a psychiatric illness. Many of these women do not consciously know they are pregnant. If they experience physical changes, they attribute them to something else. For example, morning sickness is attributed to influenza, weight gain is water retention or a tumor. More significant is that for many of these women their denial may be so strong that the normal biological changes that take place during pregnancy do not occur. They have no breast enlargement or abdominal swelling and many continue to menstruate during this time."

"Are there other characteristics of these mothers?"

"Several. Ninety percent of them are twenty-five years old or younger. They are usually unmarried and experiencing a first pregnancy, they give birth without any assistance, they have no previous involvement with the legal system, and, as I said, they have no prior history of mental illness. The behavior of these women is often marked by passivity. By and large, these women are immature for their age. But it is their denial that is most pervasive."

"Can you describe what happens to these women when they experience labor pains?"

"Many of them attribute their labor pains to intestinal gas or menstrual cramps. Or they think they are having a bowel movement. When the birth occurs, they suffer a further psychotic break from reality. As a result, they do nothing to assist their infants, who die in a variety of ways."

"For example?"

"Sometimes the mother passes out on the toilet from the strain of the birth and the infant drowns. Other times, the woman acts overtly, such as strangling or suffocating her newborn to keep it from crying out. This denial continues while the mother hides the baby, often in strange or bizarre places such as a closet, a refrigerator, or a dumpster. Sometimes a mother will toss a baby out a bathroom window. Once the baby is gone, the mother returns to her pre-labor activities as though nothing happened. She denied her pregnancy, and once she is no longer pregnant and the evidence of her pregnancy, i.e., her child, is gone, the psychosis disappears because she no longer has anything to deny."

"Do these women remember what they've done?"

"Some describe what's happened as though they were in a corner of the room watching the birth but not participating. Others remember the birth long after it happened. Still others, in particularly severe cases of denial, never remember it."

"What is the cause of this denial?"

"Most pervasive is the fear of becoming a social outcast or being rejected by one's own family, although there are other reasons."

"Such as?"

"If the pregnancy occurred as the result of rape or incest, sometimes those mothers never remember the birth."

"How would evidence of the neonaticide syndrome help a jury understand the behavior of a woman accused of murdering her newborn?"

"Most people assume that a woman who gives birth to a child that dies through her neglect, or by her own act, is a murderer. They assume she needs to be imprisoned for what she has done. The reality is that there is a pattern of behavior exhibited by these young women who commit neonaticide. A jury must be educated about that pattern, that syndrome, so they can better understand the motivation and behavior of the accused."

"Have you studied the evidence in the case of *The State of Michigan versus Calliope Faith Thomas?*"

"I have. Miss Thomas fits the profile of the women whose behavior is consistent with the neonaticide syndrome. To go forward with her trial and fail to disclose this information to a jury would be a grave injustice."

"Doctor, many people who commit homicide objectify their victims, isn't that true?" Barrett stood at the podium, on which he'd placed a clipboard with pages of typed questions.

"It is. But the women I am referring to suffer a break from reality. They dissociate."

"Are you referring to dissociative amnesia?"

"Yes."

"So you're telling us that these mothers who kill their babies"— Barrett's assistant handed him a photocopied page—"have an amnesia only for the traumatic event." He studied the page, looked up at Dr. Allen. "And that event is the pregnancy?"

"And sometimes the birth, correct."

"There are ways in our society to deal with unwanted pregnancies besides killing your newborn, aren't there? I'm referring to adoption, safe havens, even abortion?"

"The young women I am describing are incapable of weighing those options and making an informed decision. They are both consciously and unconsciously terrified of what will happen if their pregnancy is revealed. It would be a form of suicidal behavior in their eyes."

"So they hide their pregnancies."

"That's an oversimplification, Counselor. These women fear they won't survive if their pregnancy is revealed."

"Doctor, many of your colleagues do not accept the theory of the neonaticide syndrome, isn't that correct?"

"Many do. But, yes, many do not."

"Isn't it true that the reason many of your peers do not accept this theory is that they believe these women simply do not want to face up to the consequences of their actions?"

"The realization of what they have done is what leads to their denial. That is a different matter."

Barrett reached out a hand and his assistant slapped another page on it. "Are you familiar with Dr. Kevin Althorpe?"

"He is a psychiatrist at the University of London."

"Highly regarded?"

"Yes."

"In fact, Dr. Althorpe has written a paper on neonaticide syndrome for the American Psychiatric Association in which he states that the women who commit neonaticide are consciously trying to cover up or hide their pregnancies. Are you familiar with this argument, Doctor?"

"I am. I disagree with his conclusions."

"Isn't it true that what were formerly known as rape trauma syndrome and battered woman's syndrome are generally accepted by the psychiatric community?"

"That is correct."

"In fact, the criteria for a diagnosis of these syndromes, although they are known by other names, is in the *DSM-5*?"

"Yes."

"It's also true that the neonaticide syndrome has not been generally accepted by the psychiatric community?"

"That is correct. However, there is increasing data that supports it."

"But the scientific community does not agree on it?"

"Correct."

"In fact, the *DSM-5* does not recognize this syndrome, correct?"

"That is currently the situation. But that treatise is continually updated based upon research and studies."

"I have no further questions."

During the lunch break, I didn't eat. Jean and Callie shared a roast beef sandwich and Jean entertained Callie with stories of her cats. When court reconvened, I presented the second motion I'd scheduled: to exclude the photos of the baby's body.

"Those pictures will only inflame the jury and unduly prejudice them against my client," I argued. By then, only one reporter remained in the courtroom.

"Photos of the baby. It's a *baby*, Counselor," Barrett said.

"It's still a body—"

"Okay, folks," Osbourne interrupted, "you both made your positions clear. Mr. Michaels, what exactly is your motive for introducing these photos?"

"First, to show that the child is dead, and second, to link the infant's death to his mother dropping him in an icy river."

I stood to rebut, but Osbourne raised his hand, his signal that he'd heard enough. "My turn, Counselor. Your medical examiner will testify that the child died by drowning in this river, isn't that what you said, Mr. Michaels?"

"Yes, sir."

"And you have the DNA evidence that says this child is the child of the defendant, correct?"

"That's correct, your honor."

"Then you'll have to give me another reason why I should allow the jury to view these photos."

"They demonstrate the defendant's intent as well as her state of mind: to kill her newborn by exposing him to not just the frigid water but the creatures that live in that water."

Osbourne frowned. "I'm ready to rule on both motions."

I poised my pen above my legal pad and reminded myself to breathe.

"I'll begin with the easy one, defense counsel's motion to exclude the photos of the victim's body," said Osbourne. "I am no less horrified by this crime than anyone. But it is my job to see that both parties receive a fair trial. And I agree with defense counsel that if these photos are shown to the jury, it may be difficult, if not impossible, for the jurors to separate these gruesome photos from any other evidence they hear. Therefore, I grant the defendant's motion to exclude the photos of the baby's body. You may take an order to that effect, Miss Stephens."

"One down, one to go," Jean whispered.

"The second motion before me today is a *Daubert* motion, which requires that I determine the reliability and relevance of scientific evidence which the defendant proposes to admit at trial in this matter. That evidence is called the neonaticide syndrome. If I decide in favor of the defendant, evidence of the syndrome will be admitted in the trial scheduled to begin next week.

"It is the defendant's burden to establish by a preponderance of the evidence that I should admit this testimony, that it will assist the jurors in understanding or determining a fact in issue. Based on today's hearing, I find that the defendant has not met that burden."

Osbourne waxed effusively about Eleanor Allen's credentials but concluded he just could not allow testimony about the syndrome to be presented to a jury. I listened to the rest of his ruling in a fog. Something about the lack of scientific testing in the psychiatric community and how the profession may be on the edge of acceptance but that didn't help him in today's hearing. I didn't bother to take notes. Barrett's weasel could take down Osbourne's words and prepare the written order that memorialized them.

I heard Osbourne say, "Court's in recess," and felt Dr. Allen's hand on my shoulder. "I'm sorry," she said.

I stood. "Judge Osbourne?"

He'd started for his office but turned back, lowered his chin and frowned over the top of his reading glasses.

I said, "If you deny my motion, the jurors won't understand."

"Miss Stephens, I *have* denied your motion," Osbourne said. "That's all."

He'd made it as far as his office when I barged in. "Judge, did you hear what Dr. Allen said?"

"I heard the testimony, Counselor, all three hours of it."

Barrett stood behind me.

"But the law gives you the discretion to allow it. Without this testimony, I have no case."

"If you're unhappy with my ruling, take me up."

"You know the appellate court won't overrule you. You're my only hope. This girl is being railroaded by a prosecutor who's using her to win an election. And now she's being railroaded by you."

"You're dangerously close to contempt, Counselor."

"Please," I begged. "I'll file a motion to reconsider."

"This trial will go forward as scheduled. Jury selection begins next week. That's all." Osbourne stepped into his private bathroom and closed the door.

I stormed past Barrett into the courtroom. It was nearly empty. Dr. Allen was checking her phone and Jean sat with her arm around the back of Callie's chair.

"What does this mean?" Callie asked.

"It means we have to regroup before next week," Jean said calmly. "Focus on Plan B."

But our Plan B needed Callie to admit she'd been raped. And

even if she did, our chances of convincing a jury she suffered PTSD were slim. The reality was, we had no Plan B.

That night, Callie sat outside with me while I finished my fourth glass of wine. "I'm so sorry," I said. I was slurring my words, but I didn't care. "I can't believe we fucking lost."

Callie reached over and patted my hand. "Don't feel bad, Victoria."

"Right."

"You should probably get some sleep. Do you want me to help you into bed?"

I waved her away. "I'm good," I mumbled, as three fishing boats sped past on the water's shiny darkness.

But she took my arm and led me inside. "You need your sleep," she said before she turned down my bed and tucked me in.

THIRTY-TWO

THE *SENTINEL* PRINTED A SHORT ARTICLE ABOUT OUR HEARING on an inside page, a piece that wouldn't draw any serious attention to Dr. Allen's testimony. Jean tossed the paper on my desk after she read it. "If they have to explain it, they think it's too complicated," she said.

"Maybe I should've sent them a copy of my brief."

"Do you really think they'd bother to read it, let alone print it? Vultures." Jean practically spat the words. "So, now we prepare for trial."

"With what? No syndrome? No rape?"

Jean lifted her knitting from her lap, straightened the stitches on the needles. "I was hoping this case would break through the prejudice toward these poor, scared girls." She worked a row with thick red yarn as I watched.

"What do you do with all those things you knit?"

"Donate them, mostly, to shelters in Detroit. Give them to people who wouldn't otherwise have a nice piece of clothing or something to keep them warm. Mostly knitting keeps me from screaming about the craziness in the world I can't change."

We sat quietly for a long time. Jean slipped the yarn between her work, then slid a stitch from one needle to the other and started again.

I said, "My dad used to preach about always keeping a professional distance from your clients. But I can't stomach how she's being scapegoated. I mean what she did was wrong, but if she didn't know . . ." My chin trembled. "If she didn't know what she was doing, should she be locked up for the rest of her life? Is she really a danger to society? Really?"

"They're making an example of her."

"They don't know her. They don't want to know her. Did I ever tell you she has nightmares? Or that she sleeps with a teddy bear?"

Jean finished her row, then curled her shoulders forward and back. "You've become attached to her. Too attached?"

"Who else does she have?"

"But if we lose at trial—"

"I can't think about that."

"Maybe you should prepare yourself for that possibility."

"What if I can't?"

"You know, Victoria, when I lost Angela's case, I started taking in stray cats. I guess I thought if I couldn't save Angela, at least I could rescue a few lost cats." She chuckled. "My kids thought I'd gone over the edge."

"You have kids?" I'd always thought of Jean as a crazy cat lady, not a mother to actual humans.

"Three. By two different dads, both deadbeats. I enrolled in law school after I got sick of paying lawyers to collect the child support I was owed." She pointed into the air with an empty needle. "Okay then. Let's talk about what's left of our case. First. Barrett can't prove the baby wasn't already dead when Callie took him to the river. So, we claim he drowned in the toilet, that she thought the baby was dead."

"That won't work. The medical examiner's report says the baby's lungs contained river water. Which means he had to have been breathing when he was placed in the river. Besides, why would Callie take a dead baby to the river? It's five miles from the parsonage to the boat launch. Even if she wanted to hide the body, that doesn't make sense."

"That's number two. The prosecutor can't prove for sure that Callie took the baby to the river. He hasn't found the raincoat, right?"

I'd never told Jean I had it, let alone that I'd hidden it on my boat. I said, "But he has an eyewitness that saw somebody who sure looked like her. We're already claiming dissociation and possibly PTSD; I'm reluctant to add anything else to the mix. My dad used to say that's like throwing a bunch of shit against a wall and hoping some of it will stick. Juries don't like it."

"We could put Callie on the stand."

"That's unthinkable," I snapped. "She'll deny she was pregnant and everyone knows that isn't true. Barrett will chew her up and spit her out." I rose from my chair and gazed out my tiny window. Some kids were ignoring the posted city ordinance prohibiting skateboarding. I swallowed hard and wiped mascara from beneath both eyes with my index finger. I imagined Callie telling the jury, when Barrett asked, that she did own a black raincoat and that she had given it to me.

"We have one week to shape this into something," Jean said, as I watched a skinny kid push off and scoot across the asphalt.

I spoke into the glass. "We have nothing."

I was always on edge when preparing for a big court hearing. Gail knew enough to walk on eggshells around me. This trial was no exception. During that last week, Callie kept to herself in the library while I tried to organize what remained of my strategy.

It didn't help that I'd screwed up by relying so heavily on Eleanor Allen being allowed to explain the neonaticide syndrome to the jury. Now I was left with a PTSD claim dependent on Osbourne letting Eleanor testify that Callie was raped, which Callie'd never admitted. I knew Barrett would object like hell to any testimony she gave that was based on speculation. And if Osbourne ruled in Barrett's favor, I only had the dissociation defense, with no neonaticide syndrome to support it.

Jean kept me somewhat grounded during those difficult days. She suggested we divide our trial preparations. She wrote the cross-exams of Barrett's witnesses, and I focused on jury selection, my opening statement, and the questions we hoped I'd be allowed to ask Dr. Allen. She prepared a profile for what she'd dubbed "TPJ" (The Perfect Juror), a professional woman who could relate to Dr. Allen and who would be open to the idea that Callie suffered from dissociation or PTSD during the pregnancy and birth.

As we finished our assigned tasks, Jean and I exchanged and refined each other's work. Dr. Allen made herself available by phone as often as her schedule permitted so I could go over her proposed trial testimony. But each time I hung up, I was more frustrated than before. How was I going to explain Callie's behavior to a jury if Dr. Allen couldn't testify about the neonaticide syndrome? And worse, what if she wasn't allowed to speculate that Callie was raped? How could I convince twelve jurors that Callie wasn't just a scared girl who murdered her baby so no one would know she'd been pregnant?

I sat in my office with Jean and vented. "If only Callie would admit to being raped," I said for the thousandth time.

"You keep saying that. Like you know she was raped," Jean said. Her knitting needles clicked furiously.

"But that's the only thing that makes sense. If Callie was raped that would corroborate Dr. Allen's testimony and explain her lack of memory. We need a damn miracle," I said.

That same afternoon, I handled a short hearing up in Port Huron for another client. Outside the courthouse, I ran into Joyce Ballinger. She looked as disheveled as ever, her hair messy and her cheap brown suit tight on her lumpy body.

"Victoria, I wanted to thank you for referring that extradition case to me." She shifted her briefcase to her other hand. There were crayon scribbles on its leather finish. "God knows I can use the fee. I just found out my two oldest kids need braces. How's your big file going? Barrett still playing hardball?"

"Um-hmm."

"He should spend just one night in Huron Valley. The old women's prison used to be these cute cottages with fences anyone could crawl over. The inmates would go home for supper and make it back before bed check. Not Huron Valley. When the state built it, they made it hardcore. With all that goes with it."

"So I've heard."

"Last week I got a nasty reminder of just how ghastly things really are there. The mother of one of my former clients came to see me. Her daughter got seven to fifteen for dealing coke. She wasn't in Huron Valley a month before some kid didn't like how my client looked at her. So this other gal and her friends broke my client's cheekbone and put out her left eye. They're being prosecuted. Still." Joyce shifted her briefcase back. "I gotta run. Anything I can do to help, you let me know. We women gotta stick together." She scuffed away in her flats.

My dad always preached that it was a terrible idea for criminal defense attorneys to worry about possible sentences or prison conditions, that it muddied professional boundaries. And I knew that what happened to Joyce's client was an anomaly. Stuff like that wasn't common in women's prisons the way it was in men's prisons. But that afternoon every time I looked at Callie, I couldn't help picturing Joyce's client. The girl with the broken face. The ruined life.

That afternoon, I was edgy, unable to concentrate. Nor could I fathom another night of sitting on my deck with Callie, watching the river traffic, much as I'd come to appreciate those quiet evenings. At five o'clock I told Callie to pack up, and we sped down I-94 toward my favorite mall, the one with the most expensive stores in Michigan. I spent the evening ushering Callie in and out of the shops, searching for outfits that flattered her, regardless of how much she protested and regardless of the cost.

All that weekend I craved a glass of wine but didn't let myself indulge. I had to stay sharp for Callie and what was coming. I kept busy by braiding Callie's hair and convincing her to model her new clothes for me so we could select her outfit and accessories for each day of trial. I convinced her to try a tiny bit of my mascara and blush, telling her it would make her face come to life. When she saw herself in the mirror, her eyes lit up and I saw traces of a smile.

On Sunday night, she roasted a chicken with veggies. After dinner, we sat on my deck, each of us wrapped in a thick blanket. Dark clouds roiled overhead, and the few boats that were still on the water headed for cover. Before long, the rain began. When Callie headed to the shower, I stood at the window and watched the drops flatten the dark water.

I'd done my best to make her last days with me special, to give her some good memories before the ordeal ahead. After she was in bed, I stepped in to say good night. "Tomorrow won't be easy, but you need to remember everything we talked about," I told her. "Some of what the prosecutor's witnesses say about you may be hurtful. You just sit quietly and watch. I'll defend you."

"I trust you, Victoria." Callie nodded, her dark eyes meeting mine.

I leaned down and hugged her.

Back at my corner perch, I stared at the Canadian shore, my jaw clenching and unclenching. My entire body felt like one big wire with a jacked-up electrical current running through it. I tried taking a few deep, slow breaths, squeezing my hands into fists and opening my fingers wide, techniques I'd read that were supposed to help relieve stress. Nothing worked. I needed a drink but I didn't dare uncork a bottle. Once I started, I knew I wouldn't stop.

THIRTY-THREE

PEOPLE THRUST BOTH CRUDELY PAINTED AND PROFESSIONALLY printed signs into the air. I tried not to read them as we pushed through, but it was impossible to ignore their venomous words: GOD PUNISHES BABY KILLERS, TIME FOR JUSTICE, and GOD KNOWS WHAT YOU DID. A girl who looked about Callie's age held a sign in front of her obviously pregnant stomach that read, BABIES ARE GIFTS FROM GOD.

Head down, Callie clutched her drawing pad to her chest, flinching whenever someone shouted her name. I dragged my wheeled briefcase with one hand and kept Callie moving forward with the other. When the crowd began hollering taunts and insults, Art Jones and a deputy, a young man with a buzz cut and acne scars, strode from the courthouse and positioned themselves on either side of us.

"Lovely morning, Counselor," Art said, his hand on my back. He and the deputy escorted us inside, where a line of waiting spectators hushed as we neared. I kept my eyes fixed on a point ahead, but it was difficult to ignore the stern faces and judgmental stares of the people who'd come to watch these proceedings.

At the metal detector, another deputy made a cursory search of my purse and briefcase, then motioned us through the temporary frame erected in the center of the hall. I stepped across the threshold, into the world I'd known since I began shadowing my father back in high school, a place where I'd always been welcomed and respected, a world that now seemed unrecognizable, its edges blurred and its once familiar halls dark and menacing. Except for the squeaking of Art's holster on his leather belt and our footsteps on the granite steps, there wasn't a sound.

Once upstairs, I took Callie to a conference room in a back hallway. "I need to go over some preliminaries with the judge and the prosecutor. Jean will be here soon."

"Will my father come today?" It was the first she'd mentioned him in weeks.

"Today we have to select a jury. We discussed this," I said. "Remember?"

"But my father could come for this part, right? If he wanted to."

"This prosecutor sequesters his witnesses. That means he keeps them in a separate room so they can't hear what anyone else says before it's their turn to testify." I'd tied Callie's hair back with a pink ribbon that matched the twin set and plaid skirt she was wearing. Her bow was loose, so I retied it and said, "I wouldn't look for him today."

She frowned and slowly pulled a paper from the pages of her drawing pad. It was a pencil sketch of a sparrow, drawn on a page from the Strathmore tablet, the rendering every bit as masterful as one my mother might have made, the shading so realistic it could be mistaken for a photograph. Across the bottom, in perfect Palmer, she'd written, "God takes care of the least of his creatures, Victoria. He's the reason you're my lawyer."

My eyes blurred. *There is no God here*, I thought. But aloud I said, "It's beautiful."

"I know you tried your best, Victoria. If we lose, I don't want you to feel bad." She sniffed.

I rested my chin on the top of her head and bit my lip so hard I thought it might bleed. The law was bearing down on this girl like a runaway freight train, and I was helpless to stop it. And she was worried about me? I said, "I need to see the judge," and slid out before she could see my sprouting tears.

In the hall I mumbled, "Get a grip, Victoria," but by then I knew I'd lost my way. This whole mess, the *Daubert* hearing and now this trial, were foregone conclusions, exercises in futility. Callie would be convicted and sentenced to prison. The drawing she'd just given me would be the only piece of her remaining in my life. And every time, every damn time I looked at it I'd be reminded of how I'd failed her. I swiped my index fingers beneath my eyes, hoping to salvage what was left of my mascara, then forced myself to take one step, and another, down the hall in the direction of Osbourne's office. I felt like I was walking to my own execution.

Cynthia wasn't at her desk so I knocked on the judge's open door. "Victoria, hello," he said. "Would you like some coffee? Tea maybe?" He produced a thermos from a drawer and whispered, "I stopped for some real coffee this morning, and I'm happy to share."

"I'm good, thanks."

"Sit." He motioned to the chair in front of his desk, then poured his coffee into one of the county's Styrofoam cups, before sliding the thermos into a desk drawer and closing it. "I'm glad you got here before Barrett. I've been meaning to speak with you. To thank you for the way you've handled this case. I know this one has been a bit . . . extraordinary." He didn't mention my meltdown after his ruling last week.

"That's an understatement."

"Experiencing a few pretrial butterflies?"

"More like buzzards."

He leaned back in his chair, sipped his coffee. "Back when I started practicing, I was a nervous wreck before every trial. Of course, we didn't have pretrial discovery back then, so you never knew what was going to happen in the courtroom. Attorneys were still bringing surprise witnesses in from out of town, hiding them at the train station until it was time for their testimony." He chuckled. "Very Perry Mason. Nowadays you know ahead of time how things will go. For the most part. If it's any consolation, I still get nervous before I preside over a big case. So. How's your little roommate holding up?"

"Okay, I guess."

He held up a stapled packet of legal papers. "Your roommate is costing the county a lot of money. This psychiatrist you hired doesn't work cheap. The county commissioners are already bitching about her bill."

At my office I had stacks of unreturned phone messages on my desk from clients Gail had given up trying to placate. I needed to research the law in my newest drug cases, and I had a long list of witnesses I should already have chased down and interviewed. Weeks ago I'd stopped thinking about my other clients or what Callie's case was costing my practice.

"Another couple of months and I won't have to haggle with those tightwad politicians any more. That one part of this job I won't miss," Osbourne said as Barrett strolled in.

"Judge." Barrett nodded in my direction. "Counselor." He had on his usual trial attire, a worn plaid sport coat, grey pants, and a plain tie. He'd once told me that he wanted to come across to the jurors as an ordinary guy, the people's lawyer, not some slick suit. In contrast, that day I wore my most expensive trial suit: navy skirt and jacket, pink silk blouse, plus my diamond wristwatch and patent Ferragamo pumps. It was part of the courtroom image I'd carefully cultivated over the years: giving the jurors the impression I was successful, confident, a force to be reckoned with.

"Everybody set to begin? Anything we need to put on the record before we call the jury?" asked Osbourne.

I shook my head.

"Barrett?"

"No, your honor."

"Well then." Osbourne put on his readers and stood. "I'm going to seat fourteen jurors in case of illness or some other unforeseen event. We'll excuse two before deliberations, assuming we still have fourteen at that time. Oh, and it's my intention to seat a panel today, no matter how long it takes. I hope you brought your sleeping bags. We could be here a while."

When I returned to the conference room, I heard Callie ask Jean, "How do you know who to get rid of?"

Jean, resplendent in a cherry-red suit, said, "*Whom to excuse.*" Her cowgirl boots, chandelier earrings, and knitting needles were conspicuously absent. She nodded at me and turned back to Callie. "Some people have a bias and shouldn't sit on this particular jury."

"Like someone who already thinks I'm guilty?"

Jean said, "Well, yes. Or some people might know the prosecutor or one of the witnesses. The judge will excuse those for cause. Because there's a reason they can't be fair. But the prosecutor and Victoria each get to excuse ten people and they don't have to give a reason. Those are called peremptory challenges."

"How long does this, what do you call it, last?"

"Voir dire. As long as it takes to get a fair jury."

"Do you think we'll get a fair jury?" Callie said.

Jean shrugged. "A jury is like a sort of collective intelligence. Twelve brains figuring out a problem instead of one. Most of the time, they come to a reasonable conclusion. There are exceptions. But usually they do a good job."

"Is that what you think, Victoria?"

More than ever, I wanted to reassure her, to promise her everything would be all right. But the reality of what was happening was coming at me faster than I could comprehend. Just then, I was certain of only two things when it came to this trial. The first was that the three of us would have good seats. The second was that we had no chance of winning.

"Of course I do," I said, as I opened my briefcase and slid Callie's drawing inside, careful not to look either Callie or Jean in the eye.

THIRTY-FOUR

THE JURY POOL FILED INTO THE COURTROOM AND FOUND seats in the gallery. The press and a few spectators were already seated on benches cordoned off from those occupied by the six panels of citizens. I spotted Rose Walker sitting on the end of the third row, her hands folded in her lap. She must have arrived at the courthouse early to secure such a choice seat. She stood and placed her purse on her seat before walking to the rail that separated us from the gallery.

"Hello, honey," she said to Callie.

When Callie didn't turn around or acknowledge her, Rose poked my back with the corner of an envelope and whispered, "It's for Callie. Just a little note of encouragement with a piece of her favorite candy inside. I've been praying for you, sweetie," she said to Callie's back. "Both of you," she added, and nodded at me before returning to her seat.

"All rise."

Judge Osbourne took the bench, adjusted the microphone in front of him and cleared his throat. "This is the matter of *The People of the State of Michigan versus Calliope Faith Thomas*, the charge being Murder in the First Degree, file number 16-007742 FY(O). Is the state ready to proceed?"

Barrett stood. "Good morning, your honor. The people are ready."

"Is the defense ready as well?"

"Yes."

"Very well," said Osbourne. "Will the clerk please call fourteen names?"

One by one citizens filed into the jury box and stood before a numbered chair. "Be seated," Osbourne said, and they sat, waiting for the litany of questions he would ask.

As I'd instructed her, Callie stared straight ahead, her hands folded on her white Bible. She appeared composed, resigned. I chewed the inside of my lip and caught myself absentmindedly tapping Dad's Waterman against my cheek not once but twice. When Osbourne finished his questions, Barrett stepped to the jury box.

"Ladies and gentlemen," he began, "often, at home, I think I'm being perfectly clear when I try to explain something, yet my wife tells me she has no idea what I just said." Most of the panel smiled. "So if you don't understand my questions, you'll be in good company. Just raise your hand or say so. Fair enough?" He was off to his usual smooth start.

When he finished, I laid my typed questions on the podium, rolled it closer to the jury box, and took a breath. I still hadn't settled in the way I usually did by this point in a trial. Far from it. My hands quivered and worse, my mind raced and was unfocused. In previous trials, I always stepped away from the podium during voir dire, to let the panel see me as a person and get comfortable with me. Today I stood behind the podium, as though it were a shield, and read from my prepared list of questions.

"During this trial, I will present a witness, an expert in the science of psychiatry. This witness will testify that my client is sane now, but that previously, during her pregnancy and at the time she gave birth, she was not sane. At the end of the trial, I will be asking you to return a verdict of Not Guilty by Reason of Insanity. Would any of you have difficulty reaching such a verdict if the evidence warranted it?"

The man in seat number nine, a soybean farmer with a pasty forehead and an otherwise shiny red face, raised his hand. "You mean would I let her off on insanity? No way. She's either guilty or not guilty in my book," he said. "That insanity stuff is a bunch of hooey."

"Thank you for your frankness, Mister . . ." I checked the chart I'd made of each juror's names and their seat number. "Homer. Anyone else feel like that?"

The rest of the panel looked away. A couple shook their heads.

Barrett stood. "Your honor, may I ask this gentleman a few questions?"

"Go ahead."

"Mr. Homer, if you listened to all the testimony in this case and Judge Osbourne told you, at the end of the trial, that you had to follow the law, and that the law required you to consider the verdict the defense wants, Not Guilty by Reason of Insanity, you would obey the law, wouldn't you?"

Mr. Homer lifted his chin, looked at the ceiling, then back at Barrett. "The judge would tell me that's what I had to do?"

"That's correct."

He scratched his wide jaw, grinned. "Kinda like when the wife tells me to do something. I always do what she says. Whether I like it or not."

The gallery tension was broken by laughter.

Osbourne banged his gavel and the room was quiet. "Defense challenges for cause?" he asked.

I scanned my Court Rules. "Your honor, Rule 2.511(D)(3) requires that a juror be excused if he shows a state of mind that will prevent him from rendering a just verdict. Accordingly, I request that juror number nine, Mr. Homer, be excused for cause."

Barrett stood. "Mr. Homer has said he will follow your instructions, Judge. I see no reason to dismiss him."

"I find that this juror can render a fair verdict, and I decline to excuse him," barked Osbourne. "Peremptory challenges, the defense."

Jurors will always have a bias against an attorney who challenges their ability to be fair. My dad's voice echoed in my head. I stood. "The defense will thank and excuse Mr. Homer."

Mr. Homer lumbered from the box and found a seat on one of the benches in the gallery. There was a rustling in the courtroom, people repositioning themselves on the wooden pews, readying themselves for the next round. I made a checkmark on my tally sheet, and Osbourne instructed the clerk to call another name.

It was well past six.

"Defense." Judge Osbourne sounded weary. "Peremptory challenges?"

"A moment, your honor." I looked over my notes. I'd been keeping careful track of each side's peremptories and knew I had one left. By my count, Barrett had three. If I passed and Barrett did, too, the clerk would swear in this panel. I leaned behind Callie and whispered to Jean, "What do you think? We have three that are good fits, but I don't know about number two, Fleener." When asked by Osbourne whether she knew either lawyer, Anita Fleener had disclosed that five years before, when she was the principal of a local elementary school, I'd cross-examined her in a case where my client was accused of sexually assaulting one of her students. In response to Osbourne's questioning, Ms. Fleener claimed she didn't hold a grudge against me and said she knew I'd just been doing my job. Now she was one of three professional women currently sitting on the panel. Uncharacteristically, I couldn't remember the specifics of her cross-examination. I'd knew I'd won the case, gotten a Not Guilty verdict. It was number twenty-four in the composition book in my bottom desk drawer. But without my notebook, I couldn't recall the details. Had I maligned this woman's credibility in some way to win my case?

"Counselor?" said Osbourne. "We're waiting."

I scanned the faces in the jury box, tapped the Waterman on the page of my Court Rules, then stood. Best not to play the odds. "The defense will thank and excuse juror number two, Ms. Fleener."

After the courtroom door closed quietly behind her, Osbourne announced, "I show that the defense has no more peremptories. The people can wait until the empty seat is filled or can exercise one or more of their remaining peremptories now. Mr. Michaels?"

Evidently Barrett had been counting my challenges carefully, the way a person listens for six gunshots before raising his own weapon. "In the interests of moving the trial along, the people will thank and excuse jurors number five and six."

I watched helplessly as the remaining two professional women stepped from the jury box. There was no longer anyone on the jury who fit Jean's "Perfect Juror" profile.

I crossed the two names from my chart as the clerk called three more. They came forward, and I quickly scanned the notes I'd made when reviewing their questionnaires. One was a custodian at the ice arena, another worked the tollbooths on the international bridge, and the third managed a local bakery. Of course they could be fair, all replied in answer to Osbourne's question. Yes, they'd heard the media coverage, but they could make up their own minds.

Donna June was fifty-seven and a grandmother three times, she said with obvious pride when asked to tell the court something about herself. Harold Sanders ushered at St. Anne's on Sunday mornings. John Shaw was in his fifties, had never married, and still lived on the family farm with his elderly mother.

Although I had no more peremptories, I was allowed to ask questions. Concerned that Harold Sanders might let the church's position on abortion influence him, I was prepared to challenge him for cause if his answers showed a bias.

"I don't believe in abortion," he said. "But this wasn't abortion, was it?"

"That's true. But some people say neonaticide and abortion are the same. Do you believe that?"

"I believe abortion is baby killing, but this wasn't abortion, was it?"

"Do you want the law on abortion to be changed, Mr. Sanders?"

"I do."

"And do you think you might bring attention to the abortion issue by making an example of this girl?"

"Approach, your honor?" Barrett strode toward the bench, scowling. "We are not trying this girl because she had an abortion, Judge." His voice was low but emphatic. "Counselor's questions are inappropriate. Whatever this juror's opinion, my opinion, or anyone else's personal position on abortion happens to be, it's irrelevant in this case."

"But, Judge," I whispered, "it's not irrelevant. If this juror sees the two as comparable, he may see this as a way of promoting his position. Some people"—I glared at Barrett and turned to Osbourne—"say one leads to another."

Osbourne said, "Regardless of what those zealots and the media say, I will not let this trial deteriorate into an abortion debate. Step back." He turned to the jury box. "Mr. Sanders, will you follow the law as I instruct you in reaching a verdict?"

"Yes, sir."

"In other words, you will follow the law and not your religious or personal convictions when reaching a verdict?"

"Yes, sir."

"Is there anyone else on this panel who would answer the last question differently?"

No one raised a hand.

"The people are satisfied with this jury." Barrett sat down.

Since I had no choice, I smiled weakly in Mr. Sanders's direction. "The defense is also satisfied," I said.

A collective sigh reverberated through the courtroom. Osbourne instructed the chosen jurors to stand and his clerk administered the oath. They all swore to "well and truly try the issues in this case." Osbourne sent them home for the night with strict instructions not to discuss their day or this case with anyone.

When they were gone, I gathered up my files. Callie stood and stretched.

"Hardly the jury we hoped for," Jean said.

Art showed up to walk Callie and me to my car. Along the way, reporters shouted questions, but I kept walking, one hand on Callie's shoulder. When my car doors slammed shut, Art banged twice on the trunk and I drove away.

THIRTY-FIVE

I GRABBED SANDWICHES FOR THE TWO OF US AT A LOCAL deli. Once home, Callie set the table and arranged our food on china plates with a full complement of flatware and paper napkins.

It had been almost a week since I'd had a drink.

I said, "Did you open the card from Rose?"

"I don't have to. All her cards are the same."

"She sends you lots of cards?"

"She used to. She pretends we're buddies. She always says stuff like 'Just between us girls,' and 'Your father wouldn't understand,' and then she winks at me."

"And you don't want a buddy?"

"I don't want her."

"Have you told your father how you feel?"

"He wouldn't listen. He thinks marrying Rose is God's will."

"God's will . . ."

"If it grows his church, it's God's will. It was . . . like they weren't getting married, they were merging. The preacher and the social chairman."

It was the most revealing thing she'd said to me. I wanted to know more but thought I'd pushed her far enough that night, so we ate our dinner in silence. Callie did mention that the seed in the feeders was nearly gone and said she'd refill them in the morning before court. Afterward, she cleared the table and disappeared into her room.

I wandered to my corner chair and watched as Sister Phillip blinked and rocked in the night's easy breezes. A shiver passed through me, and I closed my eyes. When I opened them, Callie was standing beside me.

"Are you okay?" I asked.

Her voice was shaky. "Tell me about prison."

I took a long breath. "First you have to be convicted."

"Will you visit me there?"

"We're a long way from those kind of worries, Callie. But, if you want to know, I can say that I would definitely keep in touch with you, wherever you are. But we can jump off that bridge if and when we come to it."

"Victoria?"

"Yes?"

"If I was . . . raped . . . would it help you win my case?"

My mind reeled. My father would have been horrified if he knew what I was about to say. "Never suggest a defense to a client," he'd preached over and over. Even when a client asked for a clue, a hint, as to what they should reveal to him, he'd never wavered. But I was certain he'd never been faced with a situation like this.

"Yes, it would definitely help, Callie," I said. "If you were raped, Dr. Allen can explain why you can't remember being pregnant."

She said, "I've been praying especially hard to help me remember." Tears spilled down her pale cheeks. "But I can't."

I reached for her and she leaned into me and cried.

"Bailiff, you may call the jury."

Bill McKenna, a retired deputy who moonlighted as a bailiff, strode purposefully across the courtroom. His leather belt and holster squawked as though a small duck were following him. He disappeared through a side door then reappeared, holding the door for the fourteen jurors. They took their assigned seats in the box, their faces somber. I glanced around the courtroom and didn't see Rose, which wasn't a surprise. Neil Thomas would likely be testifying that day, and I didn't think she'd want him to see her there.

"Good morning, ladies and gentlemen." Judge Osbourne's voice sounded stronger today. "Nice to have you all with us. This part of the trial is known as 'opening statements.' The prosecutor will begin and the defense attorney will follow, unless she wishes to waive hers and give it when it is her turn to present her case. Mr. Michaels, you may proceed."

"Thank you, your honor." Barrett stepped around counsel table, closer to the jury, and dropped a legal pad with notes beside him. The courtroom gallery, filled with spectators, hushed expectantly.

"Good morning, ladies and gentlemen. When most of us travel to a place we've never gone before, we use a road map to guide us. That way we're not surprised when we come upon a twist or sharp turn in the road. An opening statement is like a road map. It gives you an idea of where we are going during this trial."

The jury shifted in their seats, uncoiled a bit.

"This trial," Barrett continued, "will include the testimony of two men who were salmon fishing on the St. Clair River this past April."

For the next hour, Barrett detailed the evidence he would present, never referring to his notes before stating a date, a time, or a name. He spoke from memory, as though he'd lived each event he described. I heard nothing unexpected, but my heart still pounded wildly. I kept bracing myself against his stabs, his blaming, his accusations that seemed directed not just at Callie but also at me.

"That is our case, ladies and gentlemen," Barrett finally concluded, and took his seat again. By then, most of the jurors had crossed their arms. Some looked over at Callie, their eyes narrowed and their faces grim.

"Defense?" Osbourne said.

I stood and picked up the lengthy speech I'd spent hours writing and rewriting, the one I'd rehearsed alone and with Jean, the one Gail had typed for me in large font and printed. I'd intended to tell the jury about Dr. Allen's stellar credentials, explain in great detail her examination of Callie, and her conclusion. How, in her expert opinion, Callie dissociated when she was pregnant and when she gave birth because she had likely been raped. I rolled the podium to a spot in front of the jury box and placed my speech on it.

"Good morning." I glanced at my notes. "May it please the court, ladies and gentlemen of the jury . . ." This much was written there, the polite words with which I began every opening statement in every jury trial. I turned back to Callie. She looked small and vulnerable, her tiny hands folded and her eyes looking straight ahead. She's a scared child, I thought. A *child*.

I turned back to the jury. "Listening to Mr. Michaels, if that was all I heard about this case, it would be difficult not to come to the conclusion he wants you to reach: that this girl . . . my client . . . murdered her baby." These words were not on the page in front of me, not what I'd planned to say. "You see, I, too, heard about this case . . . early on, and I also concluded that Calliope Thomas was guilty. She had to be, right? But then I was ordered by this judge to represent her. And I changed my mind."

"Your honor." Barrett stood. "I hate to interrupt counsel's opening, but unless she plans to be a witness in this case, and she has not notified the people of that intention, it is improper for her to state her personal opinion as to the guilt or innocence of the defendant in her opening."

Barrett was right. I waited to be admonished.

But Osbourne surprised me. "I'll allow you some leeway, Counselor, but don't go too far."

"And when I got to know this girl, I found out I'd been wrong.

This young girl . . . Callie, that's what everyone who knows her calls her . . . Callie. I should mention that she's a wonderful artist . . ." I reached for my briefcase, opened it, and pulled out the drawing of the sparrow and read to them what she'd written across the bottom. I held it up for them to see. "And she's a good cook. Very good."

Barrett stood, as though close to objecting again.

"Anyway," I said, "I found out that Callie was not guilty. And that this case is not as simple as it looks. It's a whole lot more complicated than it seems to be. There's a lot of solid evidence the prosecutor didn't tell you about, that I wanted to show you during this trial but I won't be able to—"

"Objection, your honor—"

"Sustained," Osbourne barked. "The jury will disregard the last statement of defense counsel. The only evidence that you will comment on, Counselor, is that which this court has ruled admissible. Is that clear? Miss Stephens?" Osbourne's raspy voice echoed into his microphone. The gallery stirred, whispered, and Osbourne banged his gavel once. "Proceed, Counselor."

I squeezed my fists, opened them, and took a breath. "I would like to show you . . . during this trial . . . who Callie really is. You see, we never contested that this child was my client's. It was her child. We do not contest that the child drowned. He did drown. But what you need to understand, if you're going to judge Callie, is how she got to a place in her life where she would do this thing. That's a problem because the court won't let me—"

"Your honor—" Barrett was back on his feet. "May we excuse the jury?"

Before Osbourne could rule, I said, "It's okay. I'm done." I walked back to counsel table and sat down, then reached for Callie's hand.

Osbourne said, "Ladies and gentlemen, let's take a ten-minute recess. When we return, the prosecutor will call his first witness."

"All rise," pronounced the clerk, and the bailiff quacked across the courtroom. The jury filed out.

Jean leaned behind Callie and whispered, "What the hell was that? You dumped your speech? When do you plan to explain our defense?"

"I went with my gut."

Jean shook her head. "You had all these reporters here and you missed your chance. Our chance." She was clearly not happy.

I'd desperately wanted to tell those people that Callie wasn't the person Barrett described. I'd wanted to convince them she was a normal, sweet girl who panicked. But if the looks on the faces of the jurors when Osbourne admonished me were any indication, I'd blown it. No one, least of all the members of this jury, cared who Callie was.

THIRTY-SIX

THE ER DOCTOR TESTIFIED FIRST, DESCRIBING HOW Callie was hemorrhaging when the ambulance brought her to Port Huron General. He'd called in an ob-gyn and, once Callie's father appeared and signed the necessary consents, Callie'd undergone an emergency D&C.

The ob-gyn testified that in his opinion, Callie had given birth an hour or two before she was admitted and that a minute piece of placenta he'd removed during surgery was the cause of her bleeding. Once she was stabilized, Callie was admitted to a ward.

The floor nurse in charge of Callie's care testified that she asked Callie about her baby and that Callie denied her pregnancy and denied there was any baby. Otherwise, she said, Callie had been pleasant and cooperative, no trouble at all.

The detective in charge of the case testified he'd been called to the hospital after Callie was admitted because the hospital staff knew she'd given birth but claimed there was no baby. He'd interviewed Callie's father, who denied knowing anything about his daughter's pregnancy, the birth, or the baby's whereabouts. Pastor Thomas "appeared to be in a state of shock," the detective testified, and agreed to accompany the police to the parsonage and provide them access, waiving his right to a search warrant. Next, the detective identified a series of photos he took of Callie's bedroom and bathroom, photos that showed no evidence of a birth other than a bit of blood on the bathroom floor. Two uniformed officers accompanied him to the parsonage and all searched the basement, yard, and garage, but found no evidence of a body and no sign that the lawn or the flower gardens had been recently disturbed.

"Did you subsequently return to the parsonage?" Barrett asked.

"On April twentieth, the same two officers and I returned with a search warrant."

"Why was that?"

"An infant's body had been discovered in the St. Clair River, and a witness had reported seeing a female in a dark raincoat place a pink bundle in the river on the date of the purported birth. We were seeking a pink bedsheet to match the fabric found wrapped around the infant. And a black raincoat. Pastor Thomas had cooperated before, but by then it was looking like we'd be seeking a warrant for his daughter's arrest and we didn't know how he'd react. We wanted to secure this evidence as quickly as possible."

"Did you locate these items?"

"Pastor Thomas showed us to his daughter's bedroom. The bed was made, like it was during our first search. When we pulled back the quilt, there was no top sheet on the bed. But there was a pink fitted sheet and matching pink pillowcases. We tagged these and removed them as evidence."

"Did you find the black raincoat?"

"We still have not located it."

Callie nudged my hip, and I placed my hand on hers.

"No questions," I said.

The heads of the people in the gallery swiveled in unison as Neil Thomas strode to the stand. His black suit hung on his lean frame. When he passed counsel table, Callie turned toward him, but he ignored her and kept walking. After he affirmed the oath and was seated, he answered Barrett's questions.

"When did you first have contact with your daughter on April fifth?"

"In the emergency room at Port Huron General."

"What time was that?"

"Around eleven o'clock."

"Can you tell us what happened when you arrived at Port Huron General?"

"A doctor came to see me. He told me . . . my daughter had . . ." He glanced at Callie and closed his eyes.

"Given birth?"

"Objection. Leading. And hearsay," I added.

"Sustained."

"Were you aware your daughter had been pregnant?"

"I was not."

"You had no idea?"

"None whatsoever." He chewed the inside of his cheek.

"What happened after the doctor talked to you?"

"I signed some consent forms for my daughter's surgery."

"Did you speak with your daughter at that time?"

"No."

"What happened after you signed the insurance forms?"

"A detective showed up and asked me some questions."

"What kind of questions?"

"He asked if I'd been present during the birth, and if I knew what happened to the baby."

"What did you tell him?"

"I didn't even know my daughter was pregnant. And I didn't know where the baby was."

"Did you subsequently return to the parsonage?"

"Yes. The detective wanted to go look for the baby."

"Did you give him permission to search the parsonage?"

"I did."

"When did you next see your daughter?"

"Around six o'clock that evening. I came back to the hospital. She'd been admitted to a room and was eating dinner."

"Did she say anything to you?"

"Only that she wanted to go home."

"Did you take her home?"

"No."

"Have you spoken to your daughter since that evening at the hospital?"

"I have not."

Beside me, Callie whimpered softly, so I dug in my purse for a tissue and pressed it into her hand.

"Your witness, Counsel," Barrett said.

Jean and I had agreed we should get Callie's father out of the jury's presence as quickly as possible and more important, just then, I wanted him out of Callie's sight. I asked only those questions I hoped would support Dr. Allen's upcoming testimony: that Callie had been a respectful and dutiful daughter before this happened, that she was a stellar student, and that she'd been a Sunday school teacher at his church. When I finished, I sat down at counsel table and put my arm around Callie. "All done, sweetie," I told her.

That night, we shared a frozen pizza. Callie cleaned up the kitchen while I sat on my deck and watched the light drain from the sky. Eventually, she wandered out in her pajamas and sat on the deck chair next to mine. With her index finger, she traced a figure on her arm.

I reached over and grasped her hand. "A penny for your thoughts."

"It's just—do you think he will ever forgive me?"

"It's possible. In time."

"He never forgave *her*."

Her. Her. Callie's mother. I said, "Why did she need forgiveness?"

"He said God punished her. For her promiscuity." Tears dripped from her chin to her pajamas. "That she didn't deserve forgiveness."

"Everyone deserves forgiveness, Callie."

"Not everyone."

"Do you?"

"Everyone says I was pregnant, that I had a baby. I must have been promiscuous, too."

"Getting pregnant does not make you promiscuous, Callie." I added, "Especially if you were raped."

She stood.

"Callie?" I had an idea, a desperate thought.

"Yes?"

"When you didn't drive to school, what time did the school bus pick you and Stella up in the morning?"

"I got on around six thirty and Stella a few minutes later. Why?"

"No reason."

She leaned forward and kissed my cheek before padding to her room. I sat on the deck and watched the black water. *What sweet, compliant teenaged girl with Callie's background wouldn't have dissociated if she got pregnant?* My own dad would have been furious if he'd discovered I was unmarried and pregnant at seventeen. Or ever. A true defense lawyer to his last day, my dad noticed everything. But unlike Callie, I could never have hidden a pregnancy from my dad.

THIRTY-SEVEN

EARLY THE FOLLOWING MORNING, I PEEKED IN AND TOLD
Callie I'd be back in time to pick her up for court. This time I
parked along the road, my car hidden by a copse of maple trees just
starting to shed their orange leaves. Around six thirty, a willowy
blonde walked out of the ranch house and stopped beside the mailbox.

I waved at her from a distance. "Stella? Can I talk to you?"

She glanced at the house, then took a couple steps toward me.

"I'm—"

"I know who you are," she said.

"I'm here because I think something happened to Callie last
summer in Kentucky. You were her best friend. You were down
there, too, right?"

"I'm not supposed to talk to you," she said.

"But if you know something, anything—"

She pinched her lips closed with her fingers.

"I can't help her if you won't talk to me," I said.

She glanced toward the house. "Even before Kentucky she was
different. She seemed . . . angry . . . but she wouldn't tell me what
was wrong."

"Did something happen in Kentucky?"

She paused, looked up and down the road and finally back at
me. "One night all of us went to a restaurant. Outside there was a
guy. A street musician. He was playing the trumpet, and his case
was open. There was money in it. Callie asked if I had any cash. I

gave her a dollar and she walked over and dropped it in his case. He stopped playing and bowed to her. Then he started talking to her."

"What did he say?"

"I couldn't hear."

"What happened after that?"

"She slept next to me on the church floor. That night I woke up, and she wasn't in her sleeping bag. Later she was back, and I heard her crying. She smelled like smoke. Cigarette smoke."

"Did she tell you what was wrong?"

Stella swallowed and shook her head. "I asked. But she wouldn't tell me."

"Did she ever tell you?"

"No."

"Did you know she was pregnant?"

She shook her head again, then glanced behind her. A yellow school bus turned a corner and lumbered toward us.

"Did you see Callie the morning of April fifth?"

"The day the baby was born? Only at school." She looked back at the bus and mumbled, "I have to go," then ran to the end of her driveway and stood with her back to me until the bus ground to a halt, its front door opened, and she climbed on.

Barrett's first witness that day was Nicholas Ostrowski, a wiry man with a salt-and-pepper beard. A mixture of spicy aftershave and cigarette smoke preceded him when he walked past. His plaid shirt was crisply ironed; his blue jeans were clean and his black buckled boots polished. Once on the witness stand, he folded his arms across his chest awkwardly. He cleared a throat thick with mucus before he spoke. "My son-in-law, Terry, and I drove over to Algonac with my boat. We heard the salmon jacks were running."

"Salmon jacks?"

"Young salmon. You put 'em in the smoker for a few hours, and they come out tasting like candy."

Barrett approached the witness stand. "Just you and I having a conversation," he'd probably told this man when he prepped him earlier. "You catch any?"

"We netted five. No, *six*. Six."

"Where'd you put your boat in?"

"The usual place. At the state park."

"Where'd you fish?"

"South of the park. On the American side. We were trolling spoons."

"Those are a type of fishing lure?"

"Yes, sir."

"So, Mr. Ostrowski, you were fishing on the river. Did you see anything unusual that day?"

"Yes, sir, we most certainly did." He raised his face. "Terry had just pulled in a line to reset it. I noticed something pink, just below the water, a few feet upstream."

"What did you do?"

"I started the motor and steered us toward it."

"What happened next?"

"I got the big net and pulled it up. Dropped it in the bottom of the boat."

"The pink thing?"

"Right."

"What happened then?"

"I saw up close what I'd seen in the water. It was an arm and a hand." He spread the fingers of his own hand. "They were tiny, a tiny baby's. And . . ." Nicholas swallowed, cleared his throat again, scowled. ". . . the hand was missing a thumb and two fingers."

Barrett paused while this visual sunk in for the jury. "What did you do then?" he finally asked.

"We opened the cloth so's we could see the rest of it."

"What did you see?" Barrett was nearly at the jury box by then. His steps backward had been barely noticeable. He wanted the witness to talk to the fourteen people seated there, not to him.

"A baby. A dead baby boy."

"Other than the missing fingers and thumb, was the rest of the body intact?"

"His face was gone. He was missing a foot. Appeared chewed off."

"Objection. Assumes a fact not in evidence." I'd been waiting to break the flow of his testimony, but I saw the jurors' faces and knew it was too little, too late. I might have kept the photos out, but this testimony was damning as hell.

"The jurors will disregard the assumption by this witness as to what happened to the body before the witness observed it," Osbourne pronounced.

Barrett paused again. He waited for the image of the body to solidify in the minds of each juror, then said quietly, "What did you do then?"

"Terry had his cell phone, so he called 911 and told them what we found."

Terry Solak's testimony was the same as his father-in-law's, except he was determined to tell the jury how he had three small boys of his own and that they were fishing for salmon jacks for the First Communion party for his oldest son, Nicholas. Barrett didn't bother to reel him in, and after I objected the third time, Osbourne instructed him to answer only the questions asked. Just as I thought he was finished telling the story of a fishing trip gone wrong, Barrett asked what they did with the salmon jacks, and he said, "We didn't want to remember anything about that day.

While we waited for the sheriff, I kept looking at the baby, brushing flies off what was left of his tiny face. Once we got our boat on the trailer, I got sick."

"Sick?"

"I puked twice in the grass beside the boat ramp. I threw all the fish in the dumpster on my way past."

I objected on the basis of relevance, but nobody in the court-room, including me, was under the illusion that it did any good.

The day's final witness was Laurel Kern, a short woman with unruly red hair. She wore a plum-colored leotard top and matching leggings that looked like they'd been painted on her chubby body. On direct, Barrett established that on April fifth, she'd observed a short female in a black hooded raincoat walk to the township park next to her house and place a pink bundle in the river.

"When did you report to the police that you had seen a female with a pink bundle?" I asked on cross-exam.

"After I saw your client's picture in the *Sentinel.*"

"So, it was after the fishermen found the baby's body down in Algonac?"

"Yes."

"You called the police fourteen days after you saw a female place the bundle in the water?"

"Yeah. I read about it and I said to myself, 'I saw that girl at the park when I was watering my plants two weeks ago.'"

"But you didn't call the police when you first saw her?"

"I didn't see any reason to. But when I saw the picture in the *Sentinel*, I called 911 and said, 'I need to speak to a police officer about that dead baby.'"

"What did the female you saw on April fifth look like?"

"I couldn't see her face."

"Did you see how she got to the park?"

"No. First I saw her was when she walked past me."

"So you can't say if she drove or walked there."

"Nope. All I saw is that she walked to the boat ramp and squatted down and put what she was carrying in the river."

"And you didn't see her walk away?"

"Nope. I got a phone call and I went inside to answer it. When I came back, she was gone. But I did see the pink bundle floating downriver."

"You did not speak to this person?"

"No."

"Nor did this person say anything to you, correct?"

"Correct."

"And you did not hear any cries or noise, correct?"

"Right."

"So you really have no way of knowing for certain whether there was a baby in that bundle, correct?"

"I guess."

"Is that a 'yes'?"

"Yeah."

"And assuming there was a baby in that bundle, you have no way of knowing if it was alive or dead, correct?"

"Correct."

"I have no further questions."

Barrett passed on redirect and Osbourne said, "I see it's past our usual quitting time. I'll adjourn until nine o'clock tomorrow morning. Jurors are admonished not to discuss this case with each other or anyone else. Stay away from newspapers, televisions, and radios during this break. Talk about the Red Wings or the Lions, whatever you wish. Just don't talk about this trial. Court's in recess."

THIRTY-EIGHT

IT WAS A LONG, EXHAUSTING DAY. I SNAPPED MY BRIEFCASE closed, and Art Jones showed up to escort Callie and me. We passed what was left of the day's crowds, and when we reached the parking lot I told Art we could take things from there. We'd nearly reached my car when a familiar voice hollered, "Victoria! Wait up!"

As I unlocked the car, Joyce Ballinger scurried over.

"I just heard! I won my extradition hearing!"

"Good for you," I said, as Callie climbed inside and closed her door.

"Extradition is so tricky. All those hoops to jump through, with no clue what you'll find on the other side. It's dependent on whether the requesting country has a treaty with the United States or whether the returning country has a ban on capital punishment. Anyway, the Moroccans, who wanted my guy, do *not* have a treaty with us, which made the whole thing kind of a crapshoot. Everything came down to whether the Department of Justice had some reason to want to make nice with Morocco. Which, luckily for my guy, they didn't. Plus the Moroccan evidence was weak. Bottom line, I got my guy off." Joyce grinned.

"Congratulations," I said. "It's always nice when the good gals win."

"Amen, sister. So how's your case going?"

"Barrett's being a prick."

"He's always been a prick, Victoria. Except to you. None of us ever figured out why you got such good offers from his office when

In Defense of Good Women 217

he treated the rest of us like pariahs. You must have pictures." She winked at me. "Anyway, thanks. And good luck."

That evening Callie drifted in and out of her bedroom while I sat at my kitchen table reviewing my questions for Eleanor Allen, questions I knew would be useless if Osbourne didn't allow Eleanor to speculate about Callie's rape. When Callie finally settled in the living room, she curled up with her sketch pad and pencil.

I craved a glass of wine. I wandered out to my deck and watched a freighter slip by on the darkening water. *If only*, I was thinking. If only she would tell me she'd been raped. I thought about my conversation with Stella that morning. I came inside and sat beside Callie on the sofa.

"I've been wondering," I began, "if you thought any more about whether you . . . you might have been . . . that is, you *were* raped?"

Her bottom lip quivered. "Is it that important?"

"It is."

She sniffled.

"And I so want to help you."

She began rocking.

"You know, I won't judge you. I love you, Callie."

She wiped tears from her face with her hand.

"Winning your case, helping you, is the most important thing I've ever done. But I can't do that without help from you."

"You want me to say I was raped."

"Were you?"

She stared at her drawing a long time.

"This morning I talked to Stella. I think something happened to you last summer in Kentucky." I reached for her hand. "You can tell me. You need to tell me, Callie. Please."

Finally she whispered, "He seemed nice."

"Who?"

"He said he'd meet me outside the church. When I came out, he asked if I wanted to take a walk. I was in my pajamas. He said no one else would see me, that we would just walk around the block and talk. He wanted a cigarette, and I thought he shouldn't smoke on the church steps. Plus he told me he left his trumpet in the bar around the corner and wanted to get it. He had a key." She swallowed, her breathing shaky. "He unlocked the door and then . . ." —she began gasping, sobbing all at once—"it happened. I didn't want to. I didn't want to." She shook her head back and forth, again and again.

"He raped you." I reached for Callie, but she stiffened and bowed her head.

"If I stayed in the church," she mumbled, "like I was supposed to . . . it wouldn't have . . ."

"It wasn't your fault."

She shook her head. "I shouldn't have gone with him." She covered her face with her hands and began to sob.

"Callie, it was not your fault." I pushed away her drawing pad, and her pencil dropped softly on the carpet. "It wasn't," I repeated, as I reached for her and began rocking her, trying to calm her.

Later, in her room, I smoothed her hair, then offered to sit with her until she slept. She insisted she'd be okay, so I hugged her one final time, then retreated to my corner chair to think.

She finally admitted she was raped.

My lawyer brain shifted into gear.

First thing in the morning I'd phone Eleanor and let her know what Callie told me. Then I'd talk to Barrett. Once I told him what really happened, I'd plead with him to dismiss Callie's case. He could explain his change of position to the voters; it would show how reasonable, how merciful he could be. Unlike before, this time I was certain he'd listen.

THIRTY-NINE

BEFORE THE SUN ROSE, I LEFT AN URGENT VOICE MAIL for Eleanor Allen, asking her to call me that morning before she left Ann Arbor. Then I drafted a press release for Barrett, one he could offer both the press and the public. In it, I explained Callie had been raped and that the trauma of the rape caused her to dissociate, that her actions were caused by the dissociation and not by any desire to hide what she'd done.

Callie and I got to the courthouse well ahead of the scheduled starting time, passing the line of spectators. Upstairs, Jean waited for us in the hall.

"Stay with Callie," I told her. "I need to see Barrett."

"Anything I should know?"

"Absolutely. I'll be right back to tell you all about it."

Inside Barrett's office, a secretary behind the glass partition phoned him, then buzzed me in. He and the weasel were in a conference room. Mugs of coffee and a paper plate of sugared donuts sat on a table between them. "What's up?" Barrett said when I walked in.

"I need to talk to you." I nodded at the weasel. "Without him."

Barrett's eyebrows shot up, and the weasel slid behind me, closing the door when he left. "What's the big secret?"

"Callie Thomas was raped. Last summer. During a church mission trip to Kentucky. Some musician, a drifter, lured her to a bar, and raped her."

"So she's got a case against some guy in the Commonwealth of Kentucky. What does that have to do with me?"

"Callie comes from a strict religious home. She was raped. You heard Eleanor Allen two weeks ago. Callie's a classic case of both the neonaticide syndrome and PTSD. Classic."

"Jesus, Victoria," he said, "you're like a one-trick pony. If your girl was raped, why didn't she say so before this?"

"Because she's got some backass notion she was responsible. She blames herself because she took a walk with the rapist. That's why."

"Even if . . . even *if* she was raped, that hardly justifies the murder of her baby."

"Callie was unable to accept her pregnancy because it resulted from her rape."

"And I suppose she told you about this so-called rape."

"Who the fuck else would tell me?"

"Isn't that convenient?"

"It's the truth."

"Have her explain it to the jury. Maybe they'll buy it. But I don't."

"I can't put her on the stand, Barrett. She'll never hold up. She thinks it's her fault—"

He slammed his coffee mug on the table and stood. "Victoria, this is not my problem. And we're due in court."

"Barrett—"

"See you upstairs."

I was visibly shaking by the time I got to Osbourne's office. Barrett strode in behind me.

"I need a continuance," I said. "I have new information. I just discovered it last night."

"Mind sharing this new information?" Osbourne did not look happy.

I repeated what I'd told Barrett, and Osbourne's eyes narrowed. "What's your position on this, Counselor?"

"Frankly, this revelation is a little too convenient," Barrett said. "I'm nearly ready to rest my case and counsel, who has no plausible defense, suddenly dreams one up."

"I didn't dream up anything, Barrett."

Osbourne said, "Why didn't your client share her little secret before this?"

"Her psychiatrist said it might happen if she became comfortable, trusted me, which she didn't. Until now."

Osbourne walked to his window and looked through the bare branches of the big maples outside.

"I'm only asking for a couple of days, your honor," I pleaded. "Please."

He held up a hand. "I assume you need to consult with your expert about this. And you'll want to do the same, correct?" He looked at Barrett.

"Of course."

Osbourne sighed. "I can give you twenty-four hours, Counselor. Your expert will have this morning to review this new information, and the prosecutor's expert can have the afternoon. This trial will proceed tomorrow morning at nine o'clock sharp. Let's put this all on the record, and then I'll call in the jury."

In the conference room, I updated Jean and then returned Dr. Allen's call. As soon as the jury was released for the day, Callie and I sped to Ann Arbor. Before interviewing Callie, Dr. Allen met with me in her private office.

"Assuming Calliope gives me the same information that she gave you, this will give greater credence to our PTSD defense. But I must remind you, jurors have never accepted the PTSD defense in a neonaticide case. It will be a risk. Will Callie testify?"

"She won't survive Barrett's cross." My phone buzzed and I read a text from Gail. "Prosecutor's expert declined to interview Callie." I asked Dr. Allen what she made of that development.

"It means they think our defense is weak," she said. "I'll see Calliope now."

FORTY

THAT NIGHT, LONG AFTER CALLIE WAS ASLEEP, I SAT IN my chair in the dark. So far, Barrett had presented his case like an experienced mason, laying brick next to brick with each question, pausing between each answer long enough to let the jury absorb what they just heard, allowing the mortar to set on the wall he was building that would soon close Callie inside.

Ten hours from now it would be my turn. Eleanor Allen would take the stand and explain post-traumatic stress disorder. She'd tell the jury how the trauma of rape caused Callie to dissociate through her pregnancy and the birth. Hadn't this been what I was hoping for? That Callie would admit she was raped, so I would have a chance at presenting a defense to the charge of murder?

A *chance*. For the first time in eight days, I opened a bottle from my cellar and poured myself a full glass. My father believed in the justice system, trusted it, told me the law could sort things out so that, at least most of the time, the guilty would be convicted and the innocent set free. I'd believed that, too, until recently. Somewhere during this journey with Callie, the faith I had in the courts had dissolved and I saw this trial for what it was: a game of chance—like roulette or blackjack—but instead of cash or casino chips, the justice system was playing with Callie's life.

Sister Phillip blinked a calm rhythmic greeting to a thousand-footer pushing through a layer of marine fog.

No matter what Eleanor Allen testified to, no matter how clearly she explained her conclusions, when this trial was over, Callie would stand next to me at counsel table while the jury filed into the courtroom. We'd wait in the unbearable silence until the clerk spoke, asking the jurors if they had agreed upon a verdict and, if so, who would speak for them. The foreman would stand. "We have and I will," he would say.

"On the charge of Murder in the First Degree, what is your verdict?" the clerk would ask, and I already knew, despite Eleanor Allen's testimony about Callie suffering a severe form of PTSD, we would lose. At best, the foreman would state, "We, the jury, find the defendant, Calliope Faith Thomas, guilty of Murder in the Second Degree." Murder Two could mean decades in prison for Callie.

After the verdict was pronounced and the jurors excused, Callie would be immediately remanded into custody. A convicted murderer, she'd get no reprieve to return to my cottage and pack her few possessions—her art supplies, her new clothes, her pink teddy bear. She'd be whisked away from the courtroom by the deputies, and she'd be gone.

Like everyone else I ever cared about.

The freighter sounded its foghorn, and Sister Phillip blinked and rocked easily on her tether. I stared into the cloudy darkness toward the Canadian shore as Sister Phillip opened her single eye and closed it again.

Why wouldn't Barrett listen to me? Help me? He could have dealt this file. He owed me that. I drank a second glass of wine, then a third. Afterward I closed my eyes and let it come back to me. For the first time in years, I let myself remember.

Three weeks after he called and told me he was ending things between us, I was late. I wasn't concerned, at least not at first. My periods had never been regular and I assumed the trauma of my dad's illness was wreaking havoc with my system. But days later

In Defense of Good Women   225

my breasts became tender and swollen, and I was nauseated most mornings. I continued to go to classes and come home on the weekends to be with Dad, but inside I was numb, disbelieving.

If I had this baby, I'd need to leave school and return home. I pictured the disappointment on Dad's gaunt face if I confessed my pregnancy to him, the shame he'd feel at what I'd done. It would be the last memory he would have of me, that I was a disappointment. All because of one unguarded moment. My mind raced crazily, trying to figure out a way to make this pregnancy go away, to get back my normal life.

On a rainy November day, I skipped my afternoon class and drove myself to the City of Flint, to a part of the city where I was certain I wouldn't run into anyone who might recognize me. The clinic wasn't much better than a back alley joint, but at the time I was so desperate to rid my life of this problem that it felt like I was in precisely the right place. The receptionist was behind a window that looked like it once slid open but was now locked, with a slit at the bottom so forms and cash could be passed in and out. Plastic signs on the walls read, NO DRUGS OR MONEY KEPT ON THESE PREMISES OVERNIGHT.

I paid the seven hundred dollars in cash, handing over bills I'd withdrawn from my small savings account at an Ann Arbor bank. Then I waited in the grimy lobby with the others, a few teenagers and their mothers and a couple other women I guessed were in their twenties, like me. No one made conversation. The others looked as lost and alone as I felt.

While I waited, I wondered about the stories of these women. A passionate spring night in the back seat of a car? A party they couldn't remember? A boyfriend who wasn't ready to be a father? A husband who couldn't cope with another mouth to feed? Had these women told the fathers what they were about to do?

I felt a hand on my arm so I followed a nurse to the back where the smell of antiseptic was pungent and the linoleum floors only marginally cleaner than the floor in the lobby. She led me to a room and opened a metal locker. "Put your things in here. Then cover yourself with these." Paper top, paper sheet. No gown. Paper on the table. "Shoes, everything off. Wait here and the doctor will be in to take care of you." She handed me a clipboard. "You'll have to sign this form."

I read the waiver of liability. It said I wouldn't sue the doctor if anything went wrong and my legal antennae went up.

"My attorney would advise against signing this," I said. I was afraid to admit I was a law student because I'd heard stories about doctors refusing to treat attorneys. When she left the room in a huff, I undressed. I could hear her in the hall telling someone, "She's smart enough to have an attorney but not smart enough to use birth control."

I sat on the table covered in blue paper, my shoulders hunched. I was scared and humiliated, trying not to think about what I was about to do. I kept telling myself I'd be fine, that this whole thing would soon be forgotten and my life would return to normal.

After two quick, short raps on the door, it opened. "The doctor said he'll go ahead with the procedure," the nurse said curtly. "There's no anesthetic. You might need a Tylenol afterward. If you experience any bleeding other than minor spotting, call us or go to your local emergency room."

The doctor, a fifty-something man in a white coat and surgical mask, stepped inside and scrubbed his hands at a corner sink. "We ready?" He spoke more to the nurse than me as he pulled a pair of latex gloves from a cardboard box.

The nurse helped me lie back on the table, guided my bare feet into cold metal stirrups. "Slide toward me," she said.

"You'll feel a sucking sensation, some light pain, nothing serious. Then it'll be done. All set?" It was the doctor.

I nodded, turned my head to the side, and tried to pretend I was somewhere else.

On the drive back to Ann Arbor, I debated calling him to tell him what I'd done. But by the time I got to my apartment, all I wanted to do was crawl into bed and forget any of this ever happened. Besides, I'd fixed everything for both of us. During the coming years, whenever I ran into him, he'd ask how I was doing. "Never better," I'd always say. It was the same thing I told myself. And my father never knew.

When I opened my eyes, the river was swathed in fog. Across the river the Canadian countryside was a black mass.

Canada. I stumbled to my laptop and googled "extradition from Canada," then leaned closer to the screen. An hour later I was in Callie's room, shaking her arm.

"Callie, wake up."

She squinted into the overhead light I'd flipped on. "Is it morning?"

"Not quite. I need you to get up, get dressed." I pulled her suitcase from the closet and opened it. "We need to pack your things."

"Is something wrong?" She sat up and rubbed her eyes, yawned.

"I'll explain on the way."

"Where are we going?"

"Please. We don't have much time." I pushed her tangled hair behind her shoulders. "You need to trust me. Okay?"

She frowned, pushed back the covers, and stepped to the bathroom. The toilet flushed, and she returned. I handed her one of her skirt and sweater sets and pulled her Michigan sweatshirt from the closet shelf. "Put these on," I told her.

FORTY-ONE

THERE WASN'T MUCH TRAFFIC ON THE BRIDGE TO CANADA. No one would have seen us turn around. I could have sent Callie back to bed and curled up in my corner chair, maybe managed a couple hours of sleep before we needed to head back to the courthouse. But I couldn't shake the picture I had of Callie, Jean, and me standing at counsel table in just a few hours, or maybe a few days, listening to the pronouncement of the verdict, the verdict I knew was inevitable, no matter what we said or did.

I kept driving, my hands welded to the steering wheel. The tires of my Mercedes wriggled when they crossed the metal grates at the apex of the bridge, a grid constructed to expand or contract during Michigan's extreme temperatures. I activated our seat heaters and punched the red arrow on the car's ventilating system as we started our descent. Approaching the border, we passed a queue of big rigs idling in the right lane, awaiting inspections by Canadian customs. Their cloudy exhaust, along with the fog, obscured the overhead lights.

Callie's forehead rested against the side window. "Victoria? Didn't that judge say I wasn't supposed to leave Michigan?"

"This is what's called a legal maneuver. And you're with me, so it's okay. I have a passport, but you don't," I continued. "I don't think they'll ask for ID if they think I'm your mother—"

"You're not my mother."

I'd been telling myself that for days, weeks even. *You're her lawyer*, I'd reminded myself one last time before I woke her from a sound sleep. I said, "I know I'm not. But when the customs agent asks, you need to say your name is Stephens, like mine. Calliope Stephens."

"You're telling me to lie?"

I swung behind the longest line of cars, braked more quickly than I'd intended. "I guess I am," I said.

"But—"

I inched the car forward. People in vehicles ahead were questioned, waved on. "You need to trust me, Callie." I pronounced those words automatically, reflexively, the way I did when I was reminding a client that I was the legal expert, the one in charge. I pulled forward, stopped beside a printed sign that instructed me to wait there until the car in front of mine was released. When a gloved hand from the booth motioned, I pulled ahead, stopped next to the opening.

"Please," I pleaded, then lowered my window.

"Citizenship?" The young man in uniform leaned out, checked the front seat, then glanced toward my trunk.

"Both US." I handed him my passport. He scrutinized the photo, my face, then twisted his neck to get a look at Callie.

"Passport, young lady?"

"I keep meaning to get her one, but so far, when we make this trip, we haven't had any trouble," I offered.

"How about a birth certificate? Or driver's license?"

"I didn't think to bring her birth certificate, and she's too young to drive. She's only fifteen."

He frowned. "What's the purpose of your visit to Canada?"

"Actually, we're on our way to Stratford," I said, "to see a couple of shows."

"Season still going?"

"Um-hmm. Tickets are cheaper this time of year. My daughter

and I thought we'd get an early start, check into a room, and see the town."

"Any alcohol, tobacco, or firearms in the vehicle?"

"None."

"What's your name, young lady?" He looked past me again, at Callie. I leaned back slightly, held my breath.

"Calliope Stephens," she said, as naturally as if it were the truth.

The agent snapped my passport shut and handed it back. "Have a good trip."

FORTY-TWO

THE KEY WAS STILL BENEATH THE FOURTH STONE. I unlocked the wooden door and pushed. The cottage reeked of mildew. It had probably been closed up for months. He wouldn't have had time for a getaway during the campaign. I raised a shade covering a picture window, and Lake Huron appeared, like liquid mercury, waves sliding up and away on the white sand beach. To the east, the sun was beginning to peek over the horizon.

Callie had followed me inside.

"I'll help you get settled." I hauled her suitcase to the cottage's only bedroom, then opened the fridge and turned it on, lit the pilot for the gas stove, and stowed bread, milk, cans of soup, and cereal I'd picked up at a gas station along the way. In one of the cabinets I found an open box of Red Rose tea. Back then I'd been a tea drinker, not the diehard coffee addict I was now. On a windowsill over the sink, the ceramic sheep, the mysterious prize inside every box of the ubiquitous Canadian tea, still sat where I'd positioned it twenty years before. I slid it in the pocket of my suit jacket.

"Are there sheets on the bed?"

I passed Callie on my way to check, and she reached out and touched my arm. "Victoria?"

I kept walking. "Clean sheets. That's good. You'll sleep in here. See? And the bathroom's primitive, but it works. Shower, sink, toilet."

"What's going on?"

"You're going to stay here and I'm headed back."

"You're leaving me here?"

"Just for today. I'll be back tonight."

"But—"

"I need to talk to the prosecutor again. Don't worry. I'll build a fire to warm the place up. There's food here, everything you need. Oh, and if anybody should come by, just tell them Barrett Michaels loaned us his cottage for a few days. That your mother is here with you, but she ran to the store for some supplies."

"Wait—this belongs to Mr. Michaels?"

"It's fine." I leaned my head into the fireplace and opened the damper as I'd watched him do years ago, crumpled sections of a yellowed *Globe and Mail*, and stuffed them beneath the grate, laying kindling and logs on top. "There's plenty more firewood outside if you need it." I lit a match and was relieved when the paper crackled and caught fire. It was already six thirty. If I left now, I could be at the bridge by eight. "I've got to take off," I told her.

"Why are you doing this?"

I put my arm around her shoulder, my face close to hers. "You'll be fine. We'll be fine." I was already feeling more confident than I had in weeks. "It's beautiful here. You can walk the beach, sketch, listen to the radio. I'll be back tonight. You just need to have faith in me. You know about faith, don't you?"

The morning sun had dissolved the fog by the time I crossed the bridge. I handed my passport to the customs agent, a young woman who studied the photo, then leaned into the car to get a better look.

"How long were you in Canada?" she asked.

"I came over last night."

"Purpose of your visit?"

"To visit friends. I drank more than I should have." I shrugged, tried to appear embarrassed. This was the story I'd come up with, in case the agent questioned why I had no luggage or why I was coming home so early in the day. I squinted and rubbed my temples with my fingertips.

"Are you bringing anything back with you? Gifts of any kind? Some of that rotgut Canadian whiskey?"

I smiled sheepishly. "No. Just an aching head. Serves me right."

Twenty minutes later, I passed that day's line of potential spectators, negotiated security, and kept walking. Outside Osbourne's office, I leaned against the wall. When he tottered down the hall, I stood up and smoothed my wrinkled suit jacket.

"Everything all right, Counselor?"

"I need to speak with you."

He unlocked the outer door to his office, laid a thin briefcase on his secretary's desk, and slowly removed his topcoat. "Does it concern this trial?"

"Yes."

He shook his head. "We're in the middle of things, so we'll need a prosecutor."

"I was hoping—"

"You know that, Victoria." He turned away.

Half an hour later, Barrett showed up, and the three of us sat around Osbourne's desk. "What do you mean, your client's not here?" Osbourne said.

"She's not feeling well."

He leaned back in his chair, slid a yellow pencil between his fingers, back and forth. "We can't proceed without a defendant," he said.

"What's wrong with her?" Barrett asked.

"Flu, I think. She's got a fever and can't keep anything down."

"Have you called a doctor?"

"I'm sure it's just a stomach virus. She'll get over it."

"When do you think your client will be well enough to rejoin our little gathering?" Osbourne asked.

"Maybe tomorrow."

"Well, I just hope you don't get whatever she's got. I'll have to send the jury home again. I'll tell you I don't like the idea of another delay."

"I'm sorry, your honor."

"Counselor, I'll expect you back here at four this afternoon to give the prosecutor and me an update on your client's health."

"She's sick," I said when I found Jean in the hall. "I'll phone Eleanor and tell her not to come. Why don't you take the day off, too? I'll call you when I know something."

Jean said, "You don't look so good yourself, Victoria. Why don't you get some sleep while you have the chance?"

I perched on the arm of my corner chair. A rusting freighter chugged upriver, and Sister Phillip blinked. A couple of goldfinches, their once summer yellows now winter greys, hung upside down at Callie's thistle feeder. The maples across the river were already bare. In a matter of days, the Coast Guard cutter would show up and pull Sister from her mooring and replace her with a red pencil buoy. When winter ice clogged the river, the slim marker would dip beneath the water until the ice passed and it could pop up again.

I took a deep breath and punched Barrett's cell number on my phone. "I need to see you," I said.

"What about?"

"Come to my cottage."

"Tell me, Victoria."

"I need to see you. In person." I hung up, then stood at my big window and continued to watch the river.

"What do you want to tell me that's so damned important?" he said, when I let him in.

"I have a resolution for this case. It'll be a win for both of us." I chose my words carefully. "Are you aware that Canada has a five-year max in neonaticide cases?"

"So?"

"If Callie were to . . . escape . . . to Canada, you could extradite her. I've done some research and I'm pretty sure Canada would put conditions on her return, maybe a sentencing cap, like they have over there in these types of cases. In the meantime, you'll look like the tough guy who dragged her back."

"Have you lost your fucking mind?"

I held up a hand. "No, see, once the election's over, I promise to plead her. To something with a sentence cap. Maybe two years max. This case will be old news by then. You'll be on the bench, and no one will think anything more about it."

He glanced around my kitchen suspiciously. "She's still in this jurisdiction, right?"

When I didn't answer, he shook his head. "Forget it. I'm not going to be a party to that kind of craziness. Let your bigwig doctor testify. Let the jury decide."

I thought about telling him then. Instead I said, "Please, Barrett, I'm asking you as a favor."

He slid his key ring along his index finger, shook his head again. "Let the system run its course, Vic."

I thought again about saying the words, telling him how I'd panicked, the way Callie had. That my situation had been different, but the same. But I couldn't. I dropped into a chair at my kitchen table and slammed my hand on the table so hard my palm stung. "Please."

He let the door bang shut behind him.

I showered, dressed in a clean suit and blouse, and ate a cheese sandwich and an apple from the bowl Callie set out on my kitchen counter the weekend before. "You need to eat healthier," she'd said, before she added apples to our grocery list.

In the back of my closet, I found my dad's old army duffel. I'd have on a suit and heels when I stopped by the courthouse, so I tossed in jeans and two sweatshirts, my tennis shoes and underwear. I wouldn't need much else. From my bookshelf in the kitchen, I grabbed *The Joy of Cooking*. I had a momentary vision of us eating thick stew in bowls before a fireplace and afterward Callie sketching while I read a novel and drank a glass of expensive red.

I pulled an old savings passbook from my lingerie drawer, the end of the life insurance money Dad left me. The balance was fifteen thousand and change. I drove to two different branches and made separate withdrawals, neither for more than $10,000, since under Michigan's drug laws that would raise questions. I asked for the money in Canadian funds.

FORTY-THREE

IN RETROSPECT, I SHOULD HAVE LEFT THAT MORNING, but some part of me was hoping Barrett would change his mind, that I wouldn't have to go through with this, that I could bring Callie home and there'd be no consequences for either of us. Instead, that afternoon promptly at four, I strolled into Osbourne's office. Barrett was already there; the foot across his knee was jiggling. I could sense the tension in the room.

"Your client recovered?" Osbourne asked.

"She's a little better," I lied.

Osbourne frowned. "What I'm about to say troubles me a great deal." He leaned back in his chair, tapped its arm with his pencil, a slow, deliberate beat. "But I need to address it, since the prosecutor has brought it to my attention."

Barrett's foot was still, then started up again. I did my best to keep the same expression on my face, but I could feel my neck and face heating up, my jaw tightening.

"The prosecutor has filed a motion." Osbourne held a stapled set of papers. "Have you served Victoria, Barrett?"

"No." Barrett slid papers from a red file and handed them to me.

"Motion to Produce Defendant?" I faced Barrett. "What's this about?" I flipped through the pages, scanned the affidavits that supported the warrant, one from Barrett and one from the teller at the bank.

238   Marilyn J. Zimmerman

```
That the aforesaid Victoria Stephens did state
to your affiant that the said Calliope Faith
Thomas would receive different treatment in the
Dominion of Canada, which is outside the
jurisdiction of this court. . . .
That the aforesaid Victoria Stephens did
withdraw the sum of $15,236.00 in two
installments. That in both cases she requested
that she be given her money in Canadian funds.
```

"You followed me?"

"Ed Mueller has an interest in her case."

"I hope Barrett's wrong about all this, Victoria." I heard Osbourne's voice as though I were inside a tunnel.

Barrett pulled another document from his file, pushed it toward me. "Victoria Stephens, you are under arrest for knowingly aiding and abetting the escape of a person under bond to this court."

A uniformed officer stepped into the room as I reached for the warrant and glared at Barrett. "You sonofabitch," I said.

At the jail Art hovered while a young deputy unlocked the cuffs and inventoried the contents of my purse. Art's eyes narrowed when he saw the wad of Canadian bills in my wallet. "Count it," he snapped at the deputy. When he finished, the deputy asked for my jewelry. I removed my rings and my diamond wristwatch and handed both to him. He scribbled, his hand curled around his pen, then turned the paper so it faced me. I didn't bother to read it before scrawling my name.

"I must say, I'm disappointed, Madame Counselor," Art began, and I thought about saying I didn't need a lecture, but decided against it.

"Things aren't always as they seem," I said.

"Apparently not." He stood and opened a door. "Okay, Millie," he hollered. "You can take it from here."

The portly female led me to a changing room and stood close by while I stripped. "Soles of your feet." I lifted each and she ran a stick along them. "Bend over." I shut my eyes and cringed as she slid her gloved fingers into my vagina, and then my rectum. When she was finished, she snapped off the gloves and tossed them in a nearby bin. From a metal locker she handed me floppy grey panties, an orange jumpsuit, and a pair of plastic slippers. She stuffed my worsted suit, silk blouse, pumps, and lingerie in a clear plastic bag on which STEPHENS and a number were scrawled in black marker, then pulled its cotton drawstring tight.

"When's my arraignment?"

"Probably first thing tomorrow."

"Not tonight?"

"You probably want dinner, too. The others got fed an hour ago."

"You don't need to worry about feeding me. But I'd like to speak to the bondsman."

"No dinner?" She seemed skeptical, but pleased. "I guess I could see if he's hanging around."

Half an hour later, Ed Mueller joined me in my cell.

"Where's my girl?" he asked.

"She ran away last night. But I think I know where she is."

He mouthed one word, "Where?"

"She just got scared. I'm sure of it."

"Barrett says she skipped to Canada."

"Barrett's crazy when it comes to this case. He inferred that from something I told him. Actually, I think she's in Ann Arbor."

"What makes you say that?"

"She and I went there for a couple of visits with our expert. Callie seemed to like the campus. I think that's where she is."

"How exactly would she have gotten herself to Ann Arbor?"

"I'm not sure. A bus, maybe a friend."

"What's with all the Canadian money?"

"When this trial is over, I'm headed to Canada for a long overdue vacation. It's been more than I bargained for."

"They don't take credit cards in Canada?" The bushy brow above his left eye rose.

"I'm going to the wilderness to do some hiking before the snows come. I've got a cabin north of the Soo." I'd read a feature in the *Sentinel* not long ago about the Agawa Canyon area. "It needs a few repairs, and it's easier to pay cash up there."

He chewed his lower lip and tilted his head: I hoped he was considering my story.

"I'm telling you, Barrett's nuts with the election so close," I added.

Now he leaned so close I could have counted the pores on his nose. "I'll write the bond on one condition. That I go with you to Ann Arbor to find your girl."

When I hesitated, he shrugged. "Looks like we can't do business." The molded plastic chair scraped the concrete cell floor as he stood.

"Okay, fine. Whatever you say." I put up my hands in surrender.

"What I say is that you and I will go together and pick up your client. Do we have a deal?"

"Sure."

"I have your word?"

This time I didn't hesitate. "Of course."

FORTY-FOUR

THE NEXT MORNING IN THE JAIL'S HEARING ROOM EARL peered over the top of his readers. "A plea of not guilty will be entered on behalf of the defendant. Anyone care to speak to the matter of bail?"

"The People ask that bail be denied in this case. Given the circumstances." The weasel was there in Barrett's place. A reporter I recognized from the *Sentinel* crouched in a chair at the back of the room, his pen poised, his eyes darting between me and his notebook.

"Which are?" Earl settled his chin on his thick knuckles, waited.

"Which are that the defendant's client, who was living in the defendant's home and who is charged with a capital offense, is believed to be in Canada. This defendant"—he pointed a long finger at me—"who withdrew over fifteen thousand dollars in Canadian funds from two local banks yesterday, represented to Mr. Michaels that her client, who has not been made available to this court, was in Canada. We have reason to believe this defendant may have transported her there."

Earl interrupted. "You don't need to try your whole case here, Counselor. Defense?"

Jean said, "Your honor, we all know the Constitution guarantees bail unless one of two things is likely to occur. First, there must be a risk of flight, which means flight by this defendant, not her client. Second, there must be a risk of harm to the community if the defendant is released." I relaxed a bit. Jean could probably make this argument in her sleep. "Even, and I say *even*, if this defendant were to be convicted of the crime with which she is charged, she's only accused of assisting her client's flight from the jurisdiction. Miss Stephens is not charged with fleeing, ergo she does not pose a flight risk. In addition, she has longstanding ties to this community. She owns a home here and has maintained a law practice in this county for over twenty years. Her father previously practiced law in this county." Jean referred to the notes I'd handed her when she showed up. "She has donated time and money to various charitable and philanthropic organizations in this community. The idea that she would risk her career and her reputation by fleeing this jurisdiction is unthinkable. She has other clients to represent, other cases to handle, besides the appointed case of *People versus Thomas*."

Earl scratched his chin. "Response, Counselor?"

"It is my information that this defendant has recently been acting in a bizarre and unprofessional manner. First, she let her client, Calliope Thomas, live in her home."

Earl smirked, just a little. "Inviting a criminal client to live in her home is unusual, but it's a stretch to call it bizarre, Counselor." He leaned forward and checked to make sure his recorder was picking up. "I'm going to set bond in this case at five hundred thousand dollars, cash or surety."

"Your honor," Jean began, but I stopped her. I could give up five of my fifteen thousand, but I'd need to come up with forty-five more. I had some money in my office account from the last few clients who'd hired me. It'd be a violation of professional ethics to take unearned fees for personal use, but just then I didn't care. I figured I'd cross that bridge later, if I needed to.

"Usual conditions of bond," Earl continued. "I'll set the preliminary exam for"—he raised his head, surveyed a calendar—"nine a.m. on Thursday the tenth of November. Anything else?"

In Defense of Good Women 243

Two hours later I met up with Jean in the jail parking lot. Ed Mueller slid the check Gail brought me into his wallet and hovered a few feet away.

"Do you mind telling me what's going on?" Jean said.

"I've revised our strategy."

"Do you know where Callie is?"

I fiddled with the wrinkled lapels of my jacket. "I'm pretty confident I'll find her."

Ed stepped forward. "I'll drive you home, Counselor."

"Not necessary. My car is here. I said I'd take you with me when I go look for her. I'm good for my word, Ed."

"I'll drive you to your car. I'm just protecting my investment, Counselor."

I found my Mercedes in the lot where I'd left it the previous afternoon with a parking ticket courtesy of the City of Port Huron on my windshield. Before I got out of Ed's Lexus, I said, "When I get home, I plan to take a shower before I go anywhere."

"No need to be so touchy, Counselor. I'll follow you and wait outside. When you're ready, we can head out. Together."

I pulled forward in my driveway, and Ed parked behind me, his Lexus blocking my exit. I got out, my ignition key between my front teeth, and Ed lowered his car window.

"You planning on getting any lunch?" he asked.

"I'm not hungry," I said through the key. I stood beside his Lexus and searched my purse for my house key. "So, you wait here if you feel you need to. Oh, and are you bringing your cuffs? In case we find her and she gives us trouble?"

My question had the intended result. Ed raised both eyebrows. "Sure, I got 'em." He paused. "Listen, maybe while you're getting cleaned up, I'll run into town and grab a burger. Meet you back here."

"Whatever." I found my house key.

"I'd feel better if you gave me your car key, Counselor."

"My car key? What for?" I wiped it on my sleeve for effect, then slapped it on his open palm. "Feel better?"

He grinned. "I'll be back in twenty minutes."

When I was certain he was gone, I reached inside my car and popped the trunk, grabbed my duffel, and hauled it inside.

There wasn't a cloud in the sky, but there was a chop on the water. I'd grabbed my peacoat and a stocking cap, so I put those on. *Tuque.* I'd have to remember to call the hat that, once I got across. I'd grabbed my dark glasses, too, so I slid them on my face. Although the sunlight on the river alternated as glint and glare, I could see my way clearly. Up ahead, I spotted the arch of the Blue Water Bridge. *You only need to get that far, Victoria*, I reminded myself. *Ten miles.*

I was passing Riverside when I spotted Ed's silver Lexus on the road, heading toward my cottage. My hands froze on *Margaret Ann's* steering wheel. Despite the inboard's rumbling, I heard my pulse in my ears, drumming madly. By then, my little boat bumped and rocked against the waves and the current, but I didn't slow down.

I knew Mueller would be at my house by then. If he got suspicious and knocked on my door, he'd use his cell phone to call the police. I told myself I was being paranoid, that he was parked behind my Mercedes, nursing his Whopper and fries, listening to talk radio while he waited for me.

"Sit there," I said aloud, both willing him and wishing. "Sit there as long as you want. I'm not coming out."

FORTY-FIVE

JUST SHORT OF THE BRIDGE, I MOTORED *MARGARET ANN* into a channel on the Canadian side, a dry dock for freighters and the entrance to a public marina for smaller boats. NO WAKE signs on tall posts dotted the weedy shoreline. I throttled back, grateful I'd made it. A stately powerboat approached on my left, and I casually dropped a blanket atop my duffel. If anyone noticed me, I wanted them to think I was just poking around, no one to be paid any attention.

Along a series of T docks, a smattering of boats were lined up, waiting to be pulled for the winter. I passed the stern of a cigarette boat called *Smokin'* and a tall-masted sailboat named *Feng Shui*, plus a bevy of wide-sterned powerboats with plastic covers snapped over their cockpits. Most of the slips in the marina were empty, their boats already on tall wooden cradles in an adjoining field.

The few dock workers were busy hoisting a dismasted sailboat into a sling. The office at the far end of the marina appeared deserted, and the gravel parking lot held only a couple cars. I maneuvered my craft into an empty well and tossed lines to a couple cleats, then used my cell to call a cab. I hefted the duffel to a walkway, stepped on, and adjusted my sunglasses. When I reached the vehicle entrance on the main road, I waited for my ride.

"I've got a navy blue 2005 Impala?" The plump woman behind the desk spoke with crisp diction and that Ontario lilt where every sentence sounds like a question. I'd told her my car broke down at the casino up in Port Edwards, so I thought I'd visit friends in Toronto while it was being repaired.

"I should only need a car for a couple of days." She asked for a credit card, so I told her I didn't carry one. "I have cash and can pay ahead," I quickly added. "I had a good morning at the blackjack table."

The woman scowled. "I'll need an extra deposit if you don't have a card?"

"Sure." I pulled a few large Canadian bills from my wallet. "As long as I get it back when I return the car. I'll need it to pay for the repairs."

The 402 wasn't busy, just smooth pavement running east until it would merge with the 401, the highway to Toronto. I cruised along, the heater in the outdated Impala struggling to keep me warm. Not like my Mercedes, the decoy I hoped was keeping Ed Mueller tied to my house. Periodically I checked the rearview mirror for flashing lights; seeing none, I began imagining the commotion at the jail and in Barrett's office when Ed Mueller told them I was gone. Part of me sympathized with the deputies back there. I'd worked hard to build relationships with them, and I liked most of them. Art Jones, in particular, would never understand why I betrayed his trust.

At my exit, I turned north on the two-lane pavement, slowing when I approached Forest, the town where Barrett and I used to stop for supplies. At the local LCBO I picked up a bottle of pricey red, then stopped at a grocery store for the fixings for a couple of simple meals. I added a package of Ontario's ubiquitous butter tarts for our dessert.

The skies were dark by the time I turned down the lane leading to Barrett's cottage. All the summer places I passed looked empty, closed up for the winter. When I pulled into Barrett's drive, his cottage appeared deserted, too, but as I got closer, I saw a light inside.

"Hello?" I pushed open the door. Callie was sitting on the couch. "Jesus, Callie, it's freezing in here. What happened to the fire?" I bent down and gave her a quick hug. "You're as cold as ice."

"Where were you? You promised to come back last night."

"Let me get a fire going," I told her. "Then we'll talk."

The fire crackled, and the aluminum pan from the frozen macaroni and cheese I'd heated was empty, most of it eaten by me. I sipped wine from a scratched Canadian Tire tumbler and explained Canada's five-year maximum for neonaticide and my theory that Canada was not likely to extradite Callie without a fight. "My plan is to hire a good lawyer over here, one who will negotiate a plea for us before we agree to go back."

"But I didn't kill my baby—"

That again. "But I can't prove that, Callie," I said. "Anyway, once I hire a Canadian lawyer, she'll need to convince the Canadian government that since Canada doesn't recognize a Murder One charge for neonaticide, the Canadian government should refuse to extradite you to the United States. See, under the terms of Canada's extradition treaty with the US, Canada has the right to refuse to return a fugitive to the US if the fugitive's conviction will result in capital punishment. Do you know what capital punishment is, Callie?"

"Of course I do." She picked up our dishes and carried them to the sink.

"Well, the State of Michigan doesn't have the death penalty, but certain crimes are still considered capital offenses, like Murder One, because they're punishable by life in prison with no possibility of parole. We just need to convince the Canadian government that Michigan's punishment for neonaticide is equivalent to capital punishment and that, ergo, Canada's law regarding neonaticide should be followed in your case."

"How long will all this take?"

"I'm not sure. When we go back, you might have to plead to some lesser crime and spend a little time in prison, but nothing like you would have faced if we'd stuck around for the conclusion of that joke of a trial."

She filled a dishpan with soapy water and immersed our dishes and cutlery. With her back to me, she raised a plate and pushed a dishrag around it slowly, then slid it back in the water. "I have a question," she said without turning around. "If someone had a baby and someone else took the baby, would that person be in trouble with the law?"

"Of course. Why?"

"I was just wondering."

"What you've described could be kidnapping, depending on the circumstances. Kidnapping's a pretty serious crime."

"How serious?"

"The kidnapper could get life in prison. Why do you ask?"

"No reason." She scrubbed melted cheese from the second plate.

"So, are you okay with my plan?" I asked, but her only reply was a shrug.

Later, I found her sitting cross-legged on her bed, wrapped in a wool blanket. "It's warmer out by the fire," I said, but she didn't move. When I tried to push a stray lock of hair behind her shoulder, she jerked her head away from my hand.

Perplexed, I left her there and drifted back to the sofa near the fireplace. I drained the last of the wine bottle into my glass. Although I was having trouble thinking straight, I questioned why she would ask me about someone taking a baby. It was the second time she'd mentioned that possibility, once when I'd visited her in jail and again tonight.

My brain drifted, and my gaze floated over the spines of some old paperbacks nearby. I spotted an Erle Stanley Gardner and pulled it from the shelf. The edges of its pages were curled and yellowed, the print was faded, and, to my surprise, the distinct signature of my dad was scrawled on the flyleaf. This novel, *The Case of the Black-Eyed Blonde*, had evidently been part of Dad's collection. Why was it here?

After opening it to the first page and reading the familiar, clipped dialogue between Perry and his secretary, Della, it occurred to me that I'd brought this book with me the last time Barrett brought me to this cottage.

It was the end of that summer, before I returned to Ann Arbor for my final year of law school. Barrett and I had been dating, fairly seriously I thought, when I wasn't busy looking after Dad's needs and helping lessen his workload. So when Barrett phoned and invited me to come along, I'd hesitated, unsure whether I wanted to leave Dad for an entire day. But when I ran it by Dad, he'd insisted I go. Because Barrett said he was bringing some work with him, I'd grabbed this novel.

That particular day was chilly, and the beach was practically deserted. The two of us resembled burritos, wrapped in separate blankets, lying on the soft sand, Barrett writing witness exams and me reading this book. By late afternoon Barrett finished his work and smiled over at me. He lifted the book from my hands and studied the blurb on the back.

"It's lame, I know," I said quickly. "But my dad loves all these books. He thinks they're clever, with one exception. Perry Mason never gets past the prelim, so the judge always makes the call.

There's never a jury verdict. Never. Dad says no witness ever breaks down on cross during the prelim and that's totally unrealistic."

"Those witnesses just haven't seen me in the courtroom," Barrett grinned. He looked up and down the empty beach, then unwrapped my blanket and snuggled closer, covering the two of us with his blanket. "But just now I want to concentrate on you."

Until that afternoon, I'd faithfully used my diaphragm whenever Barrett and I made love. It would have only taken a minute to grab it from my duffel. But for some unknown reason, I didn't bother. My periods were unreliable back then and I told myself I couldn't possibly get pregnant.

FORTY-SIX

BRISK WINDS SWIRLED AROUND THE COTTAGE AND echoed down the chimney, like someone was blowing across the top of an enormous pop bottle. I pushed slowly off the couch, dropped two logs on the dying embers in the fireplace, and stumbled to the window. A gibbous moon leaked enough light for me to see the waves riding each other's backs on their way to the white sand beach.

Returning to the sofa, I curled up small and wrapped myself in a wool blanket to get warm, then squinted into the glowing ashes and shivered. The enormity of what I'd done was sinking in. I'd made a lot of assumptions: assumed I could save Callie, assumed the Canadian government would take our side, assumed Barrett would back down, assumed Barrett would work with the lawyer I planned to hire, and assumed Canada would extradite Callie and me on my terms. What if one of those assumptions turned out to be wrong? Was I prepared to hide out in Canada with Callie and become a wanted person? Give up my practice and my reputation?

My option, the professional choice, would have been to stand stoically at counsel table and watch as Callie was led from the courtroom following the Guilty verdict I knew was coming. Was that really a choice?

I rolled over and closed my aching eyes, drifting back to sleep and waking later to noises in the kitchen, cupboard doors squeaking, the clicking of the gas burner, the scratching of a match tip.

"Callie?"

She appeared in her nightgown, her hair messy and snarled.

"What time is it?"

"Almost ten thirty. I'm making hot cocoa. Do you want some?"

"No thanks."

"You had a lot to drink last night."

"I know." I deliberated a minute and pointed to the end of the sofa. "Sit. Tell me what's going on."

She plunked down and tucked her feet beneath her nightgown. "Why would the prosecutor make a deal with you now?"

"Is that all that's worrying you?" I untangled a bare foot from my blanket and pushed it against her hip. "Relax, kiddo. I'm a big-shot lawyer. I can handle this."

She scowled, then slid off the couch and went back to the kitchen, returning with her cocoa and settling into a rocking chair.

I dozed again, then woke and reached for my glasses and checked the time on my watch. Gail would be at the office, fielding calls from impatient clients or reporters clamoring for a story. How would she respond? Would she lock the front door and pull down the shade? Or invite the reporters in so she could hold her own press conference? If anyone from *People* magazine showed up, who knew what she'd say? Or a bigwig from one of those court television programs?

At the window I watched the waves swell and retreat. I'd been going back and forth in Callie's case, like those waves, flailing for weeks as I searched the law and the facts for a way to help her. I'd come up with one plan after another, but none of them had worked. What I needed was a strategy to save Callie that was foolproof, certain.

I pictured Barrett's face when he served me with that warrant in Osbourne's office two days ago. He'd been smug as he ambushed and humiliated me. I remembered the last time he'd treated me that way.

I was back in Ann Arbor that final year of school. He'd phoned me one night while I was studying, sounding gleeful and giddy. He asked about Dad but seemed distracted when I answered. Then he told me about Melissa. She was the daughter of a federal judge, he kept repeating, as though that explained and excused why he was ending our relationship. At first, I was disbelieving, but when the cold truth sunk in, I was stricken. And a few weeks later, I realized I was pregnant. Despite everything, I managed to take care of it, of us, so he'd never be bothered, he'd never have to know. Neither Barrett nor my dad had ever known what I did.

My dad was dead, but why was I still protecting Barrett?

I closed myself in the tiny bathroom. Cell phone reception was sketchy in this remote area, but I managed to get a feed, probably from a tower across the lake in Michigan. I scrolled through my news app and found a CNN headline: MICHIGAN LAWYER AND CLIENT ESCAPE DURING MURDER TRIAL.

I clicked on the link. Callie's yearbook picture appeared next to an unflattering photo of me raising an arm to fend off a pushy reporter. There was a video with the story so I waited impatiently for a couple of ads to end and then saw Barrett standing before a collection of microphones. The captions were out of sync with his moving lips.

VICTORIA STEPHENS DISAPPEARED AFTER SHE WAS CHARGED WITH AIDING AND ABETTING HER CLIENT'S EARLIER DISAPPEARANCE. SHE WAS GRANTED BOND OVER THE OBJECTIONS OF MY OFFICE BECAUSE SHE PROMISED TO HELP FIND HER MISSING CLIENT. BEFORE HER OWN ARREST, SHE HINTED THAT THE DEFENDANT FLED TO CANADA AND THAT SHE ASSISTED IN THE DEFENDANT'S FLIGHT. WE BELIEVE MS. STEPHENS AND HER CLIENT ARE CURRENTLY STILL IN CANADA.

Barrett's face was replaced by that of a chisel-jawed reporter with a microphone. The caption beneath him read: ALL EFFORTS ARE BEING MADE TO CAPTURE THE ATTORNEY AND HER TEENAGE CLIENT WHOSE DROWNING OF HER NEWBORN RESULTED IN A CHARGE OF MURDER ONE. WE'LL HAVE MORE ON THESE DEVELOPMENTS ON THE *LINDA GEORGE SHOW* TONIGHT AT EIGHT O'CLOCK.

I emerged from the bathroom, pulled on a pair of jeans and a sweatshirt from my duffel, then cleaned the smeared lenses of my glasses. I warmed a can of tomato soup and made a grilled cheese sandwich for Callie's lunch. I wasn't hungry. As she ate, I pictured the string of antiquated tourist motels I'd passed on the way here. Like the summer cottages, they'd all been closed for the season.

But I knew where I could find a television with American cable. Turns out we'd be going to Stratford after all.

FORTY-SEVEN

CALLIE SAT IN THE CAR WHILE I REGISTERED US AT THE Prince Albert, a tired but functional hotel in the City of Stratford. The desk clerk was a large efficient woman whose name tag read ELLEN.

I signed my mother's maiden name, Margaret Ann Fraim, on the abbreviated form.

"I'll need a credit card for incidentals," Ellen said.

"I pay cash for everything."

She glanced from side to side. No one else was around so she whispered, "If you ask me, too many people who can't afford credit cards think they have to have one. Next thing they know, they're in debt up to their eyeballs. But, you know, carrying around cash can be dangerous, too. Especially for a woman." She jotted something on the form, then said more loudly, "Just the one night, then?"

"Yes."

She pressed a room key into my open hand. "Room thirty-four is on the third floor. Right off the elevator."

During the past twenty years, Molly and I had met in Stratford numerous times to attend the Shakespearean productions the town is famous for. But the only Shakespeare play offered that night was *King Lear*, which I quickly dismissed. Cordelia's apparent betrayal of her own father, however she was redeemed in the last act, might hit too close to home for Callie. A production of *The Music Man* was also playing that night, and I quickly decided that could keep Callie entertained while I did what I needed to do. After picking up take-out soup for us from a Tim Horton's drive-thru at the edge of town, I drove to the Festival Theatre and purchased two tickets for the eight o'clock performance.

At seven thirty, I dropped Callie in front of the same theater. "The ushers will help you find your seat, and I'll meet you inside in an hour. Don't talk to anyone. Okay?" She seemed reluctant to leave me, so I added, "I just have a little business to take care of, and I'll be back. I promise."

She looked back at me as she walked slowly toward the gathering lines in front of the auditorium, so I gave her a thumbs-up and smiled. She was back to wearing the clothes she'd brought when she came to live with me, but I noticed that her odd wardrobe blended with that of the theater crowd. She'd be fine for the hour my plan would take.

At the hotel, I punched up the pillow on one twin bed and leaned against it, then stood and dragged the straight-backed desk chair between the two beds. I tried sitting on that with my legal pad on my lap and decided it would suffice.

Linda George had a huge viewing audience, I knew, because Gail jabbered about her on a regular basis, replaying what this lawyer or that psychologist on the show said about some big case. Linda did her best to rile up the public, encourage a lynch mob mentality. But tonight, she'd be my mouthpiece so I could tell Barrett what I needed to say. I was certain he'd be on Linda's show. He wouldn't be able to resist this pre-election publicity.

I checked the time on my phone, stood, then sat down again. I was more nervous than I thought I'd be. This wasn't how I felt at the start of a jury trial, even one as serious as Callie's. This feeling was different. Tonight, I'd be playing by Linda George's rules. And

In Defense of Good Women   257

if I wasn't careful, Linda George would be judge, juror, and jailer for both Callie and me.

Promptly at eight Linda appeared on screen, a Botoxed thirty-something brunette with a California drawl. "An attorney and her client, who's charged with murder, disappear in the middle of the trial. What causes an attorney to cross the line from representing to rescuing her client? That's our subject. Stay with us."

I waited through ads for upcoming interviews, news programs, the drug Lipitor, until the show came back on. I jotted the 800 call-in number from a yellow band across the bottom of the screen on my legal pad and waited.

It didn't take long. Linda introduced him first, then a perky-looking prosecutor from Las Vegas, then a mustached psychologist from Atlanta who resembled a large walrus. The screen split into four sections, each with a guest and the last with Linda.

"Two months ago," Linda began, "Victoria Stephens, a Michigan defense attorney, was appointed to represent Calliope Thomas, a young woman charged with First-Degree Murder. In April, Miss Thomas was charged with tossing her newborn infant into the St. Clair River so he would drown. At trial, Miss Stephens told the jury she intended to prove her client was insane during her entire pregnancy and when she killed her baby. But when it came time for Miss Stephens's expert witness to testify, Miss Stephens and her client disappeared. *Vanished.* Barrett Michaels, the prosecutor in this case, is in our Detroit studio. Mr. Michaels, do I have the facts correct, sir?"

Barrett's face filled the screen now. He wore a dark suit, white shirt, and an expensive-looking tie. "You do." He seemed comfortable in front of the cameras.

"Mr. Michaels, is it true that before this incident, Miss Stephens was a respected attorney in your community?"

"Linda, as far as I was aware, she had no prior problems drawing a line between her personal and professional life. Until this case."

"Tell us about that."

"For one thing, during a bail hearing, Ms. Stephens surprised us all by inviting the defendant to live in her home after she was released. Naturally my office tried to dissuade Ms. Stephens, but we're on opposite sides and technically there is no prohibition against an attorney housing a criminal client while she represents her."

"Any idea why she allowed Calliope Thomas to live with her?"

"I'm not certain, but I surmised that Ms. Stephens was overly concerned about keeping her client out of jail. Perhaps the court system should have seen that as a warning sign, but as I said, Ms. Stephens was a well-respected attorney, so no one suspected she might go too far."

I punched the numbers on my phone and held it to my ear while I kept an eye on Barrett's face.

"Now, Mr. Michaels, you charged Calliope Thomas with First-Degree Murder for the death of her baby. Is that the usual charge for this kind of crime?"

"Given the horrific nature of this defendant's actions, I felt I had no choice."

"Ladies and gentlemen"—Linda's lower lip stuck out and her spidery eyelashes fluttered—"the prosecutor proved that this tiny infant . . ." She paused, her eyes watered, and her voice trailed off. "I can hardly say these words. I'm sorry."

"You'll manage," I muttered into my phone as I listened to the ringing on the other end of the line.

"This baby," Linda sniffed, "was wrapped in the defendant's bedsheets and thrown, like a piece of garbage"—she squared her shoulders, looked directly into the camera—"into the deep shipping channel between Canada and the United States. This tiny baby boy was found two weeks later by two fishermen with parts of his limbs and his face"—she swallowed and closed her eyes—"chewed off. *Eaten.*" She took a long, dramatic breath. "Well. Back to tonight's topic. Let's ask our expert, Dr. Joseph Shevron, what he can tell us about why an attorney would flee with her client in the middle of a jury trial. Dr. Shevron?"

The big eyes of the walrus widened. "Yes, good evening, Linda. My concern here, frankly, is for the young woman, Calliope Thomas. I fear she may be impressionable or even mentally unstable. I'm concerned that she may have been influenced by her attorney to flee the jurisdiction rather than stay and face the consequences of what she did."

"And what would cause an attorney to persuade her client to run from the law like this?"

"Well, Linda, attorneys are bound by a code of conduct that prohibits them from becoming emotionally involved with their clients."

"And why is that a problem?"

The walrus spoke slowly, as if he were addressing a jury. "The client has the right to rely on the advice of her attorney. She depends on that advice because the attorney is the expert. The attorney is the client's lifeline, so to speak, and must be steady, rational, clear thinking. If the attorney becomes emotional, that legal advice is likely to be tainted."

"Interesting. But what causes the attorney to behave this way?"

"Numerous factors, Linda. There may be something in the attorney's past that is triggered by this particular client or this particular case. The attorney could have what lay people call a 'savior complex,' wherein she feels she is the only one who can save this client. Any number of things."

I heard a voice from my phone. "This is Bridgette from the *Linda George Show*. Who am I speaking with?"

"Victoria Stephens."

A pause.

"I'm the attorney Linda George is discussing."

"Oh. Okay. Hold on, please?"

I heard a click. I ran a finger down my legal pad, checked my notes again as advertisements dragged across the screen: people danced on green lawns, dogs licked the faces of their owners. By then, my heart was pounding. Finally, another voice came on the line; this one authoritative, stern. "This is Meredith, Linda's producer. You are?"

I told her. Then I added, "You might not want to tell Mr. Michaels I'm on the phone. An on-air meeting between Barrett and me might do great things for your show's ratings."

"Hold on," she said quickly.

The commercials ended, and the box of the perky defense attorney was highlighted on the screen. She shouted about ethics and oaths, as though the louder she spoke, the more sense she made. I half-listened to the rant, and when Linda's eyes became more expressive, I knew her producer had told her. Then the toll-free number on the yellow band disappeared, replaced by the words AWOL ATTORNEY ON LINE WITH LINDA. EXCLUSIVE.

Linda's eyes flashed at the camera, and she interrupted. "Ladies and gentlemen, I have Victoria Stephens on the line, the lawyer who fled the jurisdiction with her client midway through a murder trial. Miss Stephens, what in the world would cause an otherwise respected attorney to fly the coop, so to speak, with her client?"

I cleared my throat. "I left because it was the only way my client's predicament would be understood. The prosecutor was being overzealous and, frankly, using my client to parlay his way into a judicial seat in the upcoming election."

Linda's eyes narrowed into dark beads. "Mr. Michaels, are you on the line?"

Barrett's jaw became rigid. "I'm here." Barrett and Linda were the only faces on the screen.

"Mr. Michaels, what do you say to Miss Stephens's claim that you are being overzealous?"

"As I said earlier, Linda, I acted completely within the bounds of the law when I charged this girl."

I broke in, "Come on, Barrett, you know you had plenty of discretion. Some girls in her situation are charged with manslaughter. Some get probation. If Callie is convicted, she goes to prison for life. *Life.*"

"Well." Linda's eyes flashed; she was obviously relishing this exchange. "But still, Miss Stephens, given what your client did—"

"A young girl becomes pregnant. She panics. She can't accept the guilt and embarrassment of what she's done. She goes into shock."

"Miss Stephens, we're aware that your client was claiming she was insane through this whole process. But that doesn't explain *your* behavior."

I took a nervous breath. "What my client did is no different from any unmarried woman, an attorney like me, for example, or a law student, who becomes pregnant but is abandoned by the father of the child. Dumped. The woman panics. In the law student's situation, her panic takes a different form than my client's. That woman, the law student, has the child aborted, and then has to live with what she did."

Linda's lips became pouty, as though she were planning a chess move. "I may not agree with abortion, Miss Stephens, but the two are very different. I mean, abortion is legal in this country. Infanticide is not."

"That's a distinction without a difference, Linda. In both cases the woman cannot cope with what has happened. In different circumstances, perhaps if both women had been in loving relationships, lasting relationships, neither one would have felt compelled to do what they did. One would not have committed infanticide, and the other would not have committed abortion."

"I don't see your point," Linda interjected.

"My point is that the law student, in my example, walks away with only her own conscience to answer to, while the young girl goes to prison for the rest of her life. Is that fair? And in both cases, Linda, what happens to the father? Where is the father of the child in both these cases?" Barrett was staring into the camera. He looked confused.

"The father?" Linda huffed. "Miss Stephens, setting your fictitious case aside, there is nothing in your real case that says the father had any part in the killing of the infant. Isn't that correct, Mr. Michaels?"

Barrett said, "Yes, Linda, that is correct. We have no evidence about the father's behavior that would have led us to charge him. We don't even know who he is at this point."

"And Mr. Michaels made no effort to find out who the father of this child was, Linda. Even though I have informed him that my client's pregnancy was the result of a rape."

Barrett said, "I think we're mixing apples with oranges here. First of all, there was no abortion in the case of Calliope Thomas. Her child was born."

"You make my point," I snapped. "It's a sliding scale on the continuum of unwanted pregnancies. In both cases, the woman," I paused to regroup, "or I should say the women were left alone to contend with their pregnancies. And the fathers . . . in both cases, the fathers got off, walked away."

I saw Barrett's eyes open wide, and I knew he knew.

Linda shook her head. "I think we're getting off topic here." She sounded annoyed.

"We're not," I persisted. "I'm saying that if the public were to know about that abortion and who the father of that child was, it might be harmful, shall we say, not just to this woman but to the father. Maybe even to his career."

Barrett's eyes flickered away from the camera, and Linda raised her eyebrows as best she could and shook her head a final time. "Well, my, my. This is quite the discussion. Miss Stephens, you seem to have twisted this conversation from your own behavior to something else entirely. I heard you had a good reputation in the courtroom. Now I see why. But it still begs the question. Why not let the jury decide your client's fate?"

"I couldn't take that chance."

Linda smiled her phony smile. "Miss Stephens, would you say you might have overreacted just a tad when you ran away?"

"Are you asking me if I panicked?" I said. "I'd say I responded to the situation the best way I could."

Linda took a long breath, stared into the eyes of her devoted viewers. "I'm going to ask you one more time, Miss Stephens. Why are you doing this?"

I pushed the red button on my phone.

FORTY-EIGHT

I SLID INTO THE AISLE SEAT NEXT TO CALLIE AND SQUEEZED her hand as the lights dimmed for the second act. The River City boys danced down the aisles of the theater, waving and tooting dented trombones. Callie seemed immersed in the action and songs, but my mind was on what I'd just finished, the first phase in my new plan to help Callie. As soon as the play ended and the house lights came on, I switched on my phone to check for calls and messages, but there was only one. At the hotel, when Callie headed to the bathroom for a shower, I returned it.

"Victoria. Holy Jesus, Victoria." Molly sounded upset. Beyond upset.

"Hello, Molly."

"What in hell is going on? Your face has been all over American television. I saw that god-awful show tonight, Linda-what's-her-name. After it was over, he called here."

"Barrett? He tracked you down?"

"It wasn't hard. My brother still lives in Barrett's neighborhood. Anyway, he wanted to know whether I'd heard from you. He wanted me to talk some sense into you. He sounded concerned."

"The only thing he's concerned about is how this makes him look."

"Actually, I told him that. Also that he'd been selfish, thoughtless, to dump you when your father was so sick. I told him the list was a lot longer than that. But he says he's worried about you. He said . . . you might not be . . . stable right now."

"That's me. Crazy as a loon."

"Vic." Molly's voice softened. "What was all that stuff about infanticide being just like abortion?"

"Not *just like*. I said they were different ways to react to a similar situation."

"Having the baby and giving it up for adoption is another way, Victoria. I don't hear you making that argument."

"Callie panicked, Molly."

Molly was silent for a long time. Finally she said, "And so did you."

In the bathroom, the water stopped.

"Victoria, I don't care about him or his career. But I care about you. And if what you're doing with Callie is a way of punishing yourself—"

"It's not. It's only because I understand her. What she did."

"What she did is not what *you* did."

The hair dryer clicked on, whooshed. "It's not? It's not? No. It's worse. I had choices, alternatives, not that I saw them back then. All I could think of was how I would disappoint my dad, how *embarrassed* I'd be when he found out. And I didn't want Barrett to think of me as the woman who ruined his career, *our* careers."

"So, you did something you regret."

"You don't know about regret, Molly. You've always been the good girl. The one who knew who was, what she wanted. You didn't make stupid choices like I did."

"We're not talking about me here. Honey, sometimes people have to choose between two alternatives, neither of which they like. Once they choose, they need to get on with their lives."

"What if I can't?"

"*Mortalem te esse memento.*"

"Meaning?"

"'Remember that you are mortal.' Forgive yourself."

"What if I can't?"

"Why? Because you're not perfect?"

"I don't know. Maybe because this is the first time in a long time I know, just a little, what it's like to have . . ." I started crying, hiccupy sobs.

"To have . . . ?"

"Someone who needs me. Someone to whom I'm more than a hired gun. I thought it was never going to happen to me. I didn't think I ever wanted a child. Then she came along."

"But to give up everything—"

"I know, I know. But it's like I didn't have a choice."

"You always have a choice, Victoria."

"I made plenty of bad decisions during my life, Molly. But saving Callie doesn't feel like one of them." The dryer stopped, and the room was suddenly quiet. "I have to go."

I turned off my phone and grabbed a tissue to blow my nose as Callie stepped into the room, humming "Goodnight, My Someone." She paused, tipped her head. "Are you okay?"

I sniffed, waved a hand in front of my face, smiled. "Sometimes the ventilation systems in these old hotels make my sinuses nuts."

Callie crawled into her bed and propped up the pillows, pulled out her playbill and studied it. Pleased that her mood had shifted, I headed to the bathroom, turned on the shower, and stood beneath the hot water, letting my tears flow.

By the time I crawled into my bed, I heard Callie's soft breathing, so I checked my phone again. Gail and Jean had left messages. Jean wanted to know if I was okay, and Gail wanted to know if I'd lost my mind. "I heard you on Linda George, boss. I got so excited I spilled my Diet Pepsi down the front of my pajamas. After you hung up, women called into the show from all over the world. They either beatified you or condemned you. You're famous now."

There'd been no other calls. I slid the phone beneath my pillow and tried to sleep.

FORTY-NINE

THE NEXT MORNING I WAS UP AND DRESSED BEFORE SIX, but Callie stayed in bed with her sketch pad and playbill. She was copying Marian the Librarian's dress in the last act, the one she wore when she followed Harold Hill to the train station to confess her love.

"I might have liked the costumes best of all. I mean, the songs were kind of corny. Seventy-six trombones? Really?" She giggled and I was pleased with the continued change in her mood.

I praised her sketch, then said, "I'm going for a short walk. How about you get dressed so we can find some food when I get back?"

I shoved my phone in my jacket pocket and put on dark glasses. Callie and I would be more recognizable after Linda's show, so we shouldn't be seen together any more than necessary until we could do so without being noticed. On my way out I passed the breakfast room and heard the noisy chatter of people on vacation, long tables of laughing women and retired couples sipping tea before they headed out to explore the town and purchase souvenirs. I made my way down a shaded sidewalk, keeping my head lowered as I passed people on the street.

The stores weren't open yet, and I turned toward the picturesque Avon River. A couple of boys fished from shore, and a pair of swans dove for their breakfast, their white backsides like feathered pyramids above the water.

I checked my phone again, hoping there was a message from Barrett, but there was nothing. As I repocketed it, the revelation hit me, what my father used to call "a sudden rush of shit to the heart." Silently cursing my own stupidity, I did a mental run-through of what I'd be throwing away: the private cell phone numbers of lawyers and witnesses, addresses and emails for my clients, contact information for several judges. And Barrett would have no way to reach me. But if he got really crazy and wanted to locate us, the Canadian Mounted Police could trace the GPS on my iPhone in minutes.

Glancing around, I saw an elderly couple with their arms linked and their backs to me, strolling along the riverbank. An emaciated-looking man jogged toward me and kept running; on the water, two kids pedaled a fiberglass boat shaped like a large swan. Satisfied no one was looking, I flung my phone over the live swans, toward a small dam, then pretended to ignore the splash and walked away.

Nearing the hotel, it occurred to me that Barrett might still be able to trace my location from my phone records. I was trying not to be paranoid, but I didn't think it was smart for the two of us to remain in Stratford. If we returned to the cottage, eventually I'd need to go out for groceries. What if someone in that little enclave recognized me?

By ten o'clock we were traveling east on the 401, the outdated Impala keeping up with speeding traffic. I'd told Callie where we were going before we left the hotel, and although she seemed annoyed, she said nothing. As I drove, I tried to reassure her. "We just need to buy a little more time," I repeated.

Inside the City of Toronto, I wove around parked delivery trucks and cars and pointed out local landmarks to Callie: the Royal

York, the train station, the CNN Tower, the Pantages Theatre, Eaton Centre. She didn't seem interested. I spotted the entrance to an underground lot and parked, then led a reluctant Callie up the escalator into the crisp urban air, following the business-suited crowd down a wide sidewalk until I saw a store with large signs on its windows advertising cell phones.

The clerk looked like a college kid, but the name tag on Travis's shirt identified him as the manager. I told him I wanted a prepaid phone, and he led me to a rack of packaged flip phones.

"No contract, no long-term commitments. Just a brief interlude." He held up a small black phone. "This is our biggest seller. All the terrorists have these." He flashed a shy smile at Callie, but she looked away. "Sorry. A little cell phone humor." He demonstrated the phone's spartan features and handed me a shiny brochure with the costs and areas of service. "When you're finished, it's disposable. Of course, you should take it to a proper recycling center."

"Of course," I said, remembering my iPhone at the bottom of the Avon.

"I'll just go in the back and program it," he said, and reappeared a few minutes later to present me with my new phone. "Four hundred minutes," he said, "enough to change your life."

On Queen Street, the two of us climbed into a wooden booth at a little café called Marie's. After glancing around to see if anyone was looking at us, I replaced my sunglasses with prescriptions. "I thought we'd get a room, go out for an early dinner, then crash. Tomorrow I'll find a Canadian attorney who will take our case, and then I'd like to show you around the Ontario Gallery of Art. Smile, Callie. Honestly, your brow is so furrowed I could plant corn on it." I reached across the table and squeezed her hand. "I've been thinking. How about going to a fancy Toronto salon and getting you a new haircut?"

"What's wrong with my hair?"

"Nothing. I just thought it might be fun."

"Fun for who?" She hid her face behind her menu.

I could tell Nathan's was expensive when we walked in the door. There were no poster-sized photos of the latest hairstyles or cheap magazines showing the haircuts of Hollywood celebrities. Instead, there were white leather couches and live orchids in white pots on sleek ebony tables. A tall receptionist behind a desk peered at us through wispy bangs. "May I help you?"

"My daughter and I are in town for the day. I'd like to treat her to a cut and style."

"I'm not sure we have any openings this afternoon." She studied a computer screen. "Stay here, please?" Then she disappeared.

Callie ran her fingers through her hair, pulled a strand to her mouth and chewed on it. "I'm not sure about this."

"It's only hair. If you don't like it, it'll grow back."

The woman was gone so long, I started to fear she'd seen last night's *Linda George Show*. I considered leaving, but hesitated. Would that draw more attention to us? I was still equivocating when she returned.

"Nathan never takes walk-ins but he had a cancellation, so he can help you out," she said.

I squeezed Callie's shoulder. "Nathan, huh? Come on. Let's do this."

Callie dropped the strand of hair she'd been chewing on.

"Right this way," the woman said. "I'll find you a smock." In the back she held out the white robe, I helped Callie into it, and she led us to a room with a single station. The walls were covered in a soothing green grasscloth, and more white orchids lined a black windowsill. Shortly after, a large man with a slight overbite and blond cornrows appeared.

"So, you're the beauty I'm to have the privilege of styling this afternoon. Well, let's get started, shall we?" He wrapped a thin towel around Callie's neck and arranged a plastic cape over her smock. "And just what are we doing today, princess?"

I said, "How about chin length on one side and above the ear on the other? What would you think of something like that, hon?"

Callie's dark eyes popped. "That's so drastic."

But Nathan pulled her hair into a ponytail and tilted his head at the mirror. "That would look smashing on you, princess. This cut"—he let go of her hair—"is d-r-a-b, drab." He put his face beside hers and smiled into the glass. "Let's put some drama in your life. Whaddaya say?"

I grinned at the irony. "A new look," I said. "Let's do it."

Nathan didn't wait for Callie's response. "Great. Barb?" he called, and a hefty teenager with a hennaed bob appeared. "Shampoo this gal, will you?"

An hour later, the left side of Callie's head was shaved around her ear. The right side of her cut framed her chin. Nathan had given her a few red highlights and she looked like a different girl, chic and worldly, neither the morose kid I'd brought home from jail nor the demure teenager who'd been seated beside me during her trial.

Nathan stood nearby, admiring his work. "That left ear looks naked. Needs an earring. I can pierce it if you like. Just a small stud. I think it would finish the look, princess."

Callie stared into the mirror, expressionless. "My father liked my long hair," she finally said.

"Wait'll he sees this cut. And the new earring. Barb?" he hollered. "Bring the gun and a single gold stud. Not too big. We don't want to shock Daddy."

Out front, I handed the receptionist an exorbitant amount of cash. On the way to the car, I pushed Callie into a boutique and bought her a long wool scarf, then wrapped it around her neck. "This cut is fabulous."

She fingered the tiny gold ball in her ear.

"You look great. A real Toronto girl," I said, taking her arm and leading her up the bustling street. With her hairdo and funky clothes, she looked like another hip Toronto kid. No one would recognize us now.

FIFTY

CERTAIN THAT EVERY LARGE HOTEL IN TORONTO WOULD require a credit card, no exceptions, I headed to an old neighborhood, hoping to find a B&B, where the rules would be more relaxed. Gingerbread houses lined the streets, and two fashionably chic women pushed strollers with babies bundled against the cold. When I spotted a Victorian monstrosity with a sign hanging from hooks on its front porch that read VACANCY/CHAMBRE LIBRE, I pulled over. The siding paint was chipped and one of the second-story window frames seemed in danger of falling off, but as a place to hide out, it looked promising. I parked in the rear, removed my glasses and donned my tuque, then said, "Honey, we're home," but Callie didn't appreciate my humor.

The lobby of the rooming house reeked of curry, in another room a television droned, but the wood floors were polished and clean. There was even a small bookshelf filled with paperbacks with a sign that read, TAKE ONE, LEAVE ONE. A woman in a red sari with a matching bindi opened a creaking pocket door. When I told her my daughter and I were in town on a college tour, her dark eyes brightened.

"Then I have a room for you." She bent down and hefted an old guest register to the wooden counter. It resembled the short books used by court clerks to record details of hearings and trials, volumes in which my dad's name and then mine had been written in longhand hundreds of times.

"Which schools are you visiting?"

"York University and the University of Guelph," I volunteered the first two names that came to mind.

"So, you will leave your mother and go to college?" The woman directed her smile at Callie.

"Too soon," I said, when Callie stared at the floor and said nothing.

"My three children are away at school. Two in the United States. One at Stanford." She nodded.

"Tough school," I said.

"And expensive." She nodded again. "But worth it. When your child has ability you have to give them every chance, right? Will you pay by credit card?"

"Cash, please."

"You understand I have to charge you in advance? How long will you be with us?"

"Two nights should be sufficient." I squinted to sign my mother's maiden name and filled in a made-up address in Hamilton, complete with a phony postal code.

The woman pulled a large calculator from beneath the desk. "Includes GST," she said, when she showed me the number on her screen. I handed her more of my dwindling cash.

A two-story, stained-glass window with insets of massive golden irises rose above the landing of the wide staircase. It needed work. In places, the lead had separated from the glass and the chilly air whistled through. I shivered. "Winter will be here soon, eh?" It was my best impersonation of a Canadian mother on an outing with her teenaged daughter. We climbed a narrower set of stairs. "I hope we brought enough warm clothes, honey," I called back to Callie.

"You will be comfortable up here," the woman said when we reached the third floor. "Heat rises, you know." She pointed the way. Our room was a collection of heavy antiques mixed with batik bedspreads and curtains, a modern and old-fashioned wrestling match neither side was winning. "This is our best room." She opened a closet. "There are more blankets in here, should you need them. Breakfast is between six and nine in the dining room downstairs," she said before she left.

The room had twin beds and a tiny en suite bath. A window looked down on a side yard garden that had apparently given up for the season, now a mess of lifeless leaves, dead blossoms, and leggy trees.

Callie stood in front of a marble-topped bureau, leaned into the mirror on the wall above it, and tugged at the shorter side of her new cut.

I said, "It shows off your face. You have pretty eyes."

She fingered her earring.

"Don't fiddle with it. It'll get infected."

She glared at my reflection in the mirror. "Why did you make me do this?"

"The earring?"

"All of this." She threw up her hands.

I pulled off the tuque and shook out my hair.

"Won't they be really mad when they catch us?"

Her voice was loud, bitter, so I touched my finger to my lips and whispered, "First, we're going to go back before they catch us. And when we go back, we'll have a deal, one that's fair and reasonable."

"That prosecutor will never change his mind. You said he would before, but he didn't."

"He will now."

"Why should he?"

"He just will," I said. "Anyway, how about some dinner? I saw a Chinese place around the corner that looked interesting. And tomorrow we'll find a lawyer who can help us, and then we'll visit the museum. You can take your drawing pad. Get some inspiration."

She stared at me, her eyes steely.

I left her and closed myself in the bathroom, then pulled my few toiletries from the duffel and placed them on the marble ledge. "I know this is difficult, Callie," I said when I returned. "You just have to bear with me a little longer."

"And then what? It feels sneaky and dirty, hiding out like this."

"I'm protecting you."

"Right. That's what *she* said."

"Who said that, Callie? Please. Tell me. So I can help you."

"She said that, too."

"Who are you talking about?"

"'I'll help you, I'll be your friend, I won't try to be your mother,' but she didn't do anything for me, either. I just want to go home and see my father. I want to tell him what really happened."

"Do you remember something, Callie? Something I should know?"

"Just take me home."

"Tell me. Tell me first."

"It's just—I started remembering. Little things."

"Like—?"

"Like she was there that morning. She was there. She must have taken my baby."

"Who, Callie? Who?"

"Rose." She nodded slowly, deliberately.

"Rose Walker? Why would Rose take your baby?"

"I don't know. But she did."

I backed to the edge of the closest bed, sat. "You're telling me Rose took your baby. Why would she do that?"

"Maybe you should ask her."

"This doesn't make any sense."

Callie stood in front of me with her chin raised, her jaw set. "You don't believe me?"

"I—it's . . . well, you can understand why it sounds strange . . . after all this time . . .

It's . . . Give me a minute to think, will you?" My mind reeled. Was she finally remembering? Or had she made up this story about Rose?

"You told me over and over to trust you. So now I remember and I tell you what happened and you don't believe me."

I didn't know what I thought or what I believed just then. I knew Callie detested Rose. And if she was trying to blame Rose, well, it wouldn't be the first time a client of mine blamed someone else for a crime they'd committed.

"Isn't a lawyer supposed to believe what her client says?" She interrupted my thoughts.

"Callie, what you said about Rose . . . Well, I know you aren't fond of her—"

"She was there. In the bathroom. I saw her standing over me. I was on the bathroom floor."

"Okay." I nodded, trying my best to stay calm. "Why was she there?"

"She was always there back then. She must have taken the baby."

"And let you take the blame? Would she do that?"

"She said it would be our secret. Don't you get it?" She was shouting now.

I put out my hand, a keep-your-voice-down gesture. "I'm just saying that if you didn't want Rose to marry your father, that might be a reason to say what you're saying."

"Have you even asked her?"

"Well, no. I haven't had the chance."

"Right." Callie's voice was sarcastic. "Okay then. Take all the time you need, *Counselor*." She glared at me again, then ran out, slamming the heavy wooden door behind her. I heard her footsteps clomping down the stairs.

278   Marilyn J. Zimmerman

I sat there, stunned, and tried to get my bearings. Was it possible Callie remembered what really happened that morning at the parsonage? Or had she made up this story? Whichever it was, I needed to find her. I grabbed my coat.

Outside, it was dark and had begun to rain. Passing car lights shone on the wet pavement and splashed water as they sped down the narrow street. I scanned both sides of the street for her, but she'd vanished. She'd been wearing a red sweater and one of her long skirts, plus her usual boots. Nothing that would keep her dry in a storm like this.

I started up the street, toward the skyline of the central city, checking archways and entrances where she might have taken refuge from this driving rain. She'd been scared and upset, plus she was fragile. Maybe getting her hair cut had been too much. Maybe we should have taken our chances and stayed at Barrett's cottage for a few more days. And that story about Rose. Was that possible? Would Rose have taken the baby and then sat silently by while Callie was prosecuted?

Down a side street, I ducked inside a brightly lit laundromat. It was practically deserted, only a couple of older women standing beside metal tables, robotically folding clothes and stacking them in plastic baskets. Back on the street I kept going, but I had no idea where to look. I half-walked, half-ran, my hair dripping and my glasses fogged, hoping by some stroke of luck to spot her, to convince her to come back to our room, to talk to me.

A young couple approached, snuggling beneath a black umbrella with a purple slash on it. "Did you see a girl in a red sweater?" I called to them, but they kept walking.

I reached a block of apartment towers. People in trench coats streamed from a subway exit and hurried inside. I opened the door of every bar and restaurant I came to, scanning the room for a girl in a red sweater. I spotted a sandwich board on a sidewalk that read, "Bible Study tonight. All welcome," so I splashed through puddles on the pitted concrete steps, pulled open the front door, and peered in.

An old woman sat in a back pew. "Classes are downstairs." Her voice echoed through the cavernous nave.

"I'm looking for a girl." I was breathing hard. "Wearing a red sweater?" I spotted the structure and began moving toward it, a small pool with a ladder leading to its edge. An immersion pool for baptisms.

The woman said, "Summers we baptize in Lake Ontario, but winters we use this."

Just like Callie's father's church. "The girl?" I pressed.

"Haven't seen her."

I stepped back into the cold drizzle.

Two hours later, I walked through the rooming house lobby. My hair dripped, and my shoes squished. I heard a pocket door creak open, then close. I'd had a desperate hope that I'd find Callie sitting in the lobby or maybe asleep in her bed, but she wasn't in either place. Still wearing my rain-soaked coat, I perched on the edge of one of the twin beds.

I told myself that as soon as Callie returned, I'd tell her I believed her; I'd convince her to trust me again. Even if she was one of those clients of mine who didn't tell me the truth, it didn't matter. I was the only one who cared enough about Callie to help her. And I *would* help her. She didn't need to invent that story about Rose taking her baby.

A clock in the hall chimed. Heavy beads of water landed on the window, combining like balls of mercury as gravity impelled them toward the sill. Outside, the garden was transformed from grey to shiny black. Around midnight I took off my coat and switched on the little radio beside the bed. The CBC meteorologist apologized for being sucker punched. "We sure didn't see this coming. We could get up to six centimeters before it's done."

FIFTY-ONE

WHEN THE DOOR OPENED, I SPRANG UP AND LUNGED for my glasses. "Callie?"

But it wasn't Callie. It was the owner of the rooming house, wearing a grassy green sari and a red bindi. She stepped away, and I saw Ed Mueller standing in the hall in his black fur coat.

"Well, well. Thought I might have to forfeit this one. Spoil my perfect record. Never had a skip I didn't drag back before. Course most of my skips don't go on TV." He told the woman, "I'll take it from here," and pulled a pair of handcuffs from his coat pocket. Slamming the door with his foot, he checked our empty bathroom, his burly body between me and any escape.

"Where is she?"

"She ran away."

"Yeah, yeah. And now you just want to go find her." He grabbed my hands, snapped one cuff on my right wrist, the other on my left. Then he shoved me on the bed and stepped to the window. "Wet out there tonight." He turned around, scanned the room.

"Did Barrett tell you where I was?"

"Barrett Michaels? No," he scoffed. "He didn't have to. I was in his office when the call came. Seems your law-abiding landlady watches a lot of television. She saw you on CNN. 'The girl looks different,' she said, 'and the lawyer is missing her glasses, but otherwise she's a dead ringer.'"

"So now what?"

"We sit here until the kid comes back."

"I told you, she left. I haven't seen her."

He dropped down on the bed beside me and opened his thick coat. A holstered pistol hung from his belt.

"There's a little bar just up the street that serves great burgers—"

"Fool me once," he snapped. "I don't go anyplace without you, Counselor. So where exactly did she go this time?"

"I wish I knew."

He laughed then, a loud hawing. "She stiffed you too. Perfect. And you really don't know where she is. Perfect. You fell for this one hook, line, and sinker." He stretched his arms, yawned, and stood up. Then he grabbed my arm and jerked me to my feet. "Let's do it this way so we don't disturb the other guests." Before I realized what was happening, he pulled a handkerchief from his pants pocket and shoved it in my mouth. Unlocking one cuff, he spun me around, and locked both hands behind my back.

His Lexus was double-parked on the rainy street. He popped the trunk, pushed me inside, and slammed the lid. Laws against false imprisonment, kidnapping, assault, and battery didn't apply to bail bondsmen, so we both knew he'd get away with this. Even if the RCMP stopped him, Mueller would just show them his papers, explain he was bringing back a skip, and they'd wave him on. They might even give him a police escort.

I lay in the freezing darkness as he revved the engine. When the car lurched forward, I rolled into something sharp and warm liquid trickled down my face. The car stopped abruptly and I pitched forward again, my chin bouncing on the rough carpet as Mueller splashed through potholes on the city pavement. When the engine finally steadied, I figured we were on the 401, headed west to pick up the 402 to the bridge. Ed Mueller would be sitting smugly behind the wheel, like a cat bringing a stunned songbird to its owner.

Music echoed from inside the car, a country twang. Despite my misery, all I could think about was Callie. I could have reassured her. That's what she'd needed from me. Why hadn't I just told her I believed her?

When the Lexus slowed, I heard clanging coins in a toll trough, then felt the car ascend the bridge, the tires vibrating as they crossed the expansion grid. As we descended, the purr of idling semis told me we were passing the usual endless line for truck inspections at the Michigan border. The road leveled off, the Lexus inched forward, and the music quit. I made out two voices—probably a gullible customs officer grilling Mueller and Mueller saying what he needed to say to get me back to jail.

FIFTY-TWO

BARRETT'S BODY NEARLY FILLED THE DOORWAY. HIS HANDS were empty; he held no file and no tape recorder. Not that he needed either. Someone closed the door behind him and the two of us were alone.

"I heard Mueller was pretty rough on you." He seemed uncomfortable, awkward.

"I'd show you my bruises, but I can't raise my arms above this desk."

"Victoria, I'm sorry." He turned around the chair on the other side of the desk and straddled it, rested his forearms on its back. "But you disappeared in the middle of a jury trial. What was I supposed to do?"

"Well, let's see, maybe you could arrange for the *Sentinel* to photograph me in my cell. Or I could pose in the trunk of Mueller's Lexus. Or, even better, they could take close-ups of my bruises. That would convince the undecided voters you're tough enough."

"I just . . . You're not being rational. No matter what you think of me, *that girl*—"

"Save it, Barrett. This is *me* you're talking to."

He pushed himself up from the chair and stepped to the window. "You know it's just a matter of time before Mueller finds her. He'll never surrender her bond. And I can't do anything with your warrant until she's in custody. How would it look?"

"*How would it look?* Jesus, Barrett."

"When she's back, you pay some costs and I dismiss. With prejudice."

"*With prejudice*. What a joke."

"You can go back to practicing. This will blow over."

"Maybe for you."

He turned back to the window and spoke quietly. "What you said the other night on TV . . ." His jaw stiffened. "That was a hundred years ago. Why didn't you tell me?"

"So you could help pay to get rid of it?"

Except for the motor of a nearby air cleaner, the tiny room was eerily silent. "Did you want it?"

"I didn't know what I wanted. I was scared. I reacted. I didn't think it through. Sometimes I think that's what bothers me the most."

"I would have done something, Vic."

"Right. You and Melissa were practically engaged."

"I never would have told you to get an abortion."

"That's easy to say, isn't it? Now that the deed is done. And I suppose you think that exonerates you. That you don't bear any responsibility for it. How convenient."

"I don't believe in abortion."

"Neither did I. But decisions are always easy in the abstract, Barrett."

His nostrils flared, and his breathing became loud but shallow, his eyes focused inward. "So, you blame me for what you did?"

"For a long time, yes. Maybe I just wished you loved me enough that I could have told you, that we'd have made things right, whatever that was. But I'm a big girl, and it was my choice. I have to live with that. I'm just damn tired of carrying this burden alone."

"What's that supposed to mean?"

I took a breath, tried to think. Would I still do this? I shook my head, as though that would help the floating pieces of this mess sort themselves and settle. When they didn't, I decided it didn't matter. I'd gone too far to turn back. I said, "I have a lot of regrets, Barrett. But helping Callie is not one of them."

"So you're going to sit here and rot? Be her personal Joan of Arc?"

"No. I'm done being the martyr."

"What does that mean?"

"It means this: the election's in less than a week. You give me Callie and I'll keep quiet."

FIFTY-THREE

THAT AFTERNOON, ART'S HEAVY FOOTSTEPS PAUSED OUTSIDE my cell. "I guess it's true. The Mounties always get their man. Or I should say, their girl."

I sat up. I knew Art would tell his story when he was good and ready, not before. "She turned herself in," he finally said. "She had the sense to go to a police precinct. Didn't tell them she was a runaway felon, just a runaway. Convinced them to call her father. Barrett sent Ed Mueller to get her."

"Is she okay?"

"She seems to be. The deputy's processing her now."

"When can I see her?"

"It's not your place to give orders, you know."

"I'm still her attorney. That gives me the right—"

"Seems like this case is a bit out of the ordinary. Maybe those rules don't apply."

"You'll let me talk to her, won't you, Art? Please."

"We'll sort it all out when we've finished booking her. I just thought you might want to know." He cleared his throat and adjusted his belt before disappearing down the hall.

They brought us both to the room where I'd met with Barrett that morning. Callie's eyes were red-rimmed, not like someone who'd been crying, but like someone who hadn't slept. She wasn't wearing the earring and her hair was dirty, her ivory face even paler than usual. Maybe they'd made her take the stud out when they processed her, but I doubted it. It was more likely she'd tossed it somewhere along the way.

"Are you okay?" I asked.

She shrugged, picked at her fingers. "I guess."

"You scared me when you left."

Another shrug.

"Where did you go?"

"What difference does it make?"

"I was worried sick. If anything happened to you, I'd never forgive myself."

Nothing.

I took off my glasses and rubbed my aching eyes. "Callie, I can still help you, if you let me. I spoke to the prosecutor—"

Callie crossed her arms across her chest and sat down. Her dark eyes bored through me. "I want another lawyer."

"But I've got everything under control now."

She looked away, then back at me with dark, icy eyes. "I don't believe you," she said. Then she banged on the door to be let out.

The following day, when I was arraigned at the jail, Ed Mueller renewed my bond. "That's because your temptation to sin is locked up," he told me in the hall afterward. He also knew that earlier that morning I'd withdrawn as Callie's attorney, when Osbourne appointed Joyce Ballinger to take my place. What Ed didn't know was that Barrett had returned to the jail last night and I'd made a deal with him. Nothing would happen until after the election, and no one except Barrett and me would ever know the reason for our agreement.

The press was back in full force by then, salivating over another chapter in the story I'd practically written for them these past few days. They'd have a field day now that I was released. There'd be editorials and letters to the editor about the local justice system's Good Old Boys network and the favor I'd gotten by being released again on bond after what I'd done. When I left the jail, I kept my eyes on the pavement and didn't offer the media any juicy quotes on my way to Gail's car. That was part of my deal with Barrett, too. No comments to the media or anyone else about any of this.

Gail pulled her Prius onto the highway, and I tipped my head back and closed my tired eyes. My wrists were tender, my body ached, and I was just plain exhausted. The surge of adrenaline I'd had when I crossed the bridge with Callie was long gone. I'd gotten a deal for her, one I could live with, but I had nothing left. And now, after everything that had happened, Callie didn't want anything to do with me. Because I hadn't believed her.

"Did you even ask Rose?" she'd said.

"Can we make a short detour?" I asked Gail.

"I thought you weren't the girl's lawyer anymore," she said, when I told her where I wanted to go.

"It's probably nothing. But I need to tie up a loose end."

I recognized the red Honda in the driveway. "I won't be long," I reassured Gail, whose response was to disappear wordlessly behind the pages of an *Us Weekly* magazine. I pushed the metal doorbell three times before Rose answered. "I'd like to talk to you," I said, but she turned and walked away, leaving the door ajar as though she expected me to follow, so I did.

Inside the living room, an intricately pieced quilt hung on the wall behind a spinet; another quilt, this one in pastel blocks, hid most of a sofa. Framed Bible verses hung on the walls, and a hymnal and Bible were the only books I saw. She had her back to me. "Whose side were you on in all this, Rose?" I asked.

"What?"

I needed to satisfy myself I did everything I could. "Those bags you gave me at the courthouse, was there a black raincoat inside one of them?"

"What difference does it make?"

"Was it?"

"I always tried to help her. But she wouldn't let me."

"Callie?"

"I even tried to convince him. I told him she wasn't like her mother."

"Neil Thomas?"

"He can't stand to be lied to. Not ever. So I decided to tell him. I thought he'd understand." She swiped her eyes with the crumpled handkerchief she held in one hand.

"Understand what?"

"That I tried to save the baby. I cleaned him up and tried to make him breathe. I rocked him. I talked to him. But he never cried. Aren't babies supposed to cry if they're alive?"

Callie's baby? "You were there?"

"I wanted to surprise her with the quilt I'd made her. She was supposed to be at school."

"Did you wrap the baby in Callie's bedsheet? And clean up the bathroom?"

"She wouldn't look at me. She was so lost. I tried to help."

"What did you do?"

"I borrowed her raincoat."

"You took the baby to the river?" I sank to the edge of the nearest chair.

"I wanted to baptize him."

I pictured the woman at that church in Toronto. "*Summers we baptize in the lake,*" she'd said. "But if you thought he was dead—"

"Do you know the precise moment a soul leaves a body? He

was so little, in his pink shroud. I put his tiny body under the water and raised him up. I baptized him, just like we do at church. And that's when I decided. He could just slip away. Callie and I would have a secret."

"You let go of him."

"I thought he was dead." She looked at me as if I were crazy.

"And you never told anyone?"

"No one asked me. No one assumed I was a witness to anything. Why should they? Who was I? No one who mattered." She sniffed and wiped her nose. "Today . . . today I told Neil what I did. So he'd know he could trust me. But he said I was just like his wife. And Callie. That we all lied to him."

I was suddenly lightheaded, faint. I leaned forward and dropped my head, willing oxygen to my brain.

Callie told me the truth.

When I stood back up, Rose was gone. "Rose?" I hollered, but she didn't answer. "We need to talk." She could tell the police what really happened, that she hadn't known the baby was alive when she took him to the river to baptize him. That she'd never meant to kill him.

"Rose?" I found her in a small bedroom at the back of the house. The window shades were down. She sat in the dark on the opposite side of the bed, her back to me.

"I can help you, Rose," I said. "We can explain all this."

But she didn't answer. Instead, she leaned forward, opened the drawer of a maple nightstand, and reached inside. I didn't see the gun until it was too late.

That night, after the police finished questioning me, I sat in my corner chair at home and watched the boats. Salties and freighters, mostly. It was getting too cold for most sport fishermen to be on the river. Sister blinked as a thousand-footer passed. She'd been an old nun, stern and usually crabby. But a few days after I first came to St. Anne's, she called me into her office. She told me I could come there and read books or just sit by myself when I needed to, when I was hurting too much. She gave me my own box of tissues in case I needed to cry. I never told my dad. He would have said I was feeling sorry for myself. "Lawyers aren't entitled to bad days," he used to say, even when he was too sick to leave his hospital bed.

Now Sister nodded. Her blinking light was like a pulse, a metronome, a beating heart. I drained the bottle into my glass.

Callie told me the truth.

I called Joyce Ballinger on my landline and woke her up. I told her everything Rose told me, about Rose's suicide, and that the police were probably interviewing Neil Thomas at that moment to get confirmation of what Rose told me.

"Everything's changed," I said, my words muddled and slurred but my brain still functioning. "You can't keep that deal with Barrett. Not anymore. You have to save Callie."

FIFTY-FOUR

July 2017

I'M AT THE HELM OF *MARGARET ANN.* I'VE BEEN BOATING a lot this summer, as though I have all the time in the world, which I guess I do. This past May I was suspended from the practice of law for five years. No one filed a complaint against me, but the state bar's grievance commission sent me a registered letter that declared, "We cannot continue to ignore what you have so publicly done to disgrace our profession." I consulted a lawyer who specialized in defending these kinds of suspensions, but he wasn't optimistic about my chances of success. Plus, I couldn't manage his steep retainer. I did consider representing myself but recognized I couldn't articulate an explanation for what I'd done that anyone, including me, would be able to understand. In the end, I'd consented to the suspension.

I'm also on probation, a condition the Circuit Court set for the dismissal of my felony case, provided I keep out of trouble for a year. As part of my plea, I agreed to see a psychologist every week. Sharon Holmes is nice enough, but she keeps trying to relate everything I did for Callie to my mother's suicide, and I can't force myself into that black hole. *What if I never come out?* I did admit to Sharon that I recognized that what I did to help Callie wasn't logical, that it came from someplace other than my brain—from somewhere deeper. That not only did I think I was saving Callie, but I was also saving myself, as weird as that sounded, although after I said those words to Sharon, I quickly backpedaled. "Maybe I was premenopausal, maybe my hormones were out of whack, who knows?" I'd said and laughed. But I could tell she wasn't convinced.

I haven't told Sharon, but I also recognized that during my time with Callie, I began to have feelings for her, maternal feelings, feelings I never thought I was capable of having. And when that happened, something in me couldn't stuff my emotions or bury them while I worked ferociously on some other stranger's case. Everything changed.

As the day gives up the last rays of light, I cut the engine and let *Margaret Ann* drift downriver, surrendering to the evening breezes and the current. I reach into the pocket of my Michigan hoodie and retrieve an envelope. Joyce Ballinger stopped by my cottage late this afternoon and gave it to me, but I haven't read it yet.

"It's from Callie." She'd pushed a stack of papers around inside her messy briefcase until she found it. "I keep in touch with her, mostly because she doesn't seem to have anyone else and I feel bad for her."

I'd laid the envelope on my kitchen table. "She's not at the parsonage?"

"Stubborn bastard still won't let her come home."

"So where's she living?"

"Above the church thrift store in Port Huron."

"What does she do for money?"

"The youth pastor and his wife help her out some. The apartment's owned by the church, so she doesn't pay rent."

"Is she working on her diploma?"

"Her GED, yeah. She's a smart girl; she's breezing through it. Other than that, I think she keeps to herself."

"You did a good job for her," I said.

"Thanks to you. From a Murder One charge to a ninety-day misdemeanor with credit for time served. I told Callie you got her the deal."

"Only because Rose Walker tipped the scales. What a sad mess."

"Well," she said, zipping her briefcase. "Want to hear some good news?"

"Sure."

"I just found out I'm pregnant. Again."

"Again?" I blurted, then said, "I don't know how you manage."

"You and me both," Joyce said. "I've been exhausted since I got pregnant for my first. I don't know what it feels like to have a good night's sleep. Each one makes me nuts, and each one is the light of my life. But I'll let you in on a secret. There are plenty of days when I'd give them all up to have what you have."

"What exactly is that?"

She waved her arm toward the river. "This place, your privacy, time to yourself, freedom to do whatever you want."

Lately, I *have* been sleeping better. I've stopped drinking, not that I can afford those expensive vintages I used to crave. But it's not just that; it's something else. I think it's that, after all that happened, I reached a truce with myself about my abortion. If I had the chance to do things over, I can't say I'd make a different decision, but I like to think I'd reach a conclusion because it was right for me, not because I was afraid of disappointing someone else.

"Well, don't do what I did to get all this time to myself," I'd told Joyce.

She surprised me with a quick hug. "It'll fly by. You'll be back to the grind before you know it. And in the meantime, you'll sleep in, read books, do whatever you want." She yawned. "Sounds heavenly."

I didn't tell her I'd had to refund almost everything in my bank account, the big retainers I'd taken in. Because during this suspension, I wouldn't be able to represent anyone. Even setting foot in my office would be a violation of my suspension. So I have no income, and the little savings I have left is taking a big hit. Add to that the present I got from the county commissioners: after what I did, they refused to pay Dr. Allen's bill, so I'm stuck with it.

"Starting over again, building my practice. I'll be fifty then."

"When clients hire you, they'll brag to their friends. You'll be their celebrity lawyer. And you can always go back to handling appointed cases."

"Not where I planned to be at this stage of my career."

Joyce scratched the back of her head and didn't bother smoothing her thick hair back into place. "Life's full of surprises." She'd patted her pudgy stomach. "Many of them good." Then, "Well, it's my night to get supper for my brood. Hal and I take turns. So I'm off."

When she was gone, I tried to remember how many kids she had. Five? Six? And a law practice? I'd never thought anything like that was possible. One or the other was how I'd viewed it, never both. After Barrett dumped me and Dad died, I slammed the door on any available man who might have been interested in being close to me. For twenty years, the only relationships I had were professional: attorneys, clients, and witnesses. I'd never been willing to take another chance, to open my heart again. Until Callie.

And Barrett? He lost the election. His rigidity apparently chased a few of the undecided voters to the camp of Jim Anderson. More than a few voters interviewed outside the polls by the *Sentinel* said they'd been put off by the drama that seemed to surround him. By the time Callie entered her plea and walked out of the courthouse, the election was over and the press had moved on to some other salacious story. This past spring, he and Melissa, their boys and their new baby daughter, relocated somewhere out west. At least that's what I heard.

The winds are picking up now; they're from the south, a rarity that makes it look like the river current is switching directions. The first time I witnessed this phenomenon was the night of my mother's funeral. The winds had suddenly shifted, making it look like the water was flowing upstream, backwards. My father was already back at work, law books and files of notes splayed across our kitchen table while he prepared for one of his trials. When I'd run inside to tell him what I'd seen, he told me to sit down, and he retrieved an old atlas from a bookshelf in our living room. Using his capped Waterman as a pointer, he traced the route of Lake Huron into the river out front, then followed it through the swampy flats that emptied into Lake St. Clair, the Detroit River, Lake Erie, Lake Ontario, and the St. Lawrence Seaway. "Someday," he'd said, "the water you are now watching will reach the Atlantic. A little wind won't be enough to prevent that from happening. Use your brain, Victoria," he'd said, when he snapped the atlas closed, signifying our discussion was ending. "Beneath the surface, this river will always flow relentlessly, perpetually south. There's no changing it."

The engine in gear now, I'm working my way back to my cottage, passing summer cottages and year-round mansions on the tall slopes. A bevy of powerboats sweeps by and confuses the waves. As I rock in the slop, I finger the letter Joyce gave me again, and as I do, I can hear Callie's voice. "You don't believe me," she'd said. It bothers me that after everything I did for her, that's what she'll remember about me. About us.

I steer around a lone powerboat that can't speed fast enough on the darkening river to suit its young captain, idle the engine and drift again while I finish what's left in my thermos: warm green tea, part of a collection Molly sent me when I told her I'd given up alcohol. Then, in the dusky twilight, I slit open the envelope and read.

In Defense of Good Women 297

Dear Victoria,

Mrs. Ballinger says I have you to thank for how my case turned out. When things got so crazy, I didn't know whether I could trust you. And when you didn't believe me, I got pretty mad.

But I've been thinking about how nice you were to me when I lived with you. You cared about me when no one else did.

I have lots of time to sketch now that I'm living on my own. You said I was good at it and that meant a lot to me. So I'm sending you something that I drew from memory. I hope you like it. And I hope I see you again.

Sincerely, Callie

P.S. Are you feeding my birdies?

I unfold the second page and hold it up in the dusky light. There's a tiny pencil sketch of a hummingbird in the lower right-hand corner, but the main drawing is of me. I'm standing at the podium in the courtroom, wearing my highest heels, the pair I used to think made me a stronger, more powerful advocate. One ankle is crossed behind the other and I'm pointing Dad's Waterman toward an imagined witness. At the bottom of the drawing, Callie had printed, "My Warrior."

I'm nearing my cottage now. Sister Phillip blinks, and I push the throttle, turn the steering wheel, and head to the well. I have a flash of anger, a regret for all I gave up for Callie, and a sudden urge to tear the letter, the sketch, and the envelope into tiny bits, to toss them all in the water like wafers of fish food. How different my life, not to mention my career, would be if I'd never met Callie.

Instead I refold the picture and the letter and return them to my pocket.

Inside the well, I secure the boat with its mooring lines, close the door, and sit in the dark, listening to the water lap against the concrete walls. Except for the twice weekly AA meetings I've begun attending up at St. Anne's, I really don't have much to keep me busy these days. I've toyed with the idea of attending mass on a Sunday, although I haven't.

Now I think about going to see Callie.

That night, I sleep a deep, dreamless sleep, only waking at dawn when a freighter sounds its foghorn. I wander to my chair and sit quietly until the sun burns through the cloudy mass, the closeness of this magnificent body of water as comforting to me as if someone were whispering soft words of solace in my ear.

Later, I retrieve the envelope and unfold Callie's sketch. Though it's only a profile, she's captured my prominent glasses, my thin face, my long nose, my bushy hair. I unfold the letter and read it again, then watch as Sister blinks her greeting. In my kitchen, I brew a cup of coffee and return to my perch as a purple finch lands on my deck and tips its head to get a better look at a beetle that's crawling along the rail. I blow on my coffee to cool it and realize I'm smiling.

It occurs to me that I haven't filled Callie's bird feeders all summer.

I'll start with that.

AFTERWORD

This book tells the story of two tragedies. The desire of both main characters, Victoria and Callie, to be seen as "good women" overrode everything else, and in Callie's case, resulted in her mental illness. These two were "good women" to a fault—and that led to their tragedies.

The second tragedy was the refusal of the US criminal justice system to recognize the unique changes in women's bodies, psyches, and hormones during pregnancy and birth. In 1938 the United Kingdom recognized this and passed the Infanticide Act, which created a separate homicide category for mothers who commit infanticide if the baby was twelve months old or less and the mother satisfied certain, specific conditions. Thirty first-world countries have recognized that there needs to be a separate homicide category for the crime of infanticide and passed laws to make that happen.

Meanwhile, the United States remains oblivious and indifferent to the plight of these women and, in fact, leaves it to the local prosecutor to charge them. Those arbitrary charges range from capital murder to probation, depending on the prosecutor, the county, and the state where the crime occurred.

As you read *In Defense of Good Women*, I hope you began to see that black is not always black and white is not always white. This book is about becoming open to what lies in between and beneath, the hidden truth behind infanticide.

FOR FURTHER READING

Infanticide: Psychosocial and Legal Perspectives on Mothers Who Kill, edited by Margaret Spinelli, MD (2003, American Psychiatric Publishing, Inc.).

ACKNOWLEDGMENTS

A retired small-town attorney, I was a moth drawn to a flame when in 2001 I learned about Andrea Yates and the horrifically sad story of the drowning of her five children. I followed both of her trials on social media, and, following her final sentence to a low-security mental health hospital, her behavior and her situation continued to haunt me. Through my local library, I ordered *Infanticide: Psychosocial and Legal Perspectives on Mothers Who Kill*, edited by Margaret Spinelli, MD, PhD, and learned, among other surprising information, about the arbitrary charging of women who commit infanticide in the United States. In the chapter titled "Criminal Defense in Cases of Infanticide and Neonaticide" by Judith Macfarlane, JD, I learned about otherwise "good girls," often unmarried teenagers, who dissociate during their pregnancies and births and only cease dissociating when evidence of their wrongdoing (i.e., their infants) were out of their sight, done away with in an often bizarre fashion.

I decided to write the story of one of those "good" teenage girls and elected to tell it through the eyes of her defense attorney, a woman facing her own unresolved issues regarding mothering.

Since this was my first novel, writing this book put me on a steep learning curve. My initial writing group, Dr. Jennifer Sowle, Trudy Carpenter, Patrick McMahon, David Marshall, and our mentor, Stephen Lewis, encouraged, critiqued, and provided endless hours of entertainment during our gatherings. My once-per-year luncheon with the Northport Women's Writers Group (Dorene O'Brien, Sarah Shoemaker, Trudy Carpenter, Barbara Stark

Niemon, Pamela Grath, and Elizabeth Buzzelli) provided motivation, hugs, inspiration, and the foot in my back I needed to submit this manuscript to a publisher.

I owe a debt of gratitude to Amy Bowen, LCMHC, of Salt and Sage, who line edited and performed a sensitivity edit, but mostly helped me understand the psychology of the issues raised in my book through the defense and trial.

Pamela Grath, my copy editor and dear friend, deserves her own thanks.

Finally, I wish to thank my husband, David, for his encouragement, his support, and for reminding me, "This is a good story, Marilyn," whenever I needed to hear it. His love and kindness are more than I ever imagined or expected in a marriage.

ABOUT THE AUTHOR

Photo credit: Josh Hartman

MARILYN J. ZIMMERMAN has always been interested in social issues. She attended law school in Michigan, driving to classes at night while teaching school and working as a court bailiff. Marilyn was a general practitioner, which exposed her to many types of cases and clients. After twenty years, health issues forced her to retire. Marilyn loves to read, garden, and cook, and she has a fascination with labyrinths. In 2019 she studied to become a labyrinth facilitator through Veriditas and now leads walks in both Michigan and California, where she and her husband spend winters.

Looking for your next great read?

We can help!

Visit www.gosparkpress.com/next-read or
scan the QR code below for a list
of our recommended titles.

SparkPress is an independent boutique publisher delivering high-quality, entertaining, and engaging content that enhances readers' lives, with a special focus on commercial and genre fiction.